SIMPLER TIMES

TRISHA KOOP ABEAR

DRL
press

Enjoy!

—Trisha K Abear

AUTHOR'S NOTE

It sounds cliché perhaps, but the idea for Simpler Times came to me on an evening when the craziness of life hit me. All the stresses, daily tasks, non-stop cell phone dings, the depressing news headlines sounding in the background, the general whirlwind of the present day buzzing through my head, had all become overwhelming. As usual, my go-to escape is a glass of Chardonnay and a good book. A thought crossed my mind of a story about a young woman who yearns for a more simplistic life. After putting pen to paper I became obsessed with completing a story I could put into readers hands that would allow them an escape from reality. This, for me, is the purpose of a wonderful novel and I am anxious to give my readers this with *Simpler Times*.

*Disclaimer: This book is a work of fiction. Any resemblance to actual events, locales or persons, living or dead, is entirely a result of my active imagination.

DRL Press, Georgetown, Texas

Design and Production: Riverstone Group, LLC

CONTENTS

PROLOGUE

Evie glanced in the back seat at her eight-year-old daughter who was looking out her car window at images of tall buildings flashing by. Rose's eyes were busily focusing on each sight as their car drove through the busy city streets. Evie couldn't place if Rose was bored, disinterested or just plain tired from today's car ride. Either way she seemed almost unimpressed.

"Rose, pretty soon we are going to see the Sears Tower, one of the tallest skyscrapers in the US," Evie told Rose, attempting to build some excitement.

Evie and her husband Philip had chosen to take their daughter, Rose, on a summer road trip from Duluth, MN, where they lived, to Chicago. They had hoped to show her a big city, some iconic landmarks and impressive buildings that the young Minnesota girl hadn't seen before. So far the family of three's travels had consisted of a few camping trips up the North Shore as far as Grand Marais and a few long weekends to lake towns in central Minnesota. Those trips Rose had seemed to enjoy thoroughly. But this trip was a big deal. A bit more notable.

Rose gazed up at the Sears Tower when they stopped the car.

"Let's go in and take a look, Rosalie," Philip suggested, putting the car in park. Rose fiddled with the zipper on her jacket and yawned.

"Nah, that's ok, Daddy. It looks cool. Really tall! But can we keep adventuring?" Rose asked.

Philip frowned at Evie sitting next to him. "Well sure, although I don't know how much more impressive a landmark we will be seeing on *this* road trip, honey." Evie squeezed his hand and motioned to keep driving as their daughter scratched her head.

"We can go in the tall building if you want to, Daddy. I don't mind," Rose offered.

"Oh, angel cake, that's ok. If you want to see what else is around the bend, that sounds just fine by me. Evie?" Philip asked both his girls.

"Let's go, hon. There's plenty more out there to see. We can come back to Chicago another time." Evie winked at Philip.

"Cool! Mom, how about a game of *Would You Rather* while we travel to the next place?" Rose made herself comfortable again, flipping off her sneakers and grabbing another apple slice from her plastic baggy.

"Hmmm, ok Rose. Would you rather be the queen of your very own castle or live in the forest with all the animals and plants?" Evie posed the question to Rose.

Rose looked out her window and thought hard. "I want both!"

On the long drive back to Minnesota the family had been on the hunt for a hotel to stay for the night, but the route they were taking through central Iowa wasn't providing any visible retreats.

Evie yawned and asked, "Philip, if you spot a McDonald's or a Holiday gas station could you pull in? I need a coffee; guessing you do too?"

Rose had just finished watching the movie, High School Musical, on her portable DVD player when their car turned into a small town lit by the glow of only street lights and the moon. Rose closed her DVD player, took off her headphones and watched out her window as they drove down the very short, quarter mile long, Main Street.

Sandwiched between a bookstore and a small coffee shop was a two-story inn — white, with tall windows and an old, brick chimney.

Rose looked closely as they passed. There were flickering candles in each window and a brightly lit sign out front that read *Welcome Guests*. It was so beautiful and inviting, Rose thought.

"Daddy, can we stay there for the night?" Rose asked.

Philip didn't know what his little girl was talking about. "Honey, where? It took us thirty seconds to drive down Main Street. Where did you see a place we could stay for the night?"

"Back there. Turn around. It's beautiful. I haven't seen anything that amazing on this whole trip! Have you daddy?"

Evie and Philip looked at each other, rolling their eyes and sighing out loud. Evie finally looked back at her daughter, smiling and replied, "Ok. This is your adventure, Rose. Let's go take a look."

CHAPTER 1

The constant headlines and video clips of war on the news had become gut-wrenching for Rose to watch — the palms of her hands sweating, her head throbbing. Her husband, Flynn, a US Army soldier, had been deployed to Afghanistan only three months ago. Of course, the first few weeks were some of the worst days of Rose's life. She couldn't count the times she had cried herself to sleep, or the times she had stood staring at Flynn's bathrobe, smelling it, hugging it. But life doesn't give you an alternate option. Rose, with time, learned to live with a dull ache in her heart.

But tonight, on this cool June evening, sitting in the living room on her parents' couch, in the home she grew up in, she was ready to burst. Talk of war and the violence overseas had her brain reeling. Rose, along with her mom and dad, had been watching the news and she had seen more than she could stand.

She needed to clear her damn mind. She felt like a war of her own was going on inside herself, and it was about to erupt into full blown combat.

I need to get out of here! She silently told herself. *A drive. That would help; maybe?*

The earlier drizzle of rain had turned into a full on downpour. Not ideal for a Sunday drive out of the city.

No matter. Rose had made up her mind.

As she sat in the driver's seat of her Ford Focus, she looked at the windshield, the rain rushing down the glass like the saddest of tears.

"If only tears ended in a cheery rainbow like these droplets." She said out loud, suddenly thinking back to the day she met Flynn…

Rose had graduated from Duluth East High School on May 23rd and her dad had told her it was high time for a summer job. Philip, was a regular customer at Canal Park Diner and had put in a good word to the owners, Maurice and Flora. They had hired her on the spot and threw her a white apron, insinuating they needed her to start serving immediately. Taking a deep breath, Rose tried to ignore the sudden butterflies that were flipping around in her stomach. Philip winked at his daughter and pointed to a table of four, whispering, "There's your first order."

Since that day, two years had gone by and the job had gone well — aside from the time she dropped a large chocolate milkshake in a guy's lap. Embarrassed was an understatement after that mishap. Still, Rose enjoyed the atmosphere, her co-workers and of course her own spending money.

Though she had gotten good grades in school, she didn't know what she wanted to study in college. Her parents agreed it may be a smart choice to wait a year, perhaps two. For now, the Canal Park Diner was just fine by her.

The old clock above the shelf of coffee mugs chimed telling her it was 12:00 p.m. Like clockwork, the noon hour always started a steady stream of hungry patrons through the door. Grabbing a pen and paper from under the counter she walked toward booth #1 where three elderly women were seated.

"Hello Ladies, thanks for coming in today." The sweet, elderly ladies, all wearing different style glasses and perfectly coiffed silver curls, smiled pleasantly at Rose.

Rose continued, "Our special today is the Hot Beef Sandwich for $6.95 and our soup of the day is Chicken Wild Rice. What can I get for you?" All three women opted for a cup of the soup and coffees all around.

"Sounds wonderful. I will have that right out," Rose said, tearing the order sheet from her notepad and heading for the kitchen.

Before she could hand the order off to Patrick (the afternoon cook) a young man walked through the front entrance, stopped, and smiled at her. Rose noticed he was attractive, but also strangely familiar. Where had she seen him before?

While she pondered the question, she gathered mugs and filled all three with hot coffee for the gals at booth #1. *Had she seen this guy at the movie theater maybe? Had he been an upperclassman from her high school? A friend of a friend she met once?* As she carried the tray of coffees, it dawned on her….

The milkshake guy!

Startled by her sudden realization, she almost dropped the three coffees just as she had the milkshake. This was too humiliating. And now she had to actually walk over to his table and take his lunch order. *Would anyone notice if she just ran out the door?*

Gathering herself, Rose took a breath, delivered the coffees and brought her next customer (the milkshake guy), a menu.

"Um, hi there. Our special today is a Hot Beef Sandwich for $6.95 and our soup is Chicken Wild Rice. Can I get you a beverage to start off?"

Rose's cheeks turned rose-red as he looked up at her. He smiled softly. He had a perfectly white, toothy grin and his green eyes sparkled. He cleared his throat and asked, with a hint of humor in his tone, "Would you happen to serve milkshakes here?"

"Oh no, you remember. I am so sorry! I can be so clumsy. Honestly, I want to apologize. Lunch is on us today," Rose stammered.

The handsome stranger put his hands up, halting her continual apologies and said, "Please, it was an accident; no harm done. To be perfectly honest, I do remember you spilling an entire chocolate milkshake on me, but that's not the only reason I remember you."

Again, Rose's cheeks turned crimson. She brushed a loose strand of blonde hair from her forehead and thought, *What is it with this guy?*

Clearly noticing her reaction, he spoke again, "If it's ok to say so, your cute smile and kind of sweet personality stood out the most to me. Yes, even more than ice cream down my pants."

They both laughed, almost in a flirtatious exchange.

Shyly, Rose responded, "Ah, well thanks for saying so, Mr…?"

"I'm Flynn," he answered.

"Ok, Flynn — what can I get you for lunch today?"

Flynn pondered the menu, "What's good here?"

Rose answered without hesitation, "The Reuben Sandwich is my favorite." She didn't care if it was a giant, messy sandwich that girls shouldn't pig out on; it was to die for!

Flynn pushed the menu away and said, "Then I'll have one of those and a Coke. How about a side of onion rings too?"

"You got it," Rose replied as she walked back to the kitchen, a new smile on her face she found hard to remove.

The diner was getting busy and booths were filling up with customers. Rose was running from table to table taking orders and serving hot plates of food. Every once in a while she'd glance back at Flynn to see if he'd left or not. She had been so busy with other tables that Flora had delivered Flynn's lunch to him.

Rose jotted down a large order for a table of six and collected their menus. As she walked behind the counter to grab color books and crayons for the little ones to pass the time, she noticed the booth, where Flynn had been sitting was empty. She couldn't explain the lonely, achy feeling she felt for a split second.

She thought to herself, *Rose, many young guys have stopped into the diner, smiled at you, and said a few sugar-coated lines. You've never had a problem brushing them off like a mosquito buzzing around your head. Why did this guy, this Flynn, stir up a whole new feeling in your gut?*

Flora tapped Rose's shoulder and said, "Rosie, we're busy today. Quit daydreaming and get to table #5 please. We have hungry customers."

Rose shook her dizzy head in an attempt to rid her mind of this brand new distraction, though not necessarily unwelcome.

"Give it a rest, Rose. There's a restaurant full of people," she whispered to herself, hoping afterward no one had witnessed her using a menu to fan her warm face.

"O---k, moving on." Rose wiped her hands on her apron and managed to finish out her shift for the day.

After she cleared the last dirty plates from the tables and counted her tips, she said good night to Patrick and walked out the front door.

It was a brisk May night with a cool breeze coming off Lake Superior. She walked quickly down Canal Street toward the bus stop as she did each evening after work.

"I don't think I ever got your name Miss....?," she heard someone say from behind her. Rose jumped in surprise and spun around.

"Flynn!", she yelled with obvious excitement.

He laughed, "You remember me? I have to say, I feel a little flattered," then smiling shyly Flynn continued, "After all, the diner was packed today! There had to have been several other admiring young men trying to vie for your attention. Much like myself."

Rose looked into his gentle eyes and replied to the question he had asked.

"Flynn, my name is Rose and it's very nice to meet you."

Despite the howling wind and gushing rain still hitting her car, Rose smiled at the memory. She knew that day she would fall in love with this man. Flynn wasn't like any guy. Flynn Mitchell was special. And he was taken from her only months after their magical wedding at the Rose

Garden here in Duluth. Oh, she was proud of her soldier, appropriately so. He served his country with unwavering dedication and pride. She admired this in him from day one. But she wished he could serve his country from the mainland, close to her. Selfish or not, it was the truth.

Rose's smile faded slowly as it typically did when her reality came back into sight. The dull ache behind her eyes had returned.

Taking hold of the clutch, Rose shifted the car into drive and started off on a wet, dark road out of the city, envisioning the route could lead her someplace far away.

Her mind wandered again, back to happy days.

CHAPTER 2

Flynn and Rose spent most days together, if only for a short time. He'd pop in to the diner for a burger or she'd visit him when he got home from a day of training at Fort Briggs. He was in the Army Reserves and worked as a heavy artillery mechanic. Rose was too shy to admit, but she deliberately planned her visits to his house right about when she knew he'd just be returning from the fort simply to catch a glimpse of him in his Army attire. *What was it about a man in a uniform?* It didn't hurt either that Flynn was in impeccable shape, had jet black hair and a smile that would send any girl over the edge. Best of all, he sure knew how to treat Rose well and she was pretty certain he loved her. Though, they had not spoken the words out loud just yet.

That is until June 19th, Rose's twenty-first birthday. Flynn had told her to dress up and be ready at 7:00 p.m. He was taking her *somewhere special.* Rose was on cloud nine as she sat primping in front of her bedroom mirror. Evie came into the room and watched quietly behind her smitten daughter.

"You know you haven't stopped smiling the entire time you've been curling your hair?" Rose turned around and looked at her mom and laughed at herself.

"Mom, that's not true. Quit teasing me," Rose replied. Though she knew Evie was right. It was a rare moment in a day when she was not thinking of Flynn.

"Well, either way, you look beautiful, honey," Evie complimented her while she fastened the last button of Rose's dress behind her neck. Rose stood up, running her hands down her body to smooth any last wrinkles in her dress.

She had taken her Saturday night's tips last weekend and splurged on a LBD (little black dress). Not the *clubbing kind,* that was NOT Rose's style. The dress she wore was classic. Sleeveless, simple black velvet with satin buttons up the back. She was twenty-one today and she wanted to look like a woman. Frankly, she wanted Flynn to look at her as one this evening.

When his car finally pulled up in front of the house at 7:00 p.m. sharp, she peeked out her bedroom window to see him strolling up the walkway wearing black dress pants and a buttoned up gray shirt. Along with his tanned skin and shining black hair, the sight of him made Rose weak. What was more, he was carrying a dozen long stem roses in his right hand.

"Oh, help me...." Rose could hardly breathe.

When Flynn saw her coming down the stairway, the feeling was obviously mutual. His jaw dropped when he saw her dressed in the body hugging dress, showing off her soft curves. As if no one was there, Flynn set the roses on the bench near the front door and walked toward her. He held his hands out to take hers and for a moment was completely speechless.

Finally clearing his throat, Philip piped up, "Umm Flynn, let's remember this beautiful, uhh, woman, is my daughter. And you will take good care of her this evening I presume?"

Flynn came back to life and Rose blushed in response to her father's interruption.

"Oh, uh, of course Mr. Reichert. We will be having dinner at the *JJ Astor.* I wanted Rose's birthday to be extra special. We can see all of Duluth and admire a sunset over Lake Superior. And don't worry, I would like to treat Rose to a glass of wine or champagne for her birthday, but I will stick with club soda for the evening," Flynn promised. He was a rare gentleman, and if the overprotective Philip's approving nod wasn't enough to prove it to Rose, their handshake was.

"Have a good time you two," Evie yelled as the couple walked out the front door.

Flynn and Rose were seated at *JJ Astor*, the fine dining restaurant above the Radisson Hotel. The restaurant rotated a full circle each hour so that the beautiful skyline of Duluth could be admired by the guests through the floor to ceiling windows.

What could be more romantic? Rose thought.

But when Flynn stood up to take her hand and asked her to slow dance, in the midst of fellow diners who were enjoying their entrées, she thought she must be starring in a movie. Elvis's *I Can't Help Falling in Love with You* came on in the background and suddenly Rose could see only Flynn in the whole room. The tables, chairs, servers, other couples sharing a meal — all of it had blurred into fuzzy clouds.

At song's end, Flynn's hands held Rose's face softly and his fingertips trickled down her neckline. He leaned in, breathing in her sweet scent. Finally, with a serious stare into her eyes, he said, "Rose, I love you. I know it's fast. I know you're young. I know the odds are against us." He paused and, for a moment, looked out the window at the large ships coming into the bay, his mind deep in thought. Then turning to her with glistening eyes, said, "I also know that I have never before been more sure of anything."

Rose, being a head shorter than Flynn, leaned up, kissed his chin and smiled. "I love you too, soldier."

The two danced to a second slow melody while men and women sitting at tables nearby sighed and smiled at the scene of young love in front of them.

FLYNN

Flynn and Marty were taking their usual morning jog at 0600 like they always did when they reported to Fort Briggs, Monday through Friday, without fail. The grounds provided a large, paved trail around its border. At this time of the morning the humidity of the Minnesota summer wasn't suffocating their lungs just yet. In fact, it was fairly enjoyable. The two buddies had been doing it for so long they were in good enough shape to keep a conversation while running their five miles.

"I don't know, Marty. I think I'm in trouble. This girl is something different. She stays on my mind day and night. Makes my heart beat out of my chest. In fact, since the moment I met her I've hardly noticed other women." Flynn clenched his jaw thinking of his date with Rose, their dance — their words. "Uggghhhh, I need a drink!"

"Good idea, let's grab a beer at Little Angie's Cantina after work tonight," Marty responded.

"No, I need some water. I'm dizzy. Damn, maybe we should quit talking about this girl and focus on the run." Flynn shook his head to clear the sultry thoughts of Rose out of his mind and concentrated on his steps and his timed breathing.

"Ha. Wow, Mitchell. I gotta meet this girl. Are you bringing her to the party on July third?" Marty asked, keeping up with Flynn, but showing no struggle with the cardio exercise.

"Yes, she is coming. Don't embarrass me, dude." Flynn's timer went off on his watch. Time to shower and report to duty.

CHAPTER 3

The diner was particularly busy this Friday evening. It was July 3rd and all citizens of the US were in celebration mode in anticipation of Independence Day. Canal Street was lined with American flags, kids were running down the boardwalk near Lake Superior waving sparklers in the air. Signs were posted on every corner with information of all the weekend's festivities and scheduled events.

Even the diner specials were *All-American*. A Ballpark frank piled high with chili and cheese for $4.50, fried chicken with mashed potatoes and gravy for $7.25 and for dessert—apple pie à la mode for $2.25. Rose had served up so many slices of pie she was certain she'd dream of the dessert all night.

At day's end her heart skipped a beat, her excitement boiling over as she thought about seeing Flynn in less than an hour.

"Fifty two minutes, but who's counting," she said to herself.

That evening there was a special 4th of July party being held in honor of the Fort Briggs soldiers and Flynn had asked Rose to accompany him. When she had finished wiping off the last table, she could hardly race out the door fast enough.

She yelled on her way out, "Bye Patrick, Happy 4th of July!"

"Bye Rosie! Be good," Patrick shouted, laughing at the young, giddy girl running out the door.

Rose raced down the sidewalk to the bus stop. To her relief the bus was waiting. Out of breath, she jumped on and took the first seat she could find.

Rose hurried through the evening of primping for the party. Flynn had told her it was an informal affair, but she wanted to make a good impression on his friends and fellow comrades. She cleaned up, washing her long blonde hair and shaving her legs smooth. A touch of perfume and mascara was all the make-up she wore besides a light lip gloss sometimes. She slipped on her white lace sundress and a simple pair of gold earrings.

When she heard the doorbell ring, she stepped into her red flats and charged down the stairs. "Bye Mom, Dad. Be home soon!" she called to the living room where her parents had been watching Seinfeld reruns.

She heard her dad reply sternly, "By soon you mean by midnight, Rose. We still make the rules here." Rose just smiled. She knew her dad had a hard time accepting that she had become an adult. He still thought of her as a nine-year-old little girl, his *angel cake*. So, she and Evie didn't make much of a fuss when he talked of rules and curfews. Of course, she respected her parents, but she had been a good kid and thus earned their trust.

The always-cheery Evie popped her head out from around the corner of the room.

"Hi Flynn. Can you come sit with us for the parade tomorrow?"

Flynn responded politely saying, "Oh I'm sorry Mrs. Reichert, but us soldiers are marching in the parade. Actually, leading it. It's gonna be a hot one with all our gear on. But thank you for the invite."

Flynn led Rose to his Black Chevy Impala and opened the door for her. His gaze left her with no doubt of his admiration for her. On the way to *Fort Briggs Memorial Park,* where the party was being held, Flynn and Rose discussed the events of their day. Rose told him she would have visions of apple pie and fried chicken dancing in her head that night after all the orders she had served that day.

Flynn laughed, saying, "there could be worse things to dream about. Sounds pretty great to me. I must be hungry."

He told her they had mostly taken the day off at Fort Briggs to practice marching for the parade and that it was actually a nice break from the typical grind.

At the party Flynn introduced Rose to his sergeant and many of his fellow soldiers. His best friend, Marty, was there with his girlfriend Collette.

"Wow Flynn, you were right, Rose is pretty," Marty teased, to which Flynn responded with a punch to Marty's gut. Collette and Rose greeted one another and decided they would sit together at the same table while *their soldiers* were called on stage.

The evening proceeded with a simple, but tasty meal of grilled cheeseburgers with all the fixings, potato salad and corn on the cob. There were also coolers filled with plenty of sodas, bottles of water and beer on hand for thirsty attendants trying to stay cool in the July heat.

On stage, the brass band lent to the feel of the evening with their patriotic tunes. US citizens mingled together — black, white, Asian, Hispanic, tall, short, male, female. All proud to be serving a country that had been founded so many years ago. The Army soldiers had several awards and honors to hand out and so the announcement was given to take a seat. Rose and Collette watched the ceremony proceed and smiled when Marty and Flynn were presented framed awards for each having served for ten full years. Their sergeant, that Rose had been introduced to, was awarded a plaque for his years of service and gave a touching speech that stirred up applause from all guests. The last song ending the night was *America The Beautiful* and all in attendance stood and watched fireworks overhead. A massive American flag flapped in the breeze above the stage. Rose could see in the way Flynn stood and the look on his face — the pride and love of his country he possessed. She knew then, looking at him in that moment, with his head held high and the warm light of the fireworks surrounding his silhouette, that she had fallen for him. She could imagine a future full of happiness for the two of them.

After the fireworks show was over and goodbyes had been said, Flynn offered his arm to Rose and like never before, she gladly took it. They

25

strolled slowly to his car, hand in hand.

"What an amazing party, Flynn. I honestly started to get teary-eyed observing the pride I see in all of you soldiers," Rose said with admiration. Flynn, still looking to the sky, simply replied, "It's our job. But a job we take on with extreme pride, yes." He then smiled at Rose and tried to lighten the mood a bit, "Listen Rose, can we go for a walk down on the pier before I take you home? It's still early." Rose happily agreed.

The moon was glowing white and shone down into the dark mirror of Lake Superior. The heat of the day had subsided and a comfortable, warm breeze replaced it. A few couples walked hand in hand on the boardwalk, while some stood out on the pier watching the ships come in. The lighthouse out on the farthest point of the inlet shined its beacon for all to see. Flynn talked more about his time in the Army Reserves, working at Fort Briggs and growing up in Duluth. Rose told him of her days of playing volleyball for the Duluth East volleyball team and graduating in the top fifteen of her class. She told him of summer trips her family took to small towns in central Minnesota that had captured her heart. How her family would always stay at quaint Bed & Breakfasts and how her dream was to own and run one someday.

"Sounds perfect, Rose. I can't imagine a more wonderful life, except one that had me there with you," Flynn told her, and meant it. When Rose stopped and turned toward him she noticed he was bent down on one knee and held a small box out to her. Rose could not believe her eyes at that moment. She was twenty-one years old, she and Flynn had only known and dated each other for less than two months, she lived with her parents and Marty had been staying with Flynn. NONE of this made sense.

Except when Flynn opened the box to reveal a sparkling, solitaire diamond ring and his beautiful green eyes stared into hers, how could she say no? And when he did ask, "Rose, will you be my wife?" she left no more than a second for him to ponder what her answer would be. She said "yes" and he picked her up in an embrace and swung her round in circles.

CHAPTER 4

Missing that moment desperately, tears welled up in the corners of Rose's eyes making it even that much more difficult to focus on the road in front of her. She thought of other women going through the same heartache and worry she was. Wives, mothers, sisters. Men too — husbands, fathers, brothers. What made it so complicated was that there were true heart swelling emotions involved in being married to a United States soldier. The pride in what he was doing for their country, for the people of their country, perfect strangers most of them. The gratitude to all soldiers, stationed on the homeland or overseas. There weren't enough thanks to be put into words.

But the unknown was what was sometimes unbearable. That feeling in the mornings when you are just opening your eyes, somehow forgetting what your reality is and it suddenly hits you like a boxing glove to the chest. It leaves you gasping for air and crouching down into a fetal position. Rose lived those mornings. Mostly during the first couple weeks after Flynn's deployment. Things had dulled some, but tonight she was feeling something different. A need to escape the grief and the loneliness. Flynn would hate to see her this way. Where was his strong wife? *Where?*

FLYNN

Flynn tossed and turned with nightmares hounding him and woke up in a cold sweat. He wondered why the assault of dreams of war tonight. One violent, gruesome vision to the next. Tossing his down comforter off his legs he rose out of bed, walking down the hall to the kitchen. The light from the refrigerator blinded him when he opened the door in search of orange juice. Grabbing the jug, not taking the time to pour the liquid into a glass, he took big gulps until there was nothing left. Sleepily shuffling to the garbage, he tossed the carton in. Why was this new terror keeping him from a solid few hours of sleep? It had been this way all week. At that moment, it became obvious, and he saw her angelic face as if she stood in front of him now. Rose. Marrying her. What if he had to leave her? Leave his *wife* behind, while he was sent to war. It was not unlikely, at least at some point, down the road. He was so busy setting up camp on cloud nine he didn't acknowledge this subconscious anxiety deep inside. "God, watch over her if I am called away. She is my life." Flynn's words caught in his throat as he said them out loud. Strangely though, he felt a relief and the last few hours were peaceful until the 5 a.m. alarm went off.

CHAPTER 5

Flynn and Rose were married September 18th in a small ceremony at the Rose Garden on Lake Superior. The Rose Garden was a picturesque venue for many wedding ceremonies. As one would imagine, rose bushes revealing blossoms of scarlet red, baby blanket pink and snowy white, graced the green grasses. Intricate mazes of wintergreen boxwood weaved through the gardens while fragrant lilac trees leaned over restful granite benches. The sound of trickling waters from outdoor water fountains gave the feeling of being in a tropical location; Lake Superior teasing an oceanic body of water.

Rose wore a long ivory dress, made of antique lace and her hair was loosely pinned up on the sides. Flynn stood proud, handsome in his Army dress uniform. Marty and Collette stood up for the couple under a small white gazebo while they read their vows. When Flynn took the folded paper from his jacket pocket, where he had carefully written his promises, a gust of wind off Lake Superior stole his words, written so carefully on white notebook paper, right from his hand. All in attendance watched the page fly out so far toward Lake Superior, it began to look like a small white dove in the sky. Rose looked at Flynn with worry in her eyes.

Flynn held her hands and winked. Straight from his heart he looked at his bride and said to her, "My beautiful Rose. The most beautiful rose to grace this garden today. Since I locked eyes with you, there was no one else in the room. I had spent many years as a bachelor searching for the right one. The right woman to baby, to spoil, to protect, to take care of. After getting to know you, though still willing to do all those things for you, I see the strong woman you already are, with a mind for what you want and a passion that drives you. An energy and a thirst for life that is so refreshing to witness. You're a kid at heart but have an old soul. You're fascinated with the little things, the simple things. All of these things about you have caused me to fall in love with you. Making you happy and bringing your dreams to life is my forever vow."

With crystal tears lacing her long eyelashes, Rose kissed him and the couple was pronounced husband and wife.

That evening they toasted each other surrounded by close friends and family under a star filled sky.

Rose leaned her head into the crook of her new husband's neck and breathed in his familiar scent.

"We did it," she whispered with a small smile forming on her face. Flynn looked at her, right into those crystal blue eyes he loved so much and answered, "You're stuck with me I guess, Rose Mitchell." After Marty finished his speech, the couple clinked their champagne glasses together and shared a kiss. Rose blushed when the traditional applause from their guests followed.

The September day was unseasonably warm and the few tables set up at the Rose Garden were lit with several pillar candles glowing in large, glass lanterns. Twinkling strings of white lights hung in nearby trees and over rose bushes. They dined on one of Flynn's favorites for dinner, pan-fried Walleye pike. A local catering company set up in a white tent and served other dishes such as a Wild Rice Pilaf, Sautéed Broccoli Rabe and a Feta and Pomegranate Salad. Champagne flowed for hours. Despite Philip and Evie's concern, Rose noticed the two several times watching their daughter, their pride and joy, with admiration written on their faces.

"Mom, Dad, thank you so much for everything. I couldn't have hoped for a more perfect day." Philip hugged his daughter tight. "Aww angel cake, I admit I was concerned with your haste in planning this wedding. I didn't understand the rush but seeing you so truly happy is my favorite thing in this whole world. And you do have yourself a great guy here." Philip shook

Flynn's hand firmly, an unsaid respect evident as the two smiled at each other. Evie walked up, fixing Rose's veil and agreed.

"You look at this man like he hung the moon, Rosalie." And then turning toward her new son-in-law, Evie said, "And I think he would do it for you too, Rose. Thank you Flynn. I know you'll take good care of her." Flynn nodded, smiling, fighting back emotion. "Always, Mrs. Reichert."

The glowing new couple thanked their guests and left the celebration early. They were spending their wedding night at the Old Rittenhouse Inn, an hour's drive from Duluth, in Bayfield, Wisconsin.

When their car pulled up to the beautiful, Victorian Bed & Breakfast, Rose sighed, "Oh, I just love inns like this Flynn. How did you know?"

"I just had a hunch," he replied, winking. Rose continued gazing up at the large, three- story inn with a full wraparound porch, rocking chairs facing out toward Lake Superior.

"As you know, I've dreamed of owning an inn for years. Something about them always made me intrigued, made me wonder what kind of people had been through the front door, how they had spent their time while relaxing, dining, sharing memories. I somehow wanted to be the one who made them feel like family or friends while they stayed. I wanted to make the inn my own, put my special touches into it. But not one quite as extravagant as this. A smaller two-story with a covered porch and bench swing, set right on Main Street in a small, quaint town where everyone knows each other. I'd greet tourists with freshly brewed coffee and homemade cookies when they arrived. And I'd have a little backyard garden, not too big because I don't like to weed much, but I'd plant herbs and a few vegetable plants — just enough to cook meals for my guests. And maybe some flowers, so I could snip a few to display in vases throughout the rooms and on the big dining room table. Oh, and when they were to check out—", Rose stopped, suddenly realizing she was really rambling on. "I'm sorry Flynn! I sure get carried away with my crazy dreams, don't I?" She looked away, blushing a bit.

Flynn laughed but looked at Rose with more love in his eyes for her than she'd ever seen before that moment. "Rosebud, your passion and your imagination are what I love most about you. Well, that AND how breathtakingly beautiful you look in that wedding dress. Let's go check in and relax with a glass of champagne shall we?" Flynn suggested, smiling, as he escorted his new bride to their suite.

FLYNN

"Take cover, another ambush coming in!" Flynn heard his commanding officer call out to their battalion. It was dark. Pitch dark. The color of ink, except for the few bright explosions overhead. Deafening loud blasts shook the ground and threatened to pop Flynn's eardrums. Blindingly bright bursts of flame lit the black canvas sky above. In a strange contrast from the dry, hot desert, it was cold and damp in the trenches Flynn hunkered down in. This would typically be a welcome escape from the feverish daily temperatures. Not necessarily an appreciated detail when your life is flashing before your eyes.

"Marty, what the hell is going on?" Flynn yelled out, confused and crippled with fear. "Marty! Where are you? I can't see a damn thing!" Flynn could see nothing in front of him. His head was pounding with each crashing boom overhead. He put his hands, cold and crusted with mud, up to his forehead. His fingers were ice cold and trembling. Flynn prayed, prayed this wouldn't be how things would end for him. His heart beat out of his chest and he wanted to cry out in sheer panic. "No training prepares you for the *terror* of war," he realized suddenly or had he said it out loud? There was no one there to answer. Or *was there* someone? How was he to know? He felt completely and utterly alone in this trench watching the sky above speckled with deadly fireworks hitting too close.

"Marty? Sanchez? Collins? Is anyone here?" Flynn stood up and attempted to walk through the bumpy dug-up cavity in the earth. He stumbled time and time again. After what felt like hours of struggling forward, tripping, crawling, searching for anyone, he gave up. Flynn laid down flat in the frigid mud, hoping desperately to see the light of day soon. Behind his closed eyelids the hot sting of fresh tears began. Flynn's mind was whirling out of control and suddenly everything went still.

He could see the image of a woman. The most beautiful woman. The fog in front of her angelic face cleared and there she was, as lovely as ever. Her skin, a milky cream color, the tendrils of her long hair, golden blonde, floated in a light breeze. Her stare held his, and then she smiled, the most infectious smile he had known, and he reached for her.

"Rosebud. Ahhh, my sweet Rose — you are my happy place."

He ran his hands through her silky, soft hair and lightly caressed her cheek. All that he wanted was to hold her close. She let him.

The terror of war forgotten — the nightmare fading away.

His new wife in his arms; nothing more to fear.

CHAPTER 6

S un rays shined through their window far earlier than the couple had wanted to rise. But the sound of chirping birds outside and the smell of coffee and fragrant bacon coaxed Flynn and Rose slowly to their feet. They were given the choice to dine out on the veranda, to which they agreed happily. A table was set with hot coffee, two fluted glasses of orange juice, two plates with strips of bacon, a raspberry stuffed french toast and fried breakfast potatoes seasoned with thyme and rosemary. Maple syrup, butter and powdered sugar were set in the center of the table, each in its own dainty serving dish.

Rose laid her napkin on her lap, took a sip of steaming coffee and stared out at the lake. The sun was catching the small ripples, causing diamonds to glisten across the water. Flynn took a bite of the thick French toast and, with obvious delight, said "Wow, I've never tasted anything like this before, Rose. Try it!" He cut a piece for her and offered his fork. She too, slowly chewed to savor the taste. "Mmmm, I am going to try to copy this recipe when we get home," she said, slicing another square.

Flynn's mind had wandered back to his nightmare of last night, but he pushed the thoughts away. Nothing was going to ruin this day, their first day as husband and wife.

"What do you want to do today? We have the whole day and I want you to decide how we spend it," Flynn offered.

Rose smiled, "I don't care what we do Flynn. As long as the day is spent with you, then it's a perfect day."

After breakfast they decided to take a stroll through Bayfield. There were several shops to browse through. A candy store smelling of sweet homemade taffy, caramel apples and buttery popcorn lured in sidewalk traffic. A few shops sold necessities that tourists may have forgotten to pack for their trip to Bayfield, such as beach towels, umbrellas, sunscreen, phone chargers and bottles of water. Others displayed beautifully painted artwork, while far more just sold Midwestern souvenirs — traveling coffee mugs with an imprint of *I love Bayfield* on the front or a sweatshirt with the simple, *Lake Superior,* written in bold font. Whichever you were drawn to, every shop was filled with eager shoppers by ten o'clock that morning.

Flynn and Rose walked down the boardwalk without a care in the world. It felt so good to have the day to themselves. "Mmmm, don't you love this time of year, Rosebud?" Flynn said, closing his eyes and breathing in the crisp fall air. It was such a perfect day. The two meandered for hours. Spotting a bench overlooking the lake, Rose suggested, "Why don't we take a seat and visit for a while, hon? The sunshine feels so good and ships atop the blue waters look like a postcard." Flynn sat down on the bench and after Rose sat next to him he grabbed her feet and set them on his lap.

"What are you doing?" she laughed. Flynn unzipped her cute but impractical heeled boots. He knew after walking up and down the streets of Bayfield, her feet were probably sore. "Giving my wife's feet a rest and a little massage." He slipped each boot off and softly massaged each with his large hands. Rose looked around at a few people walking by, staring. She laughed, "You're goofy, Flynn. But ya know, this does feel good." The two sat for a while laughing and visiting. They talked about where they might go on trips someday, what they might name children should they ever be blessed with them, which movies were their favorites and if they had broken any bones as kids. They talked and talked half the day away, ships still sailing out of sight and new ships and sailboats coming into view. It was a perfect way to spend their first day as husband and wife.

After a light lunch of sliced cheese, crackers and a cup of diced watermelon, Rose suggested taking a drive to visit a winery she had heard about. Rose loved a good glass of wine, though having been so young, she hadn't had the chance to visit any wineries and the romance of it was intriguing to her. Visiting where the fruit was harvested and made into wine made sipping a glass of it that much more appealing.

This particular winery was an apple orchard that produced apple wines. The taste-testing took place in what looked like an old, red barn. The inside had been transformed into a wonderful place filled with hundreds of bottles of wines, many varieties. There were tables filled with tasty items that paired well with the wines. Samples were given out so that the customers could make an informed decision before purchasing bottles to take home. Of course, these weren't top shelf, but Rose thought their apple wines were some of the best she had tasted. After deciding the apple rhubarb was her favorite, Flynn purchased three bottles to take home.

Needing a nap before going out for dinner, Flynn and Rose made their way back to the Old Rittenhouse Inn, their home for the weekend. Rose held onto Flynn's arm as they strolled up the walkway.

"This sure is a beautiful place to stay, don't you think Flynn?" Rose asked, admiring the impressive building once again.

"It's amazing, Rosebud. I'm so glad you like it. I thought of the Old Rittenhouse when you said you loved old inns. My mom and her group of friends used to make the trip to Bayfield once a year for their annual apple festival. That's where I remembered the winery, too. Mam looked forward to her *girls weekend* every fall. I'd hear her on the phone talking with Jill or Beth, discussing what each would bring for snacks and cocktails for the room. She'd scribble little notes and head to the grocery store." Flynn looked at his feet as he continued walking up the path, suddenly deep in thought. Rose sensed the memory made him miss his mother.

"I bet I would've loved her, Flynn," she said, rubbing his arm in comfort.

Flynn looked at her with a sad smile. "You sure would have, love. You two would have been good friends, I imagine." Reaching for the heavy mahogany front door, Flynn opened it widely for his wife. "After you, Mrs. Mitchell."

"Thank you, handsome."

Their pillow top antique bed was exceptionally comfortable and sleep sounded good, but the couple didn't sleep after they laid down, though neither was sorry they missed a nap.

"How do you see your future, Flynn? I mean what dreams do you have? Goals? Aspirations? It's not all just about me, ya know." Rose rested her head on the down pillow while staring at her new husband. Flynn leaned up on his elbows and thought about her question.

"Before I met you, Rose, my plan was to finish out my career at Fort Briggs, retire from there when I was about forty five and then build houses. I enjoy mechanics, but carpentry is a passion I have as well. Wouldn't it be wonderful to find the perfect place to transform into your inn and after I retire from the military I could do projects there. Whatever needed doing. Build a picket fence around your garden or build a shed in the backyard for my mower and fishing boat. I'm not so bad at building furniture either — made a few dressers and tables with my dad. He had a knack for carpentry too. It became more of a woodworking hobby out in the garage after he was older, but I learned a lot from Pops."

Rose slid closer and kissed Flynn's bare shoulder. "You're so beautiful, Flynn."

"Rosebud, guys can't be beautiful. Guys are handsome, masculine, dashing, rugged. Not beautiful." He teased her.

Looking into his eyes, Rose replied, "You are to me."

That evening the two had reservations at Landmark Restaurant which was right there at their inn. The lights in the restaurant were dimmed and flickering of candlelight was on each table covered in white linens. The sound of crystal glasses clinking together and silverware against china could be heard a bit, but the highlight was the gentleman playing music at the grand piano in the corner of the room. The sound was out of a dream. Light tunes like *Somewhere over the Rainbow* and *Unchained Melody* were among the pieces Rose recognized.

As they were seated, Rose looked across the table at Flynn and nodded toward the piano. "You're gonna ask me to dance again tonight, aren't you?"

Flynn winked. "I just may."

Greeting them, a server brought two leather-bound menus and a wine list.

"May I start you off with a drink this evening?" the young man asked politely.

Flynn waited for Rose to decide. Scanning the wine list, she decided.

"I will have a glass of the Woodbridge Chardonnay, please."

"A brandy, neat, for me." Flynn chose.

"Very good. I will be right back with those."

"Did you ever travel much when you were growing up, Flynn?" Rose asked while she looked out the window as if there were endless roads to choose from out in the dark world.

"We did a bit. Nothing really extravagant though. My parents and I took a road trip to Yellowstone when I was nine. I'll never forget those mountains and the bison roaming the plains. Such an untouched place. It was one of my favorite memories. I have a photo album my mom made years ago of the trip. I'll have to dig that out and show you."

The server returned with their drinks, setting each on square cocktail napkins in front of them.

"Have you decided on what you would like for dinner yet?" he asked.

"What do you recommend?" Flynn asked, after taking a sip of his brandy.

"Ahhhh, I would suggest the Blackened Ribeye Steak served with a luxurious Parsnip Purée and Glazed Brussel Sprouts or the Lobster Risotto which features large flakes of lobster meat, sweet peas and micro greens. They are both my favorite and the most requested on the menu."

"Rose?" Flynn looked at her.

"Let's each order one of those meals and share. They sound so delicious, it's hard to choose," she laughed. "I'm hungry. It's been hours and hours since our little lunch."

"Wonderful. I will get this order in. You won't be disappointed with your choice."

"Mmmm, this wine is wonderful." Rose took a satisfying gulp and swirled the tart liquid in her mouth. "So, what are we toasting to? Our good fortune of meeting each other? Falling in love, almost at first sight? To our exciting future full of endless possibilities?"

"Yes." Flynn replied, holding his glass up to her.

Though the lovely weekend away had been unforgettable, Flynn and Rose knew it was time to travel back to Duluth the next morning.

Rose would be moving into Flynn's house when they got back.

CHAPTER 7

The rain continued pelting the windshield with unwavering repetition, the wipers keeping up at full speed. Despite making the road a little harder to see, the somber gray clouds and deluge felt appropriate for Rose's mood, but it was strangely ok. It felt so good to just be alone, driving away from it all, even though there was no real escape. Thinking back to her and Flynn's whirlwind of a love story was both heartwarming and made her shiver with an emptiness. It seemed her emotions these days were always contradicting each other.

Spotting a Starbucks up ahead, she pulled her car into the exit, suddenly craving some caffeine. A bathroom break, a warm vanilla latte for the road — give the rain a chance to subside perhaps? Rose hadn't any intentions of turning around toward home just yet.

Despite the less than perfect weather, a long line of customers at Starbucks waiting to place their orders was something you could always count on. Rose expected no less and took her place in line. Though the pungent smell of freshly brewed coffee with a touch of sweet caramel was thick in the air, the palpable feeling of agitation was even thicker yet.

Thirsty people, impatient and in a rush continued entering the coffee shop, filing into the line behind Rose. She noticed a middle-aged man wearing an expensive Burberry sweater checking the time on his Rolex watch, rolling his eyes. She saw two young women to her left in exercise attire, tapping their Brooks clad feet on the tile floor complaining to one another. As if their coffee craving trumped that of the remaining people in line. It was really becoming crowded and exceedingly loud. Rose loved a vanilla latte as much as the next guy, but her anxiety was returning in full force. The decision to ditch her spot in line to make a beeline back to her car through the rain was a split second one, but she felt an immediate calm when she got back in the driver's seat. *I'm still convinced city life is not for me,* she told herself.

Turning the key in the ignition and shifting her car into drive, Rose recalled the day she and Flynn had purchased this vehicle for her and the conversation they had shared on the way home.

CHAPTER 8

Mr. and Mrs. Flynn Mitchell were back to full-blown reality two days after they were married. Flynn was working full time at Fort Briggs on special training. He didn't understand why the new combat drills, but he knew there was no lack of surprises when it involved the United States military.

Rose continued working at the diner. After such a wonderful escape out of the city and their stay at the Old Rittenhouse Inn, city life just seemed to get more and more stifling. Lately, Canal Park had gotten busier with back-to-back traffic, drivers honking and swearing at each other. Daily she could hear the blaring of police sirens, which meant the authorities had been called to the scene of an accident or to a disturbance at one of the new bars that had become ever so popular down the block from the diner. Several times she had spotted police arresting men or women out front.

One couldn't really call Duluth a large city. The population was less than 100,000, there were no skyscrapers, the infrastructure of the city was fairly basic. Perhaps, over time things had just changed there. For Rose, anyway, it didn't have the same feeling anymore. The small diner she worked at had become an out of place retreat among the new, loud, wild and crowded dance clubs. The changes just didn't sit well with Rose. She realized she wasn't what people might call an average twenty-one year old. Many her age frequented these new clubs often. Not Rose. In truth, she didn't even feel all that comfortable walking to the bus stop anymore after work. Flynn said it was high time they bought her a car.

That evening they took a trip to the used car lot up on Miller Hill. Flynn let Rose do the wheeling and dealing and they ended up leaving the lot with a used, but reliable Ford Focus. On the ride home with Rose at the wheel, of course, she said to Flynn, "I'm really getting frustrated with how Canal Street has become lately. I suppose it has come on slowly, but I feel myself dreading going to work each morning."

Flynn understood, but asked, "How do you mean?"

Rose thought, and answered after a minute, "The view out the diner windows isn't the same. Customers no longer are looking at just a beautiful view of the pier and the lift bridge and people meandering around the park. It used to be that you'd see families sitting on blankets having a picnic or throwing a frisbee to their dogs. It seems, of late, the view is mostly of car accidents and hurried, angry people rushing here or there. Not to mention down right rude in the process. Bars and nightclubs keep popping up on every corner and attract what my grandparents might call *riff raff*. I can't say I even feel safe walking out the door of the diner after my shift ends."

Flynn rubbed her shoulder to comfort her and responded, "Why don't you look for a different job? There are job openings all over Duluth, Rose. Colette told Marty they're looking for workers at that clothing store she works at."

Rose sighed heavily, "I don't know if it's my job or just where we reside and the ever changing world we are living in here. I just want a change. A life less hectic I guess," she glanced over at Flynn, "Tall order huh?"

Flynn pondered her words and finally replied, "Well…we can always look for other places to live. I can commute to Fort Briggs. We don't have to be *right in* Duluth. I know you are close with your parents, but I don't think an hour's drive from them will make much of a difference. My parents have passed away leaving the house to me. That can be sold. If you aren't happy Rosebud, let's find some sunshine that will make you bloom."

Rose smiled at his analogy. Flynn was always trying to make her laugh, but in truth, he had a way of making her feel better. And even with something as big as uprooting and moving to a different town, neighborhood, house, Flynn made it seem easily possible.

Rose, on the other hand, tended to do the opposite. She usually made a mountain out of a molehill. I guess they evened each other out.

"Really? Are you serious? I think it would make me, *US*, really happy and less frazzled, less stressed to live in a smaller town. One without the constant sounds of honking horns, police car sirens, and general chaos. I love Duluth, don't get me wrong, but I think I'd be ok with just visiting for a weekend here and there and then going home," Rose affirmed.

"Then it's settled. We will put the house up for sale first thing and begin the hunt for our new home," Flynn announced, clapping his hands together.

CHAPTER 9

After the decision had been made to start looking for other towns to move to, Rose could hardly contain her excitement. She searched listings online almost daily. Nothing was jumping out at her though. Flynn had a rare day off one Tuesday in December and they decided to venture out and about for the day to scope out some other nearby towns in Minnesota. It was a pleasant winter day. Not like some in Minnesota — cold, frigidly so, and road conditions that were made for snowmobiles alone. This day was cool, but comfortable with just mittens and a light coat worn.

Rose and Flynn grabbed a couple of warm cups of coffee from the diner before leaving the city. Anxious for what was to come, Rose couldn't stop talking.

"Don't you love Christmas time, Flynn? It's such a magical time. Mmmmmm. It gives me warm fuzzies all over." She reached down to turn the radio on in hopes of something festive to listen to. Bing Crosby's voice smoothly sang *I'll be home for Christmas* and Rose's face lit up.

Flynn winked at her, "Rose, you're like a little kid. So much giddiness and anticipation of the simple treasures in life." He smiled and sipped on his coffee, enjoying the morning with his girl. "So, I know you saw a house near Grand Rapids that looked appealing and in our price range. Should we start there?"

"Yes, that sounds good to me. This particular house was a very affordable asking price, but it may need a little more work than we are willing to put into it," she answered, unsure.

"Ahhh, we want a place that we can make our own, transform into the inn you've been dreaming of, right? A little hard work will be good for us. Let's keep that in mind," the always positive thinking Flynn, answered.

"Yes, you're right. Let's wait and see. Plus, there are four others that looked promising too. One in Little Falls, one in Nisswa, and two in Lanesboro. Though, Lanesboro is quite a hike for today. Maybe we leave that trip for a weekend we can do an overnight?" Rose suggested.

"Yes, I think so. We can take our time then. How about after the first of the year? There isn't usually a lot going on during that time. It would be a nice, mini vacation for us."

"You mean you aren't taking me to Hawaii this winter?" Rose teased.

"Maybe." Flynn kept her guessing.

Continuing on the road toward Grand Rapids, Rose listened to The Carpenters sing *Merry Christmas Darling* over the radio and watched as tiny snowflakes fell from the sky. Just the type of soft snowfall that disintegrated when the flakes hit the pavement. There wasn't much for snow on the ground, the unseasonably warm temps weren't allowing for much accumulation just yet. But the sparkle of a few blowing in the air was breathtaking. Rose was happy. Sickenly so.

After about an hour's drive they saw a large sign up ahead with *The town of Grand Rapids* in large letters. Rose had been through the town several times but had never really spent any time there. Certainly not to look at houses.

"Ok, Rosebud, what's the street address? Pull it up on your phone, would you?" Flynn asked.

Rose fiddled with her iPhone, found the address and punched it into the GPS. Siri's monotone voice instructed when to turn next. After a few stop lights, left hand turns and a roundabout they were on Klondyke Rd.

"Ok hon, in a half mile the house should be on our right. 207 Klondyke Rd." Rose was anxious to see the two story turn of the century house she had seen listed online. In the photos it was clear that the house needed some TLC, but that was part of the adventure, right?

When they pulled the car to the side of the road and Flynn shifted it into park, the two looked out the car window and sighed. Not a good sigh either, like a *this is it* sigh or even a *there's so many possibilities* sigh. This was a simultaneous *well that was a waste of a trip* sigh.

"Rosebud, is this what the photos looked like online? It's…Spooky," Flynn admitted. Even in broad daylight, he was right. The place was that out of an episode of *The Addams Family*. A large, very old house was what they knew they would be seeing. What they didn't expect was a large, very old, abandoned house. One that had been left to the rodents long ago. The roof and siding had been peeling and several pieces of siding were hanging by crooked nails, the front screen door was hanging wide open and in an upstairs window there was a large crack and the gray curtain from inside the room was dangling out the window — the broken glass shredding the fabric with each gust of wind. With barely a dusting of snow, it was visible the grass hadn't been cut in years.

The disappointment took the wind out of Rose's sails. "Do you think someone listed the property years ago and just has never taken it off the market? Or is that even legal, given the condition it's in? I don't understand."

Flynn grabbed her hand. "Well, it certainly makes sense that the price was so attractive. Some folks would purchase the property, bulldoze it and start fresh."

"Eh. That's not the way I envisioned doing it."

"Ahh well, Rose. We still have lots of time to check out other places. What's the rush?"

Rose knew there wasn't a rush, really, but she was so anxious and ready to begin this chapter. After all, it had been since she was a little girl that she dreamed of this.

"Come on now, Rosebud. Turn on your Christmas tunes and let's move on to the next town. Keep the faith."

"You're right. Ok, Nisswa next. There's a little bit newer place a couple blocks from Main Street. Perfectly set in town, but out of town just enough." Rose's spirits were rising a bit.

"That's my girl."

The rainstorm was keeping a steady rhythm with no signs of letting up still. Rose leaned forward and looked up to the sky. It was a strange storm. No thunder, nor lightning, the wind was minimal, but this rain wouldn't give up. When she was a kid she remembered her mom telling her God's bathtub was overflowing. She laughed. It was best to make light of things, she had learned. Flynn taught her that.

She thought again of their day in December, with high hopes of finding their forever home. All three properties weren't what they were looking for. The house in Grand Rapids was that of nightmares, even in broad daylight. The layout of the house in Nisswa was not set up for a transition into an inn and the house in Little Falls had been close to the Freeway and far from Main Street. Nothing particularly wrong with it, but not *their place*.

Maybe, she thought, this whole fantasy of owning a sweet little inn, was a stupid idea. Though, she knew she'd never let it go. Something told her she needed to keep hoping.

CHAPTER 10

The good news was that the house had an offer within one week and for their asking price. The bad news was that even though they had been looking during all their bits of free time, the search for a new home proved fruitless so far. They wanted a new town, a new home, a new chapter, but were finding nothing.

Rose, being Rose, had become agitated. Flynn reassured her they had only been looking for three months.

"Rosebud, these things don't happen overnight. We want to be patient and make sure we feel at home in our new town, make sure it's just the right fit for us." Though they had accepted the offer of the sale on the house, the new owners weren't set to move in until May 1st.

Rose agreed there was no rush. And really, why would she want to make a rash decision about something so important. Flynn was right…as usual.

That evening Flynn and Rose were invited to her parents' house for Sunday dinner. Rose carried in a sour cream and raisin pie, Dad's favorite, while Flynn held her close on the icy walkway. She couldn't help feeling a twinge of guilt in her stomach. They had planned to tell her parents about their moving. She wasn't overly excited about the reaction she knew was coming. Flynn sat with Philip in the living room watching the remainder of the Vikings football game. Rose helped her mom in the kitchen with dinner.

Evie opened the oven to check the turkey, hot steam escaping. While Rose started mashing the potatoes, she finally got up the nerve to spill their news.

"Mom, Flynn and I are looking at relocating," she swallowed and continued. "We want to find a smaller town to live in. We don't intend to move far away; don't worry about that. But we both feel like it's something we really want."

Evie pushed the roaster pan back in the oven, whispering to herself, "another twenty minutes I think."

She looked up at her daughter and replied, "Rose, don't look so guilty. Were you stressed for days to break the news to us?"

Rose blushed and shrugged her shoulders. Evie knew her too well to deny the fact. Evie smiled at her daughter and continued, "Your dad and I have always known that you've yearned to live in a small town. We saw how you lit up when we took you on summer vacations to central Minnesota lake towns, like Crosby, Crosslake, Nisswa. And I've noticed you haven't been yourself lately. Look, Dad and I don't want you to leave, but we certainly want your happiness. But make no mistake, we will demand frequent visits from you and Flynn." They both laughed and agreed that would be a must.

Rose was so surprised by her mom's reaction to the news that she had almost forgotten she was mashing the potatoes. "Oops, sorry Mom. They're a bit thin. I guess I wasn't paying attention," she admitted. "But do you really mean it? You're ok with our plans?"

Evie confirmed, "Of course, Rosalie! We love you and want you and Flynn to happily travel your own path. And don't worry about the potatoes. We'll call them a mashed potato purée like the fancy restaurants do."

Rose smiled but felt such a twinge in her heart. She knew her mom. She knew that supporting the idea of Rose moving away wasn't something that was easy to do. But her love for her daughter was greater than pushing her to live in a city she no longer felt connected to.

"Ok, now go set the table while I pull this turkey out of the oven, would you?" Evie prompted.

Dinner ended up being completely relaxed and enjoyable. Flynn gave

Rose reassuring glances across the table while her parents helped them brainstorm about nice communities in Minnesota to live in. Again, Rose was flabbergasted by her parents' understanding and genuine eagerness to help. She knew in her heart that moving didn't mean she wasn't just a call or even a car ride away.

They finished the evening with coffee and the sour cream and raisin pie Rose had made. Philip told her (as he did *every* time she brought it) that it was, by far, the best pie she had ever made. But it always brought a smile to Rose's face.

She and Flynn bundled up in their mittens and hats. Before leaving, Rose gave her parents both a hug. "Bye you two. Thank you for a wonderful night and thank you…just for everything." Flynn too, gave a hand shake and said good night.

As she and Flynn walked down the steps to his car parked out front, Flynn gave her a side glance and said, "See, I told you it would be ok, didn't I?"

Rose took in a sigh of relief, "How do you always know when it's all gonna be ok?" Flynn squeezed her hand and she held his tight.

"Don't ever leave me, Flynn," Rose said without thinking.

"Rose? I would never! How can you say such a thing?" Flynn responded feeling like he'd taken a punch to the gut.

Rose shook her head, "I didn't mean, ugh, like divorce me or leave me for another woman. I don't know what I mean." She sighed heavily. "I just want to hold you tight and never let you go. Just stay like this forever. Do you understand? I guess I maybe don't even understand what I'm saying, so how can you?" Rose laughed, but there was no humor in its tone.

But Flynn did understand. Completely. He turned her toward him, held her close and after kissing her softly replied, "I do. It's my wish every day."

CHAPTER 11

The next morning Flynn's phone rang. He reached over to the night stand and answered it. Something in the way he was speaking to the person on the other end made Rose's stomach feel hollow. Her heart began to race. *Who was Flynn talking to? And why the serious, hushed tones?* When he hung up he dressed quickly and quietly in his work uniform then turned to Rose, "That was sergeant Nelson. We are being called in for a special meeting at 0800."

Rose felt faint. "Did he say what is being discussed?"

"No, not exactly, but I sensed some urgency in his tone," Flynn replied, now looking away from Rose's stare.

It shook her to the core when her husband showed any sign of worry.

Rose thought back to the Sunday before they were married. Flynn had packed a picnic and asked her to go for a walk near Gooseberry Falls. She was excited for another adventure with her fiancé. Rose picked daisies and honeysuckle that grew wild between cracks on the trail and pointed out the beautiful rushing waterfalls after each turn they made. She hadn't noticed right away that Flynn had been unusually *business-like* that day. It wasn't until they found a place to lay their picnic blanket, that Rose could sense Flynn's uneasiness.

She had asked, "Flynn, is something wrong? I'm used to you being the more jovial one. More energetic than a five year old after eating a bag of Skittles. More talkative than my mother after a couple glasses of wine. What is troubling you?"

Flynn knelt down on the red and white gingham blanket and began unpacking their basket. As he set out their plates, forks, napkins and a dish of Waldorf salad Rose had made, he finally sat down.

With his hands reaching for Rose he said, "Honey. Come sit by me. I want to talk to you."

Rose's heart was beating out of her chest at that moment.

"Flynn? What's wrong?"

"Nothing, Rosebud. But we do need to talk." He held her hands as he continued. "You need to understand that it is possible, even likely in the course of our married life, that I will be called to duty at some time or another. It could be a short mission--three, maybe six months? Or it could be twelve to eighteen months. Generally, that is the longest time they will require us troops to be deployed. Either way, I want you to understand this when agreeing to marry a US soldier. We can't say 'No thanks' when we get the call. And we don't want to either, as hard as that is to say. Leaving you would be the hardest thing I have ever done, but you need to understand that I serve our country and go where they need me."

Rose let go of Flynn's hands and stood up. Still holding her napkin, she walked to the railing overlooking the Falls, grabbing on to the worn wood to steady herself. She watched the rushing of white water crash down the rocky mounds and surge down the river's bend, no way to stop it. Nature's course. It was so beautiful and so--dangerous and unkind at the same time.

After several minutes, she turned back to Flynn.

"Flynn, I want to marry you. And that means in good times and bad. I love you and what's more, I will be *proud* to be your wife." Rose saw a relief in Flynn's eyes. He had smiled and pulled her down on his lap, nuzzling her neck until she giggled.

Rose remembered enjoying the day. Though, admittedly, the memory of that conversation gave her a bitter stomach ache, a festering reminder of what could come to pass.

After what seemed like several minutes, Rose shook the flashback from her mind and sat in silence.

Forcing himself to appear calm, Flynn offered her a happy-go-lucky, "Have a good day now Rosebud. I'm sure the meeting will involve some boring information from overseas. It's just protocol, as they say in the military."

Rose could only respond with a kiss on the cheek and a soft good-bye. She was in a daze and felt a certain panic building up in her chest. She had heard some of the Army Reserves were being called in to Afghanistan to assist with special forces. Patrolling the warzone had gotten to be a job that required thousands more troops be sent over.

Rose watched out her window as Flynn drove away and she said a prayer out loud, "Please God, don't send my guy…"

Rose's shift at the diner went by slowly, which made it that much harder for Rose to not worry about Flynn's meeting. Something felt wrong in her chest, sour in her stomach. She just had a feeling that wasn't sitting right. She wrote orders down that she didn't remember writing, she brought a bowl of clam chowder to a big hungry truck driver who had ordered the double cheeseburger special and the cheeseburger went to the little elderly lady who had requested the soup. Rose's brain was somewhere else.

Patrick finally asked, "Rosie, what is going on? You are walking around here like a zombie. Customers are actually staring you down. Are you ok?"

"Yea, Patrick, you're fine. I mean I'm fine. I guess I'm just tired. Don't worry."

Patrick knew Rose enough to know she was *not* fine. Something was troubling her. That was very obvious. But what? He hoped it wasn't something with Flynn.

After an early dinner rush, she was out the door and speeding home. She ran in the front door, threw her coat on the floor, not bothering to hang it up, and yelled for Flynn.

"Flynn, hon, are you home?" She ran up the stairs peeking in their bedroom. "Flynn, are you in here?" When she saw Flynn looking at their wedding photos on her dresser she gasped.

And she knew…Life was about to change.

Flynn turned to her and seeing the fear written on her face, his eyes softened, "Come sit on the bed with me, Rose."

But she wouldn't. "No Flynn, don't you do that. Please tell me the meeting wasn't a call for you to be sent overseas. Just say, No, no Rosebud, nothing like that. You worry too much. I'm not going anywhere. Say those words Flynn, please!" Rose began to choke on the tears that began to fall. Flynn tucked her into his arms and hugged her tight. He whispered words of comfort against her hair and rocked her back and forth while she cried.

"Rose. Shhhh, Rose. It's ok. It's going to be ok." He held her. Comforted her. He was the one leaving, but sometimes the one being left behind was left with a tougher battle yet. Either way, Flynn had promised to take care of her and love her. It broke his heart to see her in this pain. This agonizing worry he knew would soon be her reality.

Sniffling and wiping her eyes, she looked up at Flynn, finally pleading, "You promised you'd never leave me." She could hardly breathe with relentless sobs rushing out of her.

Flynn's voice cracked when he answered her, "God knows I don't want to. Please forgive me, Rose."

After a few minutes he collected himself and asked, "And if you can, please try to be strong for me and pray for a safe return for myself and my comrades."

What could be harder than letting him walk out that door in the morning, knowing she may never see her soulmate and best friend ever again?

Flynn packed his belongings before bed that night and neither of them got much sleep. But, without fail, the sun always comes up. And this morning, that meant goodbye.

Flynn dressed quickly and leaned down to kiss Rose. He brushed the back of his hand softly against her cheek, watching her sleep. Though her sleep was fitful it was a sight of absolute peace and an angelic glow he hoped he would take with him to war and turn to it when he desperately needed to.

When Rose opened her eyes and began to get out of bed, he stopped her. "No Rose. Say goodbye here. Don't walk me out or watch me leave. It will feel too definite. I'm afraid if I see you waving in my rearview mirror I won't have the strength to keep driving." He tried to turn away, but Rose saw him wipe one of his own tears.

Flynn tried, in vain, to lighten the mood saying, "It's only one year, Rosebud. The blink of an eye." He paused and whispered, "I love you."

Rose could only let out a soft "Love you more" before the tears fell.

Though she kept her promise and didn't follow him out, she did move the curtains and watch from their bedroom window.

She watched her soldier, her *love*, walk out their front door and drive away.

When his tail lights were out of sight, Rose fell to their bed and cried until her body could produce no more tears.

And then sleep finally found her.

FLYNN

Flynn reported to Fort Briggs in full Army fatigues, an oversized Army bag hoisted over his shoulder packed heavy with all his necessary belongings. He wore his steel toe combat boots with his green trousers tucked in tight, his garrison cap pulled tight on his head. Flynn's dog tags hung around his neck and were laid against his bare chest beneath his jacket where a photo of his Rosebud was kept safely in the pocket. She was, of course, beautiful at their wedding, but this photo was one he had taken of her at the Old Rittenhouse Inn while on their honeymoon. She was leaning comfortably against the front porch railing, watching sailboats glide the soft waves of

Lake Superior. She wore a content smile on her face and one wisp of her blonde hair had blown lightly across her cheek in the breeze. Without her even noticing, he had taken his phone out and snapped the picture before she could turn toward him. It was a moment he would never forget. It was the simple moments, the quick fleeting ones, that somehow burned themselves into a person's memory. Life's blessings were so often taken for granted. For Flynn, Rose would never be. He'd give almost anything to keep her from the heartache she was in.

A loud alarm sounded throughout his barracks, signaling it was time to load the bus for New York. A long ride with quiet, uneasy, soldiers. Soldiers who were torn between feelings of pride, patriotism, fear, heartbreak, loneliness and a strange numbness filling in the cracks. Already a longing for the comfort of their homes and loved ones. Soon the daunting reality of where they were headed would sink in like a deep, fresh wound, painful and raw.

Their flight was scheduled to leave for Bagram Air Base, Afghanistan, at 0800 on Friday.

Patting his breast pocket where Rose's photo lay Flynn whispered, "Be well, my love."

CHAPTER 12

"**P**atrick, why do the crowds down on Canal Street keep getting more destructive, more wild? I wish these all-night bars and dance clubs wouldn't keep popping up on every corner. It's nothing but trouble," Rose griped.

"You sound like an old lady, Rosie. It looks to me like a lot of the people in these crowds are about your age," he responded while flipping burger patties on the griddle.

Clearly agitated, Rose kept on her rant. "Ok, number one, just because they are young doesn't mean they need to be destructive. I've seen graffiti on benches, broken garbage cans with trash tossed down the sidewalk. I have even seen all-out brawls in the street."

Rose prepared a Caesar salad. Adding a few garlic croutons and shredded parmesan cheese she continued, "And number two, I've always had an old soul. I have *no* time for that kind of nonsense." Rose was clearly not happy about how the area kept changing, in her opinion, for the worse.

Patrick shook his head and said, "Makes sense that you married a man ten years older than you then I guess. No college frat parties for you huh Ro–," but he stopped then and apologized. "I'm sorry Rosie. I sometimes forget that bringing up Flynn makes your bottom lip quiver."

He was right, of course. The first week of Flynn's absence was the most heartache she had ever experienced. She called in sick to work more times than she had during the whole time she had worked at the diner. Her mother came over daily with her favorite treats or to just scratch her back. Any attempt to comfort her.

Finally though, she remembered her promise to Flynn and talked herself into being strong--if only faking it. Eventually it became a habit and things felt half-way normal.

Normal, with a dull ache in the pit of her stomach.

Patrick served up the plates of cheeseburgers and fries for her to deliver and she smiled at him saying, "It's ok Patrick. You can say his name, talk about him. I need to practice being a strong woman, like he asked me to be."

Throwing a few pickles on the plates, Patrick gave her a sympathetic smile and nodded his head.

That evening Rose laid in bed and prayed for Flynn and his fellow soldiers. Prayed they were safe. Prayed they would all find their way home to their loved ones. As she was just feeling herself drift off to sleep she heard more sirens in the distance. It sounded as if they were heading in the direction of Canal Street. She put her hands over her face and said to herself, "I don't know how much longer I can take it here."

The next morning Flora called to tell her that there had been a fire at the diner last night. She said they would be forced to close until further notice.

Rose didn't think her eyes still had tears left to cry, but some came.

The ditches had started filling with rain. Rose couldn't believe the downpour. The flash flood warnings would be sounding if this kept up much longer. As they should be, most people weren't out driving in such a storm. Rose agreed she should probably turn around. Her thoughts of Maurice and Flora and the wreckage of their life's work, the Canal Street Diner, flashed through Rose's mind. It was still so fresh. She didn't even like to go down to Canal Park anymore. It was just too sad and no doubt a fresh sting of tears would be sure to spring up again had she returned to the site.

But she did speak with Maurice and Flora often. Rose asked them how they were doing and if there was anything she could do. They discussed with her their settlement with the insurance company and that they had already been in contact with a contractor to both clear the debris and start new construction.

As always, Maurice and Flora were in high spirits and moving forward. They had been since the day after the fire. Rose recalled the day she stood holding Flora's hand while they all stared blankly at the disaster left behind.

Simpler Times recipe for Creamy cucumber and tomato salad

Ingredients:

3 medium sized cucumbers, peeled and sliced into rounds

1 large tomato sliced into bite size pieces

2 tablespoons mayonnaise (approx.)

A sprinkle of salt, pepper, sugar and dill weed.

Instructions:

Combine ingredients in medium bowl and enjoy.

~Refreshing summer meal paired with a pan fried walleye filet or a piece of grilled chicken.

CHAPTER 13

Of course, word traveled fast about what had happened at Canal Street Diner. Every story was different. Someone had written on Facebook that they heard the owners of Canal Street Diner had been wanting to rebuild lately and were seen there in the middle of the night and most likely started the fire themselves to file a bogus insurance claim. Her mom, Evie, had heard some women talking at the hair salon that the diner had been an accident waiting to happen and that the health inspector had warned the owners several times they needed to correct some exposed fire hazards in the kitchen. Several rumors traveled the streets of Duluth, though very few people believed the stories. Canal Street Diner had been a fixture in Duluth for decades and Maurice and Flora were known for being honest, hardworking owners. Owners that treasured their little restaurant and customers. All that was known for certain and was factual, was reported in the newspaper. The fire had occurred some time between midnight and one a.m. The bartender at Grandma's Bar and Grill had called 911. Six fire trucks, four police cars and one ambulance had been at the scene. Photos of such were included in the newspaper article. Luckily, the firemen reported to the scene quickly and were able to act fast. It wasn't a total loss by any means. The structure was still standing and repairable, it seemed.

As it turned out, the fire that had taken place at the diner was determined to be arson according to the fire inspector's report. There was no way to know who had committed the crime or why. Maurice and Flora were devastated, but as they did with any setback in life, they took it in stride.

"Life happens how it happens," Maurice said to everyone the next morning as they stared at the debris covering the kitchen and dining room.

The sight in front of her broke Rose's heart. Her favorite customer, Mr.

O'Toole, had sat up at the counter on the same stool every day at the stroke of twelve o'clock p.m. He, most times, would order what was on special for lunch, or a simple bowl of soup. Mr. O'Toole's stool was lying on the floor, black, burned pieces of plastic peeling away from the cushioned seat. Behind the counter, the pie cabinet and the silver milkshake maker lay in a pile of broken glass and shards of white dinner plates. The walls, the ceiling, all the little details that Maurice and Flora had added to make this diner theirs--all flaking away into black soot. Rose bent down to pick up a broken frame. The glass was shattered and fell to the floor. A photo of the young couple, Maurice and Flora, sitting next to a sold sign in front of the diner, was singed and ripped down the center. Though the picture was ruined, Rose still took care in setting it down on the counter.

Rose glanced over at Patrick—big, old, tattooed, tough Patrick. He had tears in his eyes. This diner had been like home to him, and Maurice and Flora like family. She knew he was probably taking it harder than they were.

"What can we do to help, boss?" Patrick finally asked.

"I don't know just yet, Patrick. We have to leave the debris until the arson case has been closed. This sometimes can take weeks. The insurance adjuster has been here assessing the damage, but again, we are at a standstill." Maurice looked at Patrick, then at Rose and finally at his sweet, petite wife dabbing at her eyes with a handkerchief.

"I'm so sorry this has happened." Rose walked over to Flora and held her hand in hers, not knowing what else she could do.

Maurice, looking around the room as Rose had been doing, finally added, "God doesn't give us anything we can't handle."

Sometimes Rose wondered.

FLYNN

"Hey, Mitchell--wake up, man. We have combat training." Flynn's best friend and fellow soldier, Marty, poked him in the neck. Flynn was crouched down on a dirty sidewalk, leaned up against a crumbling stone wall, attempting to steal a few minutes of rest. In the one hundred and ten degrees Fahrenheit heat, fatigue hit without apology and the sandstorms made his eyes so itchy and gritty, it was a welcome relief to keep them closed.

"Ugh, Marty--let me pretend I'm sleeping next to my wife and the Minnesota lakes are sparkling somewhere nearby." Flynn stood up and shoved his friend, meaning it, but not, at the same time. Marty was the brother he never had. And a Godsend here in the devil's dust bowl.

"Ahh man, don't I hear ya. Tipping back a cold Budweiser at Fitgers with my girl next to me, the smell of charbroiled burgers on the flat top and deep-fried, beer batter Walleye filets on plates being delivered throughout the bar. If I make it back brother, let's take the girls out. Doesn't that sound great?" Marty reached out his hand to Flynn, who shook it firmly. What the two friends wouldn't give to be back in their hometown, holding their girls close while sipping a cold beer. It all felt like a luxury they had never appreciated until that moment.

"Deal! Now, let's go sit on the sandy beach out there and get a tan, shall we?" Flynn joked. Sometimes, in a place without humor, it was all you could do.

Flynn and Marty rounded the corner of the seemingly deserted city block where the covered Army truck was waiting to take them to the day's training course.

Both silently picturing that cold Budweiser and their girl at their side.

CHAPTER 14

Having found a new place to live or not didn't stop the calendar from moving. Rose had been so busy since Flynn had been deployed — purposefully so. A week after his departure she had already gone through kitchen cabinets. She delicately wrapped all the dishes and glassware in between clumped up newspapers and packed them in carefully labeled boxes. She had gone through her own belongings, giving some to charity and those she couldn't part with, were packed. All shelves from the walls were taken down, framed photos were stacked carefully between kitchen towels. Books, board games, lamps, throw pillows, all were packed.

Rose was finding the last room difficult to go through. Flynn's clothes hung "military neat" in the bedroom closet. His shirts folded front side up in his second dresser drawer. His extra shoes, boots and slippers on a rubber mat next to the closet door.

Rose carried a large cardboard box into the bedroom and set it on their bed. She looked at his pillow lying next to hers. 12 months without him. How was she going to survive? And what if, God forbid, he doesn't come home safe to her? Rose was on the brink of another breakdown when the doorbell startled her out of the trance she was starting to fall into.

Opening the front door, she saw Collette standing out front, crying. "Collette?" Rose's eyes began to sting looking at Collette crumbling. "Oh Collette, I know!" Rose said as she pulled Collette into an embrace. Marty had also been deployed. The two went inside and Rose poured them a glass of wine.

"Rose, this is just too long, and I keep having nightmares of what could and maybe IS happening to our boys over there," Collette blubbered, wiping her nose with a napkin. Rose sat down across from her at the small kitchen table. "I know. I was starting to pack Flynn's –, no, staring at Flynn's things in our bedroom when you arrived. I could feel myself coming unglued again."

She took a sip of her Chardonnay. "Life just doesn't prepare you for some things does it?" Collette's eyes were red from crying, probably from days of it. "My mom and aunt are taking me on a trip out to Cape Cod where we used to go when I was young. They are trying to get my mind off things. Fat chance! But...at least it's a change of scenery," Collette sighed.

Collette wiped the corner of her eye again and took in a big breath. "Ahhh, ok. I'm fine for a minute." And lifting her glass of wine, she asked "Rose, how did Flynn decide he wanted to enlist in the Reserves?"

Rose answered, remembering when she asked Flynn this very question not long after they had met.

"Well, Flynn's family was always very supportive of the U.S. military. His father had served a short time in the Army but was honorably discharged for health reasons. He had terrible migraines and whenever he was in a stressful situation, which in the military can be often, the headaches became debilitating. Flynn's grandfather served in World War II and his uncle as well. None of them had lost their lives, thank God. But, Flynn had always wanted to make his family proud and dreamed of becoming a soldier himself. The only thing that held him back a bit was his mother. She had had such a tough time becoming pregnant with him and had even recovered from three miscarriages after having Flynn. He was her one baby. She was scared to death to let him go, with the possibility of losing him. Cynthia couldn't stand the thought. And so, Flynn decided he would put the thought aside. All through high school he aspired to perfect carpentry. He was very talented in that area. Actually, in several trades. He had a rare gift for learning quickly. Mechanics, electronics, wood work, you name it. So, that was his new mindset."

"Didn't his father still really push for him to join the military though, given the family tradition?" Collette questioned.

"No, not really. Joe had seen Cynthia go through extreme heartache and depression after losing babies and failed attempts at getting pregnant. He knew, had he pushed Flynn into enlisting, and something terrible happened, he would never forgive himself." Rose took another sip of her wine and poured Collette another glassful.

She continued her story, "So like I said, Flynn was picturing his life much differently by the time he entered his senior year at Duluth Christian High School. His new plans were to start a carpentry business after he attended Dunwoody College, studying construction management. He had aspirations of building his own house, building his parents a new house. As you know, Flynn always has dreams and goals to shoot for, regardless of which path his life takes; he always had a positive outlook and a general sense of moving forward. But…tragically," Rose struggled to keep her voice steady, "Flynn's parents were in a boating accident out on Superior one evening while Flynn was at a football game. I don't know the details of the accident, really. All I know is, Joe and Cynthia along with another couple lost their lives. As you can imagine, Flynn was devastated. He had very little family nearby. He inherited this house and lived here until he graduated. His aunt, his mother's sister, had moved in with him temporarily, until he graduated. However, he switched gears and was determined at that point to join the U.S. military. There was no other thought in his mind at that point. On his eighteenth birthday he was sworn in."

"Ohhhh, that is such a sad story. His parents passing away and Flynn, alone," Collette sympathized.

"I know. Just himself and an aunt he hardly knew. But after enlisting it seems Flynn has surely found a faithful friend in Marty. That's been a blessing," Rose said smiling. The two, then again, let fresh tears fall.

Rose and Collette sat at the kitchen table talking until midnight. They shared a frozen pizza, several glasses of wine, laughed and cried together. It did both of their hearts good to lean on someone going through the same heartache.

The next morning Rose found the strength to fold up Flynn's clothes and pack them, along with his few belongings. She did it slowly, frequently bringing his shirts to her nose and breathing in the lingering scent. He wore the same cologne every day, Stetson, since he was a teenager, and never changed. It was Flynn's scent and Rose could almost feel him nearby when she hugged his t-shirt and closed her eyes. Just the same, she went about the job with purpose. It had to be done.

And it had to be her that did it.

CHAPTER 15

May 1st came and the buyers of Flynn and Rose's house pulled up in a U-Haul truck bright and early. Rose handed them the keys with a forced smile on her face. She took one last look at the house, turned and didn't look back. She jumped in her car and drove to her parents' house. She would be staying with them for the time being.

Rose had been close with her parents growing up. She was an only child, just like Flynn. Unlike Flynn's parents, Rose's hadn't tried in vain to have more children, nor did she think her mother had suffered any miscarriages. They just were content with their one little girl, as they told her often. Perhaps there was more to the decision they had made, but to Rose's knowledge her mom and dad had become pregnant with her a few years after marrying and it had always been just the three of them.

Her most cherished memories with her mother and father were the trips they had taken together. To date, the trip that had always been her favorite was the road trip they had taken to Mackinac Island in Michigan. They had stayed in a three-story inn on Main Street. Their room had a small balcony where she spent her evenings just watching the quiet bikers ride past or listening to the clip clop sound of horse hooves as they pulled their carriages by. It had seemed like such an escape and the inn they had stayed in provided such homey comforts. Rose had been inspired since then to run her own inn someday.

Flynn had been so supportive of her dream. He was excited for her, for *them*. Rose wondered if it would ever come to pass.

As she pulled into her parents' driveway, Philip ran out to help her with the few boxes and bags she had brought along. The remaining boxes of her and Flynn's belongings were kept safely in a storage unit nearby.

"Hi, my girl. How are you? Let me carry in some of those heavy boxes for you," Philip offered.

"Hi Dad. Oh, thanks. Don't worry, the heavy boxes filled with my book collection are in the storage unit," Rose teased. The two walked to the house where Evie was standing, holding the front door open for them.

"Oh, Rosalie! I know this is all so hard, but I am excited to spend some quality time with you," Evie stated, hugging her daughter tight.

"Mom, I see you at least a couple times a week and talk to you on the phone almost daily. You're too funny," Rose replied.

"Well, I know, but for right now it's like you're a little girl in our house again. And to be honest, I like taking care of you while Flynn's away. It makes my *mom-heart* feel better."

Rose laughed. "Well, I'll take the pampering then, Mama."

"Something smells wonderful, by the way. What are you cooking?" Rose asked.

"Your favorite, Rose. Beef roast, with Yukon gold potatoes, a few chopped Vidalia onions and beautiful carrots from my garden. I've had it in the oven, slow cooking all afternoon. I also baked some fresh oatmeal bread to soak up the yummy juices." Evie sounded proud. Rose inhaled deeply, taking in the delectable smells again. "Thank you guys, for taking care of me. I miss Flynn so much, but I feel blessed to have you both at my side."

Rose, Philip and Evie enjoyed a wonderful evening together. After they had eaten all they could of the delightful meal Evie had made and the conversation began to dwindle, Rose excused herself. "I think I'm going to go upstairs, take a bath and then read a bit before bed if you don't mind. Your lovely meal made me sleepy, Mom." She winked at Evie, kissed her dad on the cheek and walked upstairs to the bathroom.

Once she filled the old clawfoot tub with hot water, she took her clothes off and eased her body down into the frothy, lavender-scented bubbles. Rose laid her head back and closed her eyes, seeing Flynn's smiling face behind her eyelids. It had been a huge mystery to Rose that Flynn had never had any serious relationships until her. Oh, there were a few girlfriends, but nothing serious. He was *movie star* good looking, as Rose described him. "How have you not been scooped up by a tall, slender beauty?" Rose had asked him. After all he was thirty-one, almost thirty-two, and single until they had met. Flynn had told her, he always knew God would send him an angel and that he would know when he saw her. He said, when the cute, little blonde waited on him at the diner he knew she was special. Even more so when she spilled the milkshake on him. He had told her, the sweet apologies and the sudden pink in her cheeks, painted a picture in his mind that, for some reason, wouldn't let him forget her. This led to his eventual trip back to Canal Street Diner where he had prayed that the waitress still worked.

Since the day they had met, *properly and minus the ice cream*, things had moved so fast. And now, already, she was an Army wife waiting on her soldier's safe return.

Rose eased further down in the water until she was underneath the bubbles covering her head. She wished the liquid could wash her memories away for a night so that she could get a full night's sleep. Possibly that would give her some relief? Some desired energy? Deciding to remain the strong wife she had promised to be, she stood up and grabbed her oversized pink bath towel and dried off. After draining the bath and putting on her soft cotton sweats and one of Flynn's t-shirts, she walked to her bedroom with the hope of a few hours' sleep.

Days with her mother and father had become routine. Rose helped Evie around the house and took her out for coffee some afternoons. They'd take walks with the family German Shepherd, Jack, or go shopping at Fitgers. She didn't like heading that way often though because seeing the Rose Garden where she and Flynn were married brought back a heartache she had been working hard on easing.

"Well, there are a few more vehicles out and about now. I thought I was the only crazy person braving the rain this afternoon." As large semi-trucks, delivery vans and SUVs passed Rose on the left, water sprayed out from their tires, splattering the windshield of her car, making it that much harder to see the road. Not just that, but there was so much water accumulating on the highway that she felt the car hydroplane from time to time; the feeling of no control made her fingers tighten on the steering wheel.

"Ok, Rose — time to pull over and then make a U-turn for home." She looked ahead for a side road to pull onto, but she could see only trees. She couldn't see much at all in front of her, but certainly no roads to pull onto.

Continuing to search, she thought back to a few hours ago at home with her mom and dad and remembered why she wanted to leave, had to. And she kept driving.

It had been a month since Rose had moved in. She and Evie sat in the kitchen assembling a lasagna for tonight's dinner when Philip called them into the living room and pointed to the TV.

"It appears more U.S troops are being sent to Afghanistan. Al-Qaeda is threatening attacks and there's so much unrest on the streets that the civilians are in danger of losing their lives," Philip briefed them as they all watched the news anchor continue. Rose and Evie observed the statistics that were shown on the screen — the news anchor's deep, grave voice reading off the facts as they appeared on the TV screen.

> To date about 2,400 American soldiers have lost their lives during the U.S war in Afghanistan. 16 of these deaths occurred during combat. What's even more revealing are the astounding numbers of service men who have been deployed to Afghanistan. Such data has been reported directly from the Pentagon. Official records show that 775,000 United States service members have been deployed to Afghanistan

at least once. Many U.S veterans of Afghanistan have served one deployment, but some have served many times. At least 28,267 US soldiers have been deployed over five times to Afghanistan. The Pentagon's largest military branch, The Army, has deployed the most troops. The number of soldiers that have served there comes to more than 491,500. This includes active-duty forces, Army reservists and national guardsmen. The air force, despite the overall number of troops decreasing, has deployed the second most, reaching around 123,000 airmen. During the height of the war between 2010 and 2011 about 20,000 marines were deployed. Though this large number was during the height of the war- overall the Marine Corps has deployed 114,000 service members. Even the Coast Guard has sent more than 100 of their own. Indeed, these staggering statistics provided by the Pentagon directly reveal the U.S military's long-time involvement in the Afghanistan war. A war's end that many feel is nowhere in sight.

When video footage of the violence came up on the screen, it all became too real and Rose couldn't breathe. "Phil! Please turn it off. She doesn't need to see this," Evie ordered, giving Philip a side look of disapproval.

"Listen Rose, honey, we would hear if Flynn was in extreme danger or if anything had happened. They are just reporting the fact that more troops are being sent to patrol the areas--to keep control. There have been no new or recent reports of lives lost," Evie reassured Rose though her tone didn't sound so sure.

At that point Rose had lost her appetite entirely and ran up to her room. She felt both panic and a new claustrophobia she hadn't felt before. She looked out her window to see a hard rainfall. A walk to the park was out of the question, but maybe a drive would be ok. She needed to get out. Go somewhere. Anywhere! She was ready to jump out of her skin. She grabbed her rain jacket from the hook at the bottom of the stairway and her purse that sat on the bench.

Peeking her head into the kitchen she said, "Mom, I'm sorry I'm leaving you to finish dinner. I need to take a drive. Just alone. I need to clear my head a bit."

Evie looked concerned, "Ok, but be careful, Rose. The rain is coming down hard."

Rose replied, "Don't worry Mom, I will. Love you."

She ran quickly to her car holding her hood over her head through the pelting rain. For a brief moment she questioned her ability to see the road clearly in the steady, blinding rainfall. But she felt like she would burst with anxiety sitting in the house, replaying the news report they had just watched, over and over in her mind.

> To date about 2,400 American soldiers have lost their lives during the U.S war in Afghanistan. 16 of these deaths occurred during combat. What's even more revealing are the astounding numbers of service men who have been deployed to Afghanistan. Such data has been reported directly from the Pentagon. Official records show that 775,000 United States service members have been deployed to Afghanistan at least once. Many U.S veterans of Afghanistan have served one deployment, but some have served many times. At least 28,267 US soldiers have been deployed over five times to Afghanistan. The Pentagon's largest military branch, The Army, has deployed the most troops.

The news anchor's voice kept repeating the report in her head; the official statistics scrolled down the screen of her parents' forty-five inch flat screen. How could she listen to the reality of war on the news and then watch an episode of *Friends* as if things were normal? Eat a plate of hot lasagna with a glass of Merlot while her husband ate a granola bar if time allowed?

"Many US troops have deployed there five or more times." Her voice was shaking. "Five or more times!"

Rose's chest felt suddenly tight.

She needed to clear her head, just focus on driving, and hope the raindrops would wash it all away.

"It's fine. I'm fine. A quick little drive out of the city and I'll feel as good as new," she told herself. Her foot hit the gas pedal and she started inching down the street. She chose a random route with no particular plan or reason for doing it.

CHAPTER 16

After hours of driving, Rose's tension returned. The news anchor's monotone voice reciting the agonizing statistics were in her head again.

It was time to turn around and go home. She looked, again, for a logical place to pull over, but a sudden feeling of panic hit her in the chest. The glare in front of her was blurry. She couldn't see well, but something wasn't right. The oncoming headlights — were they in her lane?

The rain was coming down so hard now, she couldn't tell. They certainly seemed to be and the vehicle was coming fast, the headlights blinding her!

With no time left to react, she cranked the steering wheel hard to the right, swerving off the road. She had no control. Her car was racing fast down into the ditch. She tried to steady the steering wheel, push the brakes, do something. Her eyes couldn't focus, her brain couldn't think. It felt like in those few seconds of panic a whole gamut of thoughts went through her head. *Is this it? Am I gonna die? Why did I venture out in a rainstorm? How can I stop this vehicle before I run into something? GOD, help me!* Her mind was reeling.

Something finally came over her and Rose was able to take control of the steering wheel, grasping it tight, just missing a huge oak tree. She slammed on the brakes and found she was stopped in a clearing. A large field. Sitting frozen and staring straight ahead, Rose couldn't move. Her fingers still gripped the steering wheel tightly; her foot was still holding the brake pedal down hard; the windshield wipers were still moving back and forth at full speed. It was the squeaking of the wipers on dry glass that finally broke Rose from her trance. She shifted the car into park and looked out her window at the sky.

The rain had subsided and the clouds seemed to have cleared.

She took in a breath of relief and thanked God she had missed the tree or she would probably, *most likely*, be dead.

"My God! What just happened?" Rose's hands were shaking with adrenaline and a new tension to add to her already present anxiety.

Disoriented and still trembling, she turned the key in the ignition. Only a clicking sound. She put the car in park and tried again. Nothing. Rose hit the steering wheel with the palm of her hand. "Come on!" She sat for a couple of minutes, giving her car time to revamp. Maybe it helped to give it some time? Swallowing hard, she grabbed the key and turned it. Click, click, click.

"Damn."

Rose assumed something had been damaged internally. Though what did she know of these things? She grabbed her purse and reached in for her cell phone. "You've got to be kidding me? I never leave my phone at home," she scolded herself. "Well, at least the rain has stopped."

Deciding she had no other obvious options, Rose got out of her car and began to walk. "Well, this was a nice way to end my drive. Here I thought it would be a way to ease my nerves. Ha! Fat chance! I should've just gone upstairs and taken another bubble bath and gone to bed early." Rose scolded herself for the first few minutes of her walk, realizing soon after, it was no use.

She noticed her long drive to nowhere certainly had brought her to an area of Minnesota she hadn't ever been to. This particular road wasn't deserted, cars passed by her here and there, but it wasn't a heavily traveled highway either.

Looking ahead she saw several farms in the distance and rolling fields of corn or hay perhaps? She wasn't familiar with crop farming, but her view of the clean, hard-worked fields on either side of her was that of peace and humble beauty. Just that took the edge off her anxiety.

The gentle breeze played with the loose strands of hair around her face and she breathed in the smell of damp, rich soil that made up the fields at this time of year. It was an earthy, fresh scent that was strangely cleansing. It all felt welcome and nourishing. Even her walk felt like something she had needed.

She had been so fixated on being sad, lonely and worried, rightfully so, but she had forgotten that she was still Rose, still living a life with dreams and passions. The very things that Flynn loved most about her. He wouldn't want to see her wallowing in this pity. Of course, it was only human to worry about your husband, an Army soldier, being in harm's way. But it had begun to consume her. It suddenly felt good to feel her calf muscles burn and a new full feeling of air in her lungs. Rose thought to herself, *God sure works in mysterious ways.* Here she had been at her absolute wit's end, yearning to escape for a brief moment. After a very long drive full of pounding rain, she ends up swerving off the road into a ditch, missing her death by a millimeter, and is left stranded without a working vehicle or a cell phone. And yet, at this very moment, she felt rejuvenated — almost energetic. Though unnerving, it felt great!

It had been only twenty minutes or so before she saw a road sign up ahead. It read: *the town of Cherish - 5 miles.* There was an arrow pointing east. Guessing a town five miles away was probably her best bet, she turned east and continued following that road. A road she had never traveled.

To a town she had never heard of.

FLYNN

After Flynn had written his letter he looked at it closely, reading it softly to himself.

Rosebud,

The cell service here is less than perfect (ha ha), so snail mail it is. I had to write to you. It is strange how it is a real comfort when I do. Like I'm conversing with you somehow.

How dumb is that huh? Is this a Hallmark movie? Ha. But really, jokes aside- I am getting used to it here. As best I can of course, but Marty and I are learning the skills needed if we should be forced to use them. Try not to worry about that though. To be honest, most of our time is spent patrolling the streets in full combat gear. The heat here is torturous. Our uniforms are tight and itchy. Our gear is heavy, seventy pounds heavy. It's boring most of the time here. Like 'Checkers' boring (yes we do play board games here).

But — it isn't war. Take comfort in that, Love. How are you? I know you're sad. You don't know how much I wish I could take that away. Knowing your heart hurts tempts me to jump on a plane and go AWOL, though I shouldn't joke about such a thing. I want you to be proud of us over here and continue to send prayers. We'll take em.

Anyway, have you been looking for houses for us? Scoping out other towns where we can open up an inn like the Old Rittenhouse when I return?

It sounds like heaven, Rose. It won't be long. Stay well my love.

Loving you from afar,

Flynn

CHAPTER 17

After what had felt like an hour's walk Rose spotted a big sign ahead. It was a large wooden sign that hung on two posts attached by metal loop chains and it moved with the breeze. Painted words read, *Welcome to Cherish, population 800.* The sign looked like an old antique, though in perfectly kept condition. How quaint, Rose thought. On the corner was an old gas station with a sign advertising Coca-Colas and Cracker Jack for sale. Rose was thirsty and hot after her walk and decided to go inside.

A bell above the door rang as she entered, letting the owner know a customer had come inside. A short, older fellow came out from behind a cabinet to greet Rose, "Hi there, can I help you find anything special?"

Rose replied, "Hi, something cold to drink maybe? I've been walking a while." She dabbed her forehead with a tissue she had dug out of her purse.

"Sure thing, we have sodas in the back cooler there. Help yourself," then added, "I'm Chives O'Connor if you need anything."

"Chives?" Rose thought. Strange nickname. She meandered to the back of the store, opened the cooler and grabbed a glass bottle of Coca-Cola. There was just nothing like drinking a cold soda from a glass bottle.

Setting her bottle on the front counter, she dug in her purse for a dollar. "That'll be ten cents Miss, sorry didn't catch your name?" Chives questioned.

"Um, It's Rose. And ten cents for a Coke? Is that right?" she stammered.

Chives confirmed the price. "Last time I checked ten cents was the going rate for a bottle of Cola." Chives grabbed her bottle and with a bottle opener snapped it open. The bottle fizzed. Rose took a long, refreshing drink.

"Cherish is a fairly small town. I haven't seen you around here. Are you new to our area?" he said, fishing for information.

Rose looked at her bottle of Coke and smiled. She decided on an honest, but vague, answer.

"I'm just visiting for a bit."

"Ahh, well, Welcome to our neck of the woods." He smiled at her with a jovial, genuine smile. "It was nice meeting ya, Rose. Come back anytime," Chives yelled as he headed to a shelf that needed stocking.

Rose replied, "Thank you, nice to have met you too." She grabbed her Coke and walked out onto Main Street, Cherish.

Black ornate street lights lined both sides of Main Street. Large potted plants sat at each corner and small benches were placed in front of store windows. Rose took sips of her soda as she wandered down the sidewalk admiring this charming little town.

Across the street she saw a café called, The Crystal Café (according to the sign above the front entrance). And it appeared to be quite busy inside. Walking on, she saw a flower shop called Wild Flowers. A wagon sat next to the entrance and held small bundles of bouquets for sale. Rose noticed each was priced separately. A little wooden box was set next to the wagon with a dollar sign painted on the front indicating where a customer would put their payment. Rose thought of such a trust system set up on Canal Street among the bar and club goers. The little wagon of sweet bouquets would be destroyed and money taken the first night.

On her stroll, she spotted a dry cleaner's shop, a grocery store, a hardware store, a clothing boutique, a dental clinic, a bookstore, a newspaper office, a post office, a hair salon, a bowling alley and a small movie theater. She noticed signs at road intersections indicating which direction to take to get to the school, the hospital, the police station and the small volunteer fire station.

Rose took her time and noticed several people giving her polite smiles or "hellos" as they passed by. Many children raced by her on bikes. Local business owners had started locking up their front doors for the evening.

Coming back to reality for a moment, she remembered it must be getting late. Without her cell phone she wondered where she might find a phone to call her parents. She remembered the café had still looked open and decided to go in that direction. Maybe there would be a land line she could use.

A couple with three young children were entering the café just in front of her. The gentleman, noticing Rose, held the door open for her. Rose thanked him for the unusual, but kind, gesture and stepped inside. All but two booths were occupied. Oldies played in the background and Rose could smell a slight scent of cigarette smoke. *In the restaurant? Isn't that against the law?* she thought. Rose noticed a counter straight ahead with a cash register and a stocky lady with her hair in a bun taking money from a customer. She waited her turn in line. When the waitress was finished with the customer in front of her she asked Rose, "Can I help you sweetheart? You look hungry. We have freshly made split pea soup with ham we're trying to get rid of tonight. My recipe," the waitress winked at her.

Rose smiled, "No, but thank you. Would you have a phone I could use?" she asked. The waitress, or was she the cook, answered, "Yes, there is a pay phone in the back by the women's restroom if you have a nickel."

Rose looked at her puzzled but walked in the direction she had pointed. There might be instructions posted next to the payphone. She had only heard about payphones, had never used one. Surprisingly, she managed it fairly easily, dropping a nickel in the slot. Lifting the receiver to her ear, she heard a dial tone and called her mom's cell phone. The call wouldn't connect though. The operator's voice stated, "I'm sorry, the number you have dialed could not be reached." Rose hung up, thinking, perhaps, she misdialed? Who remembered phone numbers anymore anyway. Once someone's number was saved in your phone, you never had to actually dial it ever again. She swore she knew her mom's cell phone number, but it was conceivable she didn't.

Rose was still stuck in her own thoughts when the waitress she had spoken to earlier stopped her and said, "Everything ok honey? You look lost. And hungry, I might add. Here, sit at this open table up front and I'll grab you a menu."

She grabbed a menu, poured two cups of coffee and brought both over with her. She gave Rose the menu and one of the cups of coffee. She took a seat across from Rose and sipped on the other coffee she had in her hand.

"Anything sound good? We made farm fresh egg salad this morning if that's something you like. Chopped up onion, celery and green olives with a dash of salt and pepper and dill weed. Mmmmm mmm. Spread thick between two slices of fresh baked skillet bread."

Rose thought it a bit strange the waitress was sitting down at a table, sipping from a cup of coffee when the place was busy. Wouldn't her boss frown upon her behavior with tables of customers hungry and needing her attention?

As if reading her mind the waitress responded, "I can see your wheels turning. I own the café. I like to be out on the floor helping out and yacking with new customers like yourself or catching up with my regulars. Everyone calls me Mudsie. You may as well too," she smiled at Rose, "and your name?"

She answered simply, "Rose."

"And as pretty as one I'd say," Mudsie complimented. "Now, what can I get you from the kitchen, Rose?"

"I think that egg salad sandwich sounds delicious. Thank you," Rose decided. Mudsie grabbed her menu and said "Great choice. I'll have it up in a jiffy." As she scurried away, Rose thought to herself, *what a sweet, cute little lady.* She reminded Rose of her grandma, who was no longer alive. Same short, round build, but her personality was almost spot on. Her grandma, also, wouldn't be fully satisfied until you sat down at her kitchen table with a plate of food in front of you. And she always had a cup of coffee in her hand.

Rose sighed and looked out the window again. How nice to not see traffic racing down Main Street and no alarming sounds of loud music and sirens. In fact, the only two vehicles she saw were parked down on the corner at Chive's gas station. They looked like 1950s era cars. Maybe headed to a car show out of town or something. Kind of peculiar.

Customers came and went from the Crystal Café and most gave her a smile or polite nod. Was everyone in Cherish so friendly? Mudsie returned to her table and set a plate in front of her. A sandwich piled full of yellow and white, fluffy egg salad sat upon a large lettuce leaf. Two toothpicks held the sandwich halves together. Rose was surprised at how hungry she finally felt. Lifting the sandwich to her mouth she took a big, satisfying bite. She noticed Mudsie still standing at her table almost waiting for a response from Rose. With her mouth full, Rose giggled and gave Mudsie a thumbs-up instead. It was true, the egg salad was the best she'd ever tasted. She finished the whole thing leaving only crumbs on the decorative lettuce leaf. She was waiting for her bill, but nothing came. Nor did she see Mudsie around.

Walking up to the counter where the cash register was she spotted a young waitress and asked, "Excuse me, but I didn't get my bill. Would you mind checking on that for me so that I can pay and be on my way?"

The young waitress smiled and in response said, "Oh no, Mudsie said your meal is on the house today and hopes you'll stop in again."

"Really? Well, wow. Please thank her for me. And I certainly hope to come back again soon."

Rose stepped out the front door and onto the sidewalk. Her feet were sore from her long walk earlier, but she felt a desire to keep exploring. She continued down block after block, passing an ice cream shop, a jewelry store, an insurance agency, a small toy store, and a lovely, white Catholic church with a tall steeple. A small cemetery sat just behind, and a black wrought iron fence surrounded the tombstones.

Just down at the very end of the block, on the edge of town sat a two-story, yellow house with a painted white, covered porch and a bench swing. There was a white, wooden sign out front in the yard, but it appeared the words had been painted over. In fact, it looked as if no one was living or working in the building currently and maybe hadn't for a long time.

Curiosity took over and Rose walked closer.

FLYNN

Flynn, Marty, Sanchez and Collins stood statue-still, barely breathing, as they waited for Pashtu speaking Taliban soldiers, creeping through their current station, to pass through. The four soldiers had been ordered to hide out in an old, abandoned business building. From the looks of the debris left behind, it had been a store that had sold and made luxury Persian rugs. Pieces of finely dyed fabrics and fragments of brightly colored threads were strung about like an explosion of rainbow colors. The beauty of bright purples, oranges and golds lay on the stone floor next to broken glass shards, and crushed plaster. A desk was tipped over on its side. Hundreds of papers that were once organized precisely in drawers and files, laid lifeless and unimportant.

A livelihood, a prospering business — now a skeleton of a building that would never be resurrected. Flynn started to feel a trickle of sweat drip down the back of his neck. He was sandwiched tight in a small storeroom next to Sanchez. Marty and Collins on the other side of Sanchez, just as close. They had heard the voices yell for them early that morning as they lay back to back in an attempt to get a much needed nap.

Sudden panic sent all four soldiers jumping up alert. The dialect was a strange and frantic yelling. They had been familiar, somewhat, with the language the Taliban spoke, but the tone was what was unmistakable. These Taliban soldiers were there to find, to capture, and most likely, torture whomever they found in the building. It seemed easy enough to shut your mouth, stay still and wait, but it was not. Flynn could hear Collins breathing hard and fast, Sanchez trying, in vain, to quit shaking. Marty was stone cold silent; Flynn wondering if he was still alive.

Please, let them pass through, God. Flynn said the words in his head without even a flutter of his eyes. As she did often during troubling times, Rose came to his mind. She seemed to know when to show up in Flynn's thoughts and knew how to sooth him, to let the moments pass, even the most frightening instances. He couldn't explain it or make sense of it, but whenever she was there, searching for him through the ugliness, the *terror* of war, he knew, somehow everything was going to be ok.

After what had seemed like several hours, Flynn heard a voice, an English speaking voice. A familiar voice. One that belonged to his commanding officer, Captain Silva.

"You're safe, soldiers. We cleared the area. Let's get you out of here."

The four brothers, brothers of not blood, but bond, shakenly filed out of the small storeroom they had been crammed in, shielding the blinding sun from their eyes. A sun both blinding, freeing and confusingly nonjudgmental to all who yearned for its warmth on their skin.

Flynn stepped out of the doorless entryway of the building, the sun rays shining like a beacon in his face.

He wondered, despite where he was and what he had just experienced, what Rose was doing. He hoped she was pursuing their dreams, living out life, even though he was not there with her.

He was, in *some* way, there with her. He could feel it — feel *her* profoundly.

CHAPTER 18

Rose walked down a narrow cobblestone path, which led to three wide steps. She grabbed the wooden handrail and walked onto the front porch. The boards creaked a bit under foot as she looked around. The bench swing was hung by two chains and swayed slightly in the breeze. Rose smiled and said out loud, to no one, "I always wanted a bench swing on a front porch like this." She thought back to the time she told Flynn about her dream of owning and running an inn. And how she wanted a front porch with a bench swing exactly like this house had. It was strange at that moment she pictured a couple, an elderly couple, sitting on the swing. They were covered in a checkered wool blanket and holding hands. The man pushed his feet a bit on the porch floor so that the swing would keep in motion. The woman leaned her head on his still broad shoulder and admired the front yard. As fast as she had pictured the scene, it was gone. The empty swing lonely again. She stared into the front yard where rose bushes and peonies used to be, and only brown wispy weeds now stood. She could see it full of life as it was before. Lovely, happy plants and flowers well taken care of and reaching to the sunlight.

Turning back to the house she could see that the front porch, painted white, was chipping and boards were rotting. A couple of high back rocking chairs still sat next to the front door. Rose could picture past owners sitting in them waving to passers-by.

She wanted to walk inside but didn't dare trespass. It seemed pretty clear that no one actually lived here, but still, she wasn't free to waltz through the front door. Though, why was it so tempting?

As if God was judging her and sent his messenger, a voice from behind caught her off guard.

"Hi there," and sensing he had surprised Rose, continued, "Oh, I'm sorry. I didn't mean to startle you. I'm Father Eli. Dear friends of mine left this house to me and I promised to always keep an eye on it until the perfect buyer came about. Are you interested?"

Rose stammered, "Oh, no. Just looking. I didn't mean to lurk around like some curious tom cat. To be honest, the house just has a feel to it that drew me in. Like I had been here before. Like a place I've always known about, dreamed about."

"Ahh yes. Some might call that déjà vu. Strange feeling isn't it?" Father Eli said, but he smiled as if he knew something Rose didn't.

"What's your name? If you don't mind my asking?"

"Rose Mitchell. Nice to meet you, Father."

"And you, Rose. Now, let's open up the front door and take a tour of the house. I can see you were contemplating that very thing when I strolled up the sidewalk," Father Eli said with a smirk that held no judgment behind it.

Who was Rose kidding? She desperately wanted to see what this treasure held inside. Father Eli took an old key from his front pocket and unlocked the old oak door with a click.

The door slowly creaked open. The house was still furnished with furniture dating back to the 1930s, 40s, 50s? Rose wasn't a historian, but it was clear the furnishings were not the current style. The foyer was large and she and Father Eli stood upon an antique area rug. It was faded, but the handmade intricate patterns were still visible and impressive. Next to the front door stood an old coat tree and a vintage umbrella stand. On the opposite side of the foyer a small, cushioned bench sat up against the wall. Straight ahead was a tall staircase with a wooden banister that any young child would have loved sliding down.

Father Eli led the way and encouraged Rose to follow. To her left was a sitting room, charming, with large windows letting sunshine in or a cool autumn breeze. Two lovely, emerald green armchairs sat facing a large brick fireplace. The mantel was of solid oak and still held its rich, dark color that shined. Above the mantel hung a framed colonial American flag. It looked to be quite old and despite the protection of the glass, a bit yellowed in areas.

On the other side of the large room was a long dining room table with eight chairs. Against the wall nearby was a wooden buffet where large meals could be displayed and served to guests. Rose was admiring each and every characteristic of the house. The details of the crown molding, the arches between rooms, the ceiling medallions.

Houses like this one weren't built in a week, but they sure were built to be special and admired. She gazed at the room and imagined past residents enjoying parties, holiday celebrations and quiet cozy nights in front of a crackling fire in the fireplace.

Looking to the opposite side of the foyer was a swinging door, which she assumed led to the kitchen. A long hallway led just past the staircase where other closed doors were visible.

"Where would you like to start, Rose?" Father Eli asked, interrupting her admiration of the house. "Well, the kitchen is one of my favorite rooms in the house. Can we start there?" she suggested.

"Right this way," and he pushed open the swinging door for her to enter.

It looked as if the previous owners had just walked out the back door one day and left things as is. The kitchen held all the old appliances. The small dome refrigerator sat in the corner of the room next to a counter that held tin canisters. Plates were stacked on shelves above the counter. A beautiful hutch graced the back wall. Glass cabinet doors were held shut by brushed bronze latches. Small teacups and saucers were visibly and orderly stacked on the shelves of the hutch. White cloth napkins and dish towels were folded neatly in baskets on the floor next to the hutch. The butcher block in the center of the kitchen held potato and onion drawers underneath and only a light layer of dust covered the surface.

Rose could envision herself rolling out bread dough on the clean wooden surface each morning, while bacon fried on the stove and oatmeal bubbled in a pot. She was positive no other twenty-one year olds were dreaming of such things. Though she had always known she wasn't like the norm.

They continued the tour throughout the house including the sitting room, dining room, study and bathroom on the first floor. They walked up the tall staircase to the second floor and wandered through the six bedrooms and two additional bathrooms. All rooms were furnished with exquisite antique dressers and four post beds. Handmade quilts still laid upon the mattresses and sheer white curtains hung by bronze rods above tall windows.

The scent was a bit musty due to years gone by. Rose could only stare mystified. Father Eli suggested, "Rose, why don't you stop by Wild Flowers? Violet and Daisy rent out rooms above their shop for guests. Yes, they own a flower shop and yes, those are their given names," he said, chuckling, as if he'd gotten the question before. "It's getting dark, and I assure you they are sweet, welcoming young ladies. You will be comfortable there."

Father Eli walked Rose to Wild Flowers and said good-bye, while Rose opened, yet another new door here in Cherish.

CHAPTER 19

Wild Flowers was a somewhat eclectic shop. Shelves hung on walls with Ficus plants dangling their vines. Large, colorful floral arrangements sat between tables where smaller vases of baby's breath and orchids were displayed. Boxes of tulip bulbs and packets of seeds were set throughout the shop. It wasn't exactly orderly, but Rose liked the wildness of Wild Flowers.

She finally found her way to a wooden counter near the back of the shop. There was a small written note that read, *Ring bell for Service.* Rose put her finger on the push bell and gave a quick tap. *Ding.* After a few moments she heard footsteps coming down the steps. Pushing through a curtain appeared a tall, middle-aged woman wearing a long flowing skirt. Her hair was long and auburn red curls sprung in all directions.

"Hello there! How are you and how may I help you, sweet pea?" she asked cheerfully.

"Hi, I'm Rose. I need a room for the night. Father Eli recommended, and quite literally, led me here."

"Well, he led you to the right place. Did you say your name is Rose? Oh, I just love flower names! My name is Daisy. My sister, Violet, and I own the shop together. And, as you know, rent out the rooms upstairs to guests traveling through town. I happen to have a single bed room available if you'd like to take a look," Daisy offered. Rose agreed and they proceeded up the flight of stairs.

Daisy stopped at the first door on the right and unlocked it. "Take a peek, Rose. It's a small, but comfy room. You look like you could use a night's sleep. Can I bring up a little snack before you turn in?" Daisy offered. Rose had become a bit hungry. It had been hours since her lunch at the Crystal Café.

"Actually, that would be wonderful," she replied. After Daisy closed the door behind her, Rose looked at her room. Daisy was right, it was small and simple, but not without charm. A twin bed sat against the wall with a quilt atop that had large sunflowers stitched in an intricate pattern. A nightstand stood next to the bed with a Bible and small lamp atop. Rose looked out the small four pane window and admired Cherish from above. Taking off her shoes (finally) she plopped down on the bed and groaned. She rubbed her temples and ran her hands through her long hair. What the hell was she doing here? Tomorrow she would need to try calling her parents again. By now, they no doubt had a search party out looking for her. And staying overnight in an unknown town alone — in a little room rented out by strangers? Well, this just wasn't the Rose she knew. But everything about it felt right. Like all her roads she had traveled in her life had led her in some way to Cherish. It all felt perfect and beautiful and meant to be.

Except…for Flynn. They were meant to be on this adventure together. How many times had she dreamed and envisioned a town like Cherish where Flynn and she could spend their lives together. In that instance, she became very sad and worried about her husband. Closing her eyes, the video segments and the news anchor's reports from earlier that day flashed through her mind again. *Was her husband among the soldiers being sent on missions that were unlikely to succeed without at least a casualty or two? Maybe several? Who was to know?*

When Flynn asked her to be his wife, she knew what she was getting into, marrying an Army soldier. She had accepted it and was extremely proud of her husband. But she knew it was something she could never get used to. Watching him leave, not knowing when or *if* she would see him again. She knew nothing else to do at that moment except to kneel at the side of the small, modest bed. Doing so, she closed her eyes again and said a silent prayer for Flynn's safety and his return to her.

As she opened her eyes and stood up again the door slowly creaked open. Another tall woman with long, wavy black hair walked in holding a small plate of something and a glass.

"Hi Rose, I'm Violet. Daisy is preoccupied with a large delivery we have going out tomorrow. I offered to come up," Violet said.

"Hi Violet, great to meet you," Rose replied.

"Listen hon, you need to get some rest, but here is a plate of strawberries, cheese slices and saltine crackers. Also, a glass of ice water. Nothing fancy. I left a towel and a pair of clean PJs by the bath if you'd like to wash up before bed. Down the hall, third door on the left."

There seemed to be a touch of sadness in Violet's eyes, a loneliness perhaps? It wasn't an obvious detail, but Rose thought she saw something there. She wondered why.

Violet and Daisy were both polite and seemed a pleasure to be around, but their personalities were polar opposites. Daisy was bubbly, confident and silly. Violet appeared to be quiet, meek and much more serious. But maybe there were things that had happened in Violet's past that lent a hand to her demeanor.

Rose didn't aim to pry, but should the two become friends, she hoped Violet would confide in her if necessary.

"Violet, thank you so much for your hospitality. And for the food. You make a girl in a strange town feel welcome."

Rose held the dainty china plate that held her snack, in her hands. She noticed details so closely. Looking down, the strawberries sat neatly lined next to a row of small square slices of cheddar cheese and a few soda crackers stacked on the side. The porcelain dish looked like some her mom had stored in the hutch cabinet back home. Small, lily of the valley was intricately painted around the perimeter, greens and whites on a soft ivory shine. Art work.

"Oh, we are delighted to have you, Rose. Please let me know if you need anything else."

Rose couldn't have felt more welcome and grateful. "Thank you so much for your hospitality. I sure appreciate it."

Violet smiled and quietly closed the door as she left the room.

Rose picked at the plate of food and took a long gulp of water. She laid down on the bed, still feeling heart sick over her thoughts of Flynn. *Where was he? What danger was he in at this moment? Would she ever sleep curled up next to him again?* Feeling overly exhausted, Rose began to cry.

The next thing she saw was the sun rising in her window the next morning.

CHAPTER 20

When Rose went down the hall to the bathroom there was a towel still folded next to the bath. A clean outfit replaced the pajamas she never wore last night. Realizing she slept in her yesterday clothes, she felt like a bath and a fresh outfit would be nice. She sure was being well cared for here. The warm water over her body revived her and after she put on the strangely, perfectly fitted clothing she ventured downstairs.

Violet and Daisy were busy boxing large floral arrangements to be delivered to St. Mary's church for a funeral.

Noticing Rose, Daisy gave a cheerful greeting, "Good Morning, sweet pea. How are you feeling this morning? You looked dead in your tracks last night."

Rose laughed in agreement, "Yes, I suppose you're right. Sleep and a hot bath brought me back to life. That, and your kindness."

Violet brought her a hot cup of coffee and a cheese danish. "Here you go, Rose. Take a seat and have a little bite." Rose looked around the room for a chair, finding none free. Sensing this, Daisy improvised, tipping over a crate next to a table covered with pink heather and lemon leaf bunches. Pushing the fragrant flowers aside she motioned for Rose to sit.

"Sorry, doll face. It's a little crowded in here isn't it?"

"I love it," Rose replied. She sat on the makeshift chair, and enjoyed her delicious danish, while the flower sisters worked their magic. Violet was very business-like, measuring and arranging flowers like she would work a math equation. Daisy, on the other hand, hummed a soft tune while she tucked random sprigs of baby's breath here and there. The sisters clearly had different personalities, but both were sweet in their own way. And they sure seemed to work well together. The lovely floral masterpieces were coming together in front of her eyes.

"Are you planning to stay for a few days here in our lovely little town, Rose?" Daisy asked.

"I think I might. You're right, it is lovely. And after one day, I've already met some welcoming and wonderful residents of Cherish, including yourselves." Rose winked.

Violet, being the quieter one, softly added, "Please don't be shy if you need anything. We are happy to lend a hand if needed, Rose."

"Thank you both. I really appreciate that. And, this cheese danish is delicious, by the way." Finishing her last sip of the strong coffee, Rose decided she'd take another walk around town. Possibly visit some of the shops and maybe stop and say "hi" to Mudsie at the Crystal Café. Oh, and she needed to call her parents — cannot forget that.

"Thank you, again, for the coffee and danish. I think I'm going to take a little stroll through town this morning," Rose announced.

"It's a beautiful day for it, sunshine. You enjoy," Daisy yelled from behind an armful of hydrangeas.

Stepping out onto the sidewalk Rose took a deep breath of fresh air. Town's people were milling around, in and out of shops and their own businesses. Noticing a small general store, Rose made her way across the street.

Chives O'Connor stepped out of the post office, almost knocking into Rose on his way.

"Oh, pardon me Miss…was it Rose?"

"Good memory, Chives. No biggie. You're a man on a mission this morning," she teased.

"Yes, well, running a bit late opening up shop this morning. Gas is supposed to go up to thirty cents a gallon by tomorrow. So, believe me it will be a steady flow of traffic at the pump today," he complained, but gave Rose a friendly nod before turning to leave. She smiled. Chives was sure a good ole guy. He wore old, grease stained trousers and a button up shirt tucked in. His white hair and mustache had a tint of red in it, which, along with his Irish last name, gave her an inkling of his nationality. He was rather short and round, with a hearty laugh. Rose thought, with a beard and red suit, he'd play Santa really well. She laughed to herself and then stopped, thinking for a minute.

"Did Chives say gas was going *up* to thirty cents a gallon? In Duluth it had gone up to $3.25 per gallon. Was she in a dream or on another planet? She shook the thought from her head, thinking, "Well, good for Cherish. They don't know how lucky they are."

Entering the general store, she noticed a few sundry items on a shelf near the entrance that she knew she needed. Grabbing a cart, she started shopping. A tube of toothpaste and toothbrush, a hair brush, shampoo, conditioner, soap, a razor, mascara, lip gloss and a couple hair ties. She then made her way toward the small clothing section. She hadn't planned to stay in Cherish long but needed a few changes of clothes. The flower sisters couldn't provide for her forever. She found a package of underwear, a lace bra, two pairs of shorts, a t-shirt, a light jacket, a long skirt, a pair of pajamas and a pair of sandals. Deciding on one more skirt, she placed it in her cart and was startled by a very large man, with a full black beard, who had approached her.

"Rose is it? Are you finding everything you need?"

Taken by surprise, Rose stammered, "Yes, thank you sir. Have I met you?"

"Oh, no you haven't yet. But small town people talk when there's a new face in town," he replied, "I'm Hank. My wife Millie and I own the store. Let us know if you need anything else."

He pointed toward the cash register where a tiny woman no taller than five feet stood. She had a blonde bob haircut and wore black rimmed glasses. She waved to Rose. She returned the greeting and kept browsing. Picking up a couple odds and ends she decided that she had plenty for now and made her way up to the cash register where Millie waited.

"So, where are you from, Rose?" Millie asked.

"Duluth. Not too far from here. Though I guess I can't say I've ever been to Cherish before. And too bad. It sure is a lovely little town," Rose said thoughtfully.

"Oh, thank you. We sure love it here. And happy to see new faces like yours around."

Rose and Millie visited a bit more. Then after Rose had paid and her items were bagged up she said goodbye to Hank and Millie and walked her things back to Wild Flowers.

She then, continued exploring.

Leisurely, she walked down Main Street. It was a clean, well-kept town. Townspeople were, as she had noticed the day before, exceptionally cordial and friendly, offering a nod, a wave or hello when she walked by. She noticed many children out and about riding bicycles and wooden push scooters. Some on foot chasing each other. Funny how no adults seemed to be attending them. A few businesses and front steps of nearby houses had metal crates holding empty glass bottles. Milk delivery?

Really? Rose thought. *Was Cherish this old school?* She decided she loved it and kept walking down the sidewalk. Large glass storefronts displayed fashions from decades prior, the pencil skirt and button up cardigans, men's pleated trousers, bowling shirts and penny loafers. This town was out of a story book!

Something was leading her back in the direction of the old house she and Father Eli had toured yesterday. Seeing it again in the morning sunlight brought it alive. She stood on the cobblestone path imagining what it could be; what she could make it.

The wooden sign out front was freshly painted white, as was the trim on the house and the front porch. The remainder of the house, a soft yellow. On either side of the cobblestone path large bushes of soft peach rosebuds grew. Light pink peonies stretched over metal cages, while tall hollyhocks vied for attention. Dainty white lobelia lined the path right up to the front porch steps.

A few potted plants from Wild Flowers sat up on the porch. She and Mudsie sat in the rockers on the porch, sipping iced tea while greeting guests and helping them to their rooms at *her* inn.

Though she didn't know what it would be called, she knew she wanted this vision to come to life. She knew, somehow, at that very moment, Flynn would be telling her to *go for it*. He would be pushing her to start living their dream. It would take a lot of money, work, sweat and tears (as they say). But she found herself not wanting to leave Cherish, nor this house. It felt like home already.

Feeling a bit light headed with her new aspirations, she decided her first steps would be onto the steps of St. Mary's Church. First, she could use God's strength and guidance with what she was planning (hoping) to take on. And second, Father Eli would most likely be found there.

If she truly wanted her inn to become a reality, only he could make that happen.

FLYNN

Dear Rosebud,

You're never gonna believe what we did today, in the desert of Afghanistan. We set up a game of baseball. We had some down time and were given a half-day off duty.

I'm not sure who started the game. Sanchez brought his baseball from home and was tossing it up in the air. He's a huge baseball fan; played in college too. He has three older brothers who have all played in college too. He says baseball was as much a tradition in the Sanchez house as Sunday Mass or the sons joining the US military. That Sanchez though.... nice kid. All my closest buddies here are. I tell ya, I'm sure grateful for that.

But anyway, before we knew it, someone had set out four makeshift bases (empty duffle bags I think) and we used a broken board from one of the fallen down buildings as a bat. Not ideal, but no one cared. It was a comfort from home. Hanging with the "bros" and playing an All-American game. With our shirts off and a quick splash of water from our canteens over our heads, it was almost bearable in the heat. After the game, Captain Silva even grilled up some brats and handed out cans of some foreign kind of beer. I tell you, Rose, it tasted better than any damn beer I have ever sipped on.

Somehow, us soldiers - men and women, of all backgrounds, ethnicities, shapes, sizes - actually enjoyed ourselves. We almost forgot for a brief few hours that we were at war. It brought us closer. We are family. We are all fighting as one, for our country and for our families we left behind. I slept like a baby that night too, Rose. Which, until then, had been unheard of.

I have a few minutes before I report to morning briefs, so I thought I'd write.

What are you up to? I haven't received one letter. I imagine it is because the delivery time out here is absurdly slow, if not a matter of emergency.

No matter, I write to you as much for myself as for you. As I've said, it gives me a great comfort that I am grateful for.

I look at your photo so often it has become wrinkled like

an aged polaroid from my parents' old albums. I can't help it. I miss my wife. Your smile still makes me weak, Rose. You know that, and I'm guessing you use it to your advantage sometimes. Ha.

I miss the smell of the lavender laundry detergent you wash our bed sheets in. I miss that egg dish you used to make in the mornings with the pie crust and sausage and cheese. My mouth is watering as I think of it.

I'm still curious if you have taken road trips across Minnesota in search of the perfect setting for our future inn. I hope you have. Nothing would make me happier than to come home to find you already making plans and putting them into motion. I'm on board, Love.

And I will be there soon. Counting down the days.

Until then, be safe and keep visiting me in my dreams.

Love,

Flynn

CHAPTER 21

St. Mary's was a beautiful, old white church shaded by large oak trees. Restful and serene. The very large mahogany doors at the front entrance were unlocked, welcoming all who wished to come in. Rose pushed them open and quietly entered. She dipped her fingers in the bowl of Holy Water, making the sign of the cross as she had learned many years ago at her First Communion. Several wooden pews were set in the Chapel. Beautiful stained-glass windows lined the walls, and the sun made the colors come alive.

She knelt at one of the back pews and bowing her head began a silent prayer asking advice from a friend that could listen to her heart when she didn't have the words.

After a few minutes she heard footsteps from behind and then felt a soft tap on her shoulder. Father Eli smiled at her and whispered, "Hi Rose. We have a funeral scheduled for 10:00 today, but you're welcome to stay until then."

Oh, that's right! The flower sisters had been busy putting together the arrangements.

"That's ok. I was just finishing up here Father. I was hoping we could discuss the inn we had toured yesterday, though. When you are able, that is."

"The inn?" he questioned.

"I guess I'm getting ahead of myself," Rose laughed, completely embarrassed. "I am interested in purchasing the house and my thought would be to turn it into an Inn. At least that's my wild aspiration."

Father Eli looked up at the cross on the altar and back to Rose. "I tell you what, here's the key. You go take a look again and see what work needs to be done. Sit on the front porch and picture it being yours. This afternoon I will walk down, and we can discuss the logistics. Does that sound ok?"

Rose nodded in agreement. Father Eli could sense she was feeling many emotions, none of which were settling.

"Rose, listen. Sometimes God leads you down unknown paths. They may be scary or unsettling for a bit. But the trick is to trust in His plan. In the end, if you always ask Him for the guidance you need, everything will turn out perfectly."

"Thank you Father. I will try hard to remember that," Rose promised. He handed her the key and sent her back out of the church through the double mahogany doors.

Rose was filled with a new excitement she hadn't felt in months. Almost running up the steps, she put the old key in the keyhole and unlocked the door. It creaked open and as before Rose looked inside this time and envisioned what could be hers.

Fresh paint covered the walls. The wooden floors shined, and the rugs and furniture were dust-free. A warm fire crackled in the fireplace while a couple of guests sat in the emerald green armchairs, sipping on cups of coffee. She saw herself walking in from the back; the screen door slamming behind her. She held a handful of freshly snipped herbs and in the crook of her other arm, a basket of Roma tomatoes and English cucumbers. The vision felt so real she could almost smell the smokey scent of the burning logs in the fireplace, the smell of freshly snipped rosemary sprigs and dill weed. She could feel the warm steam rising from the cups of coffee her guests enjoyed and could feel the breeze through an open kitchen window. The sound of content friends visiting, birds chirping at the window feeders and an old record player softly playing Billie Holiday songs in the background were a welcome thought.

Ohhhh, it was true, some (much) work needed to be done. But feeling like this might become a reality for Rose, made it all seem easy. Nothing seemed impossible or hard when your heart's passion was pushing you forward.

Clapping her hands together, she declared to the emptiness of the house, "We have work to do!"

CHAPTER 22

Father Eli's promised visit later that afternoon found Rose stripping bedding off the beds and pulling drapes from windows. She was so focused on her task that his presence in the doorway startled her.

"Oh my gosh Father, you scared the daylights out of me!" Rose exclaimed. Father Eli felt bad for scaring Rose, but deep inside felt a glimmer of hope that, finally, someone (the right someone) was here to do the place proud.

"I see you've dug in," he said smiling.

Father Eli was a tall, thin man, about age forty-five or so. Rose guessed about her dad's age. He had a short haircut, brown and a clean shaven face and the most trustworthy, kind eyes Rose had ever seen. She felt some sort of connection, maybe a comfort too, in him. She felt he was a friend she could come to at any time and feel no judgment. Much how she pictured Jesus Christ must've been. It made sense that the people of Cherish spoke so highly of him. He was something real, something *special.*

"I sure have. I know we haven't discussed terms, purchase price, or if you are even considering going through with the deal. But either way, I feel an obligation to clean this house up and attempt to bring it back to life."

Father Eli looked at the pile of dusty, worn drapes laying in a heap on the floor and answered, "I think that is a wonderful idea, Rose. Why don't you do just that. Do some cleaning, painting, redecorating a bit and take note of repairs that need to be done. As needed, I will pay for these improvements and count that as pay for your hard work or factor it into the sale price. We won't make any solid decisions right away. Does that sound ok?"

Rose knew she wanted the house — felt it in her bones. But, perhaps it was the more reasonable of an offer, for now. She nodded in agreement and shook his hand firmly, "I think that sounds like a perfect plan."

"Great! Now let's get these drapes and piles of bedding to the laundromat. While we are waiting on them I'll take you to the Crystal Café for an early supper," he offered.

Father Eli drove a simple sedan which he had parked in front of the old house. They tossed the dirty linens in the back seat and in the trunk. Closing the doors to keep it all in took some muscle. They both laughed and hopped in the car.

At the laundromat they added detergent and coins to three large washing machines, and then made their way to the Crystal Café.

"Well, hi there girlie cakes. You're still in town huh?" Mudsie said as Rose walked in. She greeted Father Eli in the same boisterous way, "Hi Padre. You showing Rose the house huh?"

Father Eli was used to the brassy personality Mudsie had and never took any insult to the way she acted.

The truth was, there was no better, kinder heart in the world than hers. All who knew her would confirm that, if asked.

"I am. She's doing some work on the place. Brightening her up a bit. But Rose needs a break and a good meal," Father Eli replied.

Mudsie showed them to a booth. "Well, we still have plenty of our homemade tater tot hotdish if you are a fan. We also have spaghetti and meatballs with garlic bread or a fried bologna sandwich with a side of coleslaw, on special. Anything sound particularly tasty this evening?" Mudsie asked.

Rose replied, "Wow, actually it all sounds delicious. I must be starving." In the busyness of the day she had forgotten, entirely, to eat. She decided, "I will have the tater tot hotdish with an iced tea, please."

Father Eli handed Mudsie his menu and nodded, "I will have the same. You do make the best tater tot hotdish in Minnesota, in my opinion, Mudsie. So, I can't pass it up." She smiled, always happy to hear praise for her dishes as she took their menus and order ticket back to the kitchen.

Father Eli's face became a bit more business-like and he took a small notepad and pen from his coat pocket. "Ok Rose, so far what have you noticed in the house that needs attention. Chives O'Connor is my go-to handyman. Mrs. Patches, a teacher at the school, mends upholstery and linens beautifully. And I can think of several other volunteers that wouldn't mind pitching in where needed." Rose, suddenly, became overwhelmed with the task of being the woman-in-charge.

She sighed, "I was so engrossed in my work today, I hardly took time to note the major needs. Can we come back to that question tomorrow? I plan to wake up bright and early and get back to the house."

"Of course. You take a couple of days even and when you have a list compiled, bring it my way."

Unintentionally interrupting their discussion, Mudsie set two steaming plates of her famous tater tot hotdish in front of them, along with iced teas and rolled up silverware.

"Bon appétit, my friends. Can we grab you anything else?"

Rose had already taken her fork out and was digging in, but stopped and giggled, "This looks so good Mudsie. I can't wait to try it. Thank you." She tasted the hotdish and she decided Father Eli was absolutely right. This certainly was the best of this Minnesota delight she had tasted yet. Crunchy tater tots sat atop a creamy beef filled gravy with onions, carrots, green beans and herbs swirled in the mix.

Rose took a few long drinks of her iced tea and, setting it down, asked, "So Father, did you always know you wanted to be a priest, if it's ok to ask?"

"Of course, that is a perfectly fine question. I always wonder why people think it may offend me. I like the question actually."

Father Eli set his fork down and thoughtfully began, "I was thirteen years old, seventh grade, a very awkward, introverted young guy. Not much for friends. Thick glasses, a mouth full of braces, a face covered in acne. That and teenagers are mean, to be honest. So, I had a rough time for a while. My parents weren't overly strict, but the one rule they had was to be up and at em Sunday morning for church. I always groaned. It was so boring. And our priest seemed, frankly, unapproachable. Not a regular person that you could laugh with or watch a Vikes game with. Ya know?

"Well, the summer after I had turned thirteen, it was announced that our current priest, Father Paul, was being transferred and a new priest, Father David, was coming to St. Joseph's. A new world opened up for me. Father David was young and full of excitement. He would take the time to stop and talk to everyone. He would crouch down to talk to a four year old, tie their shoe or ask them what they were going to do for fun today. He would shake hands with the guy sitting in the back pew that was wearing a dirty, ripped t-shirt; would softly hug the small elderly woman he knew had been struggling with illness.

"What I wasn't used to though, was that he took the time to say hello to me. To ask me how school was going, what sports I enjoyed, if my family had gone on any camping trips that summer yet. He made me feel like a somebody, Rose. I wanted to be like Father David. The rest is kind of history, as they say. I went to seminary school, traveled to the holy lands, have met and enjoyed many people throughout my time as a priest. Like anything, it isn't without its ups and downs, but all and all, certainly where God intended me to be."

Father Eli smiled and began eating his dinner again. Rose thought about his story and responded genuinely, "I'm glad we crossed paths, Father."

Cleaning her plate Rose became full and sleepy. Father Eli noticed and asked, "Rose, I'll go put the linens in the driers and fold them up if you would like to get over to Wild Flowers before dark. I think you could use a good night's sleep."

Rose thanked him and they left the café after one more compliment to Mudsie for a wonderful meal.

Despite the fact that the sun was still glowing bright in the summer sky, Rose was spent. She said goodbye to Father Eli and walked in the direction of Wild Flowers.

What a day! She felt full. Not just belly-full, but her heart was full. How was it, that her heart could hurt so much for Flynn and yet feel his presence in everything she was doing here in Cherish. Laying her head down that night she thought, for the first time in months, *I can't wait to start the day tomorrow.*

FLYNN

Flynn sat at Collins's side holding his hand in comfort as they sat in the back of the covered Army truck, racing for the base. They needed a medic, and fast.

A fly-by shot had hit Collins in the torso. It appeared the bullet grazed his side, hopefully missing any major organs. God willing! Though, it was hard to tell with the ripped fabric, torn flesh and grotesque blood on Collins's body.

Flynn spoke to his buddy in a soothing, comforting tone. He knew his hands were shaking, but he wouldn't let his voice follow suit.

"Collins, man, you are a tough son of a bitch. I can't believe how you barely made a peep when that sucker bit ya." Flynn held his hand tight and wiped a ripped square of t-shirt across Collins's forehead where beads of sweat flowed down his anxious brow. Marty sat across from Flynn holding another balled up shirt against Collins's wound, pressing firmly, the once white t-shirt now almost completely Merlot red.

"No shit, Dude. I would probably be crying for my girl right now if that thing hit me." Marty chimed in but gave Flynn a concerned look.

"Ah, it was nothing. I sa — I saw it com– coming," Collins coughed until he choked.

"Give me a canteen, someone! He needs water." Out of nowhere someone handed Flynn their canteen and he carefully poured a few drops of water in Collins's mouth. It was enough to stop his retching. When Collins turned his head away after a few meager sips and closed his eyes, Flynn felt a worry like none he had ever experienced.

"Hurry, we don't have much time!"

Almost seconds later the truck stopped, and four medics were there carefully pulling Collins onto a gurney.

"We'll take him from here, men. Thank you."

Flynn and Marty sat on the tail gate of that Army truck, blood soaked towels in hand, both exhausted, physically and emotionally, and unable to move a muscle.

CHAPTER 23

After a quick cup of coffee and a blueberry scone with the flower sisters (as she had come to affectionately refer to them), Rose made a trip to the hardware store. She purchased a bucket, mop, multi-purpose cleaner, a broom, dust pan and a bundle of rags. She had seen a red wagon in the front window for sale and decided that would come in handy for the supplies she would be hauling to the house. She thanked the clerk for pulling out the wagon and filling it with her bags.

The sun was gleaming high in the sky this morning and the bluebirds were singing a sweet song for the folks of Cherish. Rose felt light on her feet, greeting people as she walked. Young kids zipped by her on bikes and scooters, laughing and enjoying the summer break.

Stopping the wagon at the front steps of the house, she began to make trips in with her cleaning supplies. Rose stood in the foyer, thinking, *Now, where to begin?* She stood and pondered the question for a minute, then saying out loud, "Well. Nothing's gonna get done just standing here, Rose. Let's start in the kitchen. That room will require a little elbow grease." (Though she never really understood that phrase.)

She wiped counters clean, then scrubbed walls and appliances until her hands were red and raw. The dust on the shelves and on the top of the hutch was as thick as fur and breathing in the fragments was making Rose sneeze. The grease and dirt from under the appliances and butcher block was like tar; a tar that was glue when she attempted to scrape it loose.

Finally, sitting down on the tile floor she wiped her forehead with a clean rag, and craved a glass of cold water. Finding a drink glass in the cupboard she went to the sink and turned the knob marked *cold*. She heard a groan and a screech. After a few minutes, liquid began rushing through the pipes. Finally, dribbling out the faucet, into her glass, was a brick red sludge. She kept the water running, figuring it just needed to clear out a bit. No luck. "Well, Father Eli, I found the first repair job to start our list."

Rose sighed and decided, "I'll work another hour and walk up to the gas station for an ice cold Coke. I can also speak to Chives about repairs and when he'd have the time to take a look."

Continuing throughout the house, she shook rugs, dusted framed art, the fireplace mantel and the stairway banister. She swept the wood floors and mopped until they shined like warm honey. By the time she had finished all but the bathrooms, it had been not one, but two hours. She was beat. Being a true Minnesotan, she exclaimed out loud, "Uffda. I need a break!"

Rose was tired; this was true. But what a feeling of accomplishment.

Along with the obvious plumbing issues, it was clear the house needed new windows. The shingles on the roof, no doubt, needed to be replaced. The light fixtures were in desperate need of an electrician to do some updates and get things up to code. There were the obvious necessities such as the fresh coats of paint on the exterior and the interior of every room, every piece of trim, every teeny, little twist and turn of crown molding that she had admired from the beginning, which now was causing her headache.

She knew there must be several other things she wasn't noticing, but once she had the place *spic-n-span*, she and Father Eli would do a walk through to further inspect. Chives could accompany them at that time if he was willing.

Rose opened the heavy pine door to leave, when she saw Daisy and Violet walking up the path carrying a picnic basket.

"Hi sweet pea, we thought you might like to take a break," Daisy exclaimed. Violet smiled and said, "We grabbed some ice cold colas from Chive's gas station and made some fresh tuna salad for lunch."

How sweet these ladies were to Rose and how appreciated. Rose motioned to the chairs on the front porch and said, "Oh, that sounds wonderful. Please sit! I'll grab another chair from inside."

By the time she had returned with a dining room chair, Daisy and Violet had set out plates, silverware and red and white gingham napkins. Daisy handed Rose an open bottle of Coke while Violet dished up tuna salad for each of them. Daisy sat down and blurted out, before anyone could speak, "Now, Rose, we have taken the rest of the day off to help you out. You tell us what you need. We can go get paint and paint brushes from the hardware store and dive in with that project or scrub toilets, iron drapes and table cloths. Whatever you need."

Violet smiled at Rose gently, saying, "Why don't we let her think a minute, Daisy. Get a little something in her belly."

The ladies enjoyed the creamy tuna salad and laughed together about stories the flower sisters told of days gone by. How their mother and father had owned the building that Wild Flowers now operated in. How the sisters had been named after flowers, but never thought they would actually open a flower shop. Violet had gone to school to be a nurse and Daisy worked as a secretary down the road at the Main Street Insurance Agency. Their parents had grown old, had moved to a retirement home, but passed within a year of each other soon after.

The building was left to their daughters. Father Eli had been the one to suggest opening a shop of some kind and perhaps renting the upstairs rooms out. He had helped them get started and after ten years, they were still at it and loving this life more and more each day. It was refreshing to hear their story. It made Rose feel even more hopeful about the house and what she hoped it to be. On top of that, she felt so fortunate to have met Violet and Daisy and hoped they'd be friends for a long time to come.

Sensing the time was ticking on, Rose brushed a few crumbs from her skirt and put her napkin on the table. All three women began to clear the table and pack up the picnic basket. Daisy grabbed the extra chair to bring back inside. She lifted it and took a step toward the door when the floorboard under her crunched and broke. Daisy's left ankle twisted and went right through the board. She fell to the floor grimacing in pain. Rose yelled to Daisy, "Daisy, oh my word! Are you ok? I am so, so sorry! Is your ankle sprained? Broken? Ah, this is terrible."

Violet calmly sat Daisy comfortably against the porch railing and pulled her leg from the new hole in the rotting floorboards. She gently touched Daisy's ankle while Daisy clenched her teeth and started to form beads of sweat on her red hairline.

Violet spoke, "It looks like a bad sprain, Sis. We will need to ice this and put you in a chair with your leg elevated."

Rose exclaimed, "We should probably call the ambulance! What if it is broken?"

"No, no, that won't be necessary." Violet seemed to answer a bit too quickly. Almost as if she didn't like the idea. Perhaps, she felt like her expertise as a nurse was enough and questioning it was rude of Rose? Who knew, but Rose thought it a bit peculiar.

Letting the moment pass, Rose rubbed Daisy's back to comfort her, "I'm so sorry Daisy. I feel responsible."

Daisy, finally piped up, saying, "Well, I guess you found another repair project to add to Father Eli's list."

In spite of the unfortunate event, all three women looked at each other and began to laugh.

CHAPTER 24

After that first day, problems with the house just kept coming about. Daisy teased that the house was mad they were disturbing her slumber. Rose was getting more frustrated though. The chimney sweep said the fireplace needed repairs or it wouldn't be safe to burn wood. The plumber, after starting his work in the kitchen, found that in both bathrooms, the toilets, sinks and piping needed to be replaced. Then there was the damage done by rodents in the attic, more rotting floorboards on the porch, extensive wiring replacement needed throughout the house. Father Eli's list grew to be more of a book these days.

And then, at the worst possible time, it hit. A thunderstorm. A windy, destructive kind of thunderstorm. Rose had been busy upstairs in one of the bedrooms. She had just replaced the drawer handles on the antique dresser when she heard a loud rumble outside. Moving the freshly washed and ironed drapes, she looked out the window.

The yard was still, perfectly still. *Eerily* still. The color in the sky was strange and greenish. In the distance she could see steel colored clouds moving in.

"Oh no, not now!" Rose pleaded to the sky. Defying her, the thunder sounded again, and a blinding bright flash of lightning stung her eyes.

Rose ran to each room in the house, closing any cracked open windows. She rushed to her front porch, took in the few potted plants she had set out, and tucked her chairs inside the foyer for the night. She was anticipating some undesired storm action this evening. Luckily, she hadn't been one to fear storms. However, she had never stood up against one alone and in a new strange, very old, house.

After the few necessary precautions had been made, Rose calmly sat on her front step dabbing her head with a kitchen towel and waited. The still, humid air was not fooling her. The dark clouds had eaten up the greenish color in the sky now and were almost on top of her. Rose's long, blonde waves started floating in a new, light breeze. Putting her hand out from under the protection of the covered porch, one single raindrop splattered on the palm of her hand and rolled off. What seemed like only seconds later, the storm came to Cherish with a vengeance.

With the blinding flashes of lightning and the deafening crashes of thunder, a downpour began. "Here we go," Rose said out loud. She ran inside, slamming the front door shut tight.

Rose sat down in the kitchen pantry closet, where there were no windows. She had pulled the string of the lone light bulb above, which, for now, was working. As backup she brought a glass jar with a lit candle inside, in case the power went out.

With nothing to do, she started wiping the shelves down with her kitchen towel. Her broom was kept in the closet and so she utilized that as well, reaching for cobwebs in high up corners and sweeping old dirt and dust from under shelves and wooden boxes.

"Hmmm, maybe this isn't so bad after all. This pantry needed attention and was an easy space to ignore," Rose declared to no one. Hearing her voice echo with no response, made her kind of lonely and uneasy.

"Why didn't I get a cat, at least to keep me company in this huge, empty house? Tomorrow, I am on the hunt for Mrs. Bigglesworth." She laughed at the name she had randomly given her fictitious cat.

At that moment a loud crash outside the pantry door rudely interrupted her daydream. The house shuttered and, as she had feared, the power went out, leaving Rose alone. Alone in a dark, musty closet with only her dimly lit candle and her thoughts.

Time. Moved. Slowly.

She could hear the rapid pelting of rain, or was it hail, on the rooftop. Gusts of wind whistled through the tree branches. The crashing of thunder didn't subside. Would her house, with her in it, be sucked up and sent to Oz like Dorothy had been? Rose was beginning to wonder as the storm kept on without any end in sight.

Her throat started feeling dry after a while, and she thought she remembered setting a jug of orange juice on the third shelf on her left. It was very hard to see with such a small candle. She set the flickering candle on an empty spot near a few canned goods and reached for the jug of orange juice. On her tippy toes, she felt the jug and slid it toward her. Before she had time to realize it was the flour canister she had pulled forward, it was too late. Losing her balance, Rose slipped and fell to the floor. The canister followed and a puff of white exploded.

"Ouch!" Rose yelled, mostly in anger at her own stupidity. Now she looked like a powdered sugar donut, felt a bruise already forming on her right shoulder and to add insult to injury, she was still thirsty. This storm was relentless. Was it ever going to let up?

After another several minutes, Rose groaned, "I give up!" and sat down on the floor to wait it out.

In the cool, dark pantry, minutes ticked on, and Rose nodded off.

"Rose? Where are you?" She heard someone yell.

"Rose, where are you hiding, darlin?" That voice sounded like Mudsie's.

Disoriented, Rose had to think back to what the hell happened that evening and where was she? Why was she in a pitch black closet? Finally gathering herself, it all came back to her.

Thank God! The storm was over. And she had not been blown away to Oz.

"I'm in here!" She yelled loudly through the wooden door, trying, in haste, to find the old iron doorknob with her hands.

Finally, the door squeaked open from the outside. She squinted and saw standing before her Mudsie, Chives and Father Eli.

"Well, what in tarnation happened to you, Rose?," Mudsie asked in utter surprise.

Father Eli and Chives' jaws dropped as they saw Rose walk out of the pantry closet.

"Let's not ask. I'm sure there is a good explanation of why you are covered in flour and dust. Unfortunately, we have more pressing issues thanks to the storm, Rose," Chives' demeanor changing to serious after his initial smirk when he saw Rose.

"Oh no! What happened? Is everyone ok?" Rose asked, concerned.

"Yes, Rose. Everyone is fine. But, I can't say the same for your house. Don't worry, things can be fixed. We are just going to have to add a few extra jobs to our list," Father Eli told her.

Rose wiped her face off with the same kitchen towel she had sitting in the closet with her and ran outside.

"Oh my gosh!," She gasped, putting her hands over her mouth. A beautiful, very large, Oak tree had been knocked down in her front yard. The white sign had been crushed under it. A portion of the large branches had hit the front porch, tearing down shingles and fascia boards with it. As she eased around the side of the large tree, she could see the roof sustained some wind damage as well. Shingles lay all over her yard, along with debris of all kinds. Branches, blankets of leaves and random yard decor, were flung every which way.

"Listen, Rose. It could have been much worse. Everyone is fine. After seeing this damage, I have already contacted Tom's Tree Service as well as a roofing contractor that comes highly recommended. I'm hoping he can get here as soon as possible so that we can patch things up before another rainfall comes. Fingers crossed there isn't already water damage inside." Father Eli spoke to himself as much as the others with his last comment.

Rose worried the same and walked back inside and up the steps. She was hoping, praying there was no damage, holes, or water leaks in the ceilings. This would make for far more repairs to the house.

She was beginning to see the light at the end of the tunnel become as dim as the small candle she brought into the closet last night.

Knowing Rose was ok, Mudsie walked back to the café, but Chives and Father Eli walked upstairs to help Rose inspect the bedrooms and bathroom, each starting in a different area.

"You seeing anything, Chives?" Father Eli called.

"Both these bedrooms look dry as a bone. You Rosie?" Chives yelled down the hall.

"I don't really know exactly what to look for, but I see no obvious damage to the ceilings or walls, nor cracks or water leakage. But perhaps you guys want to come take a peek too," she requested, unsure.

The three went through each room again carefully and all appeared fine, to Rose's relief. After Chives and Father Eli (who kept reassuring Rose everything would work out just fine) left, Rose looked at herself in her dresser mirror and gasped.

"O…k. I will be needing a shower before anything else is done." Her hair was the color of her grandmother's and her clothes white washed. In spite of everything, she laughed and shook her head as she walked to Wild Flowers to use the sisters' bathroom.

She turned on the shower, letting the hot steam rise into the room and fog up the mirror. She grabbed a fluffy bath towel out of the closet and took her clothes off. Moving the shower curtain she eased under the warm streams of water. What a day Rose thought. As if enough problems with the house weren't already hounding her. Now this. Rose squirted shampoo in the palm of her hand and thought to herself, *Am I crazy? What am I doing here? How is it conceivable that I can make this all come together?*

The rest of the day, Rose was agitated and troubled as she cleaned the pantry clear of flour and, given the empty canister on the shelf, added it to her grocery list. She wandered her yard, picking up sticks and raking loose leaves, dumping them with her little wagon in the nearby woods. She felt discontent and down. Unsure if this whole plan, *this fantasy*, was a smart idea.

With her mind elsewhere and not on task, she dropped a handful of branches on her foot.

"Damn it!! You stupid fricken sticks! You are stupid, naive Rose!" She kicked a couple of the branches across the backyard, pushed her wagon hard enough to tip it on its side. She stomped off, needing a brisk walk. A walk away from this dream-turned-nightmare. A nearby path through the woods would do nicely.

Rose started off huffing and puffing, angry at nothing that made any real sense to her. She could hear Father Eli's voice in the back of her mind telling her to calm herself and understand that setbacks happen. But, what a mess things had become. Maybe even he was at his wit's end...she wouldn't blame him.

For Rose, she was getting very close to her's.

FLYNN

Dear Rosebud,

I don't have a whole lot of time to write this morning, but I want to tell you that you keep me strong here. You give me courage. You don't let me give up or lose faith. Us soldiers had a traumatic experience not so long ago here. It was something I dare not share with you, but it was a nightmare I'm afraid I won't soon forget. However, after the panic and horror wore off a bit (that and the shot of brandy Captain Silva gave me) I saw your face again. As I laid on my hard cot and closed my eyes, begging for an hour's sleep - there you were again. Thank you for visiting my thoughts over here angel. You don't know how much of a savior you have been to me. I can do nothing for you here, but I hope you are staying strong and keeping faith in whatever you are doing.

It's a journey, all of this. Whatever lies ahead, let's tackle it with the comforting thoughts of one another.

Keep smiling Sweetheart.

Love,

Flynn

CHAPTER 25

A week had passed. The tree was removed, chopped and given to a family happy for the firewood. The roofing contractor had even come to inspect the damages in need of repairs. Rose still was feeling a building sense of stress she was unable to shake.

Not surprisingly, Father Eli had remained completely level-headed and genuinely upbeat. Rose noticed this, especially, on a day the two of them had been moving the large dining room table so that the rug underneath could be cleaned. Though very heavy, the two of them were able to lift the table. Unfortunately, when they did so, the tabletop kept firmly in their grip, while all four legs of the table came loose and fell to the floor. Rose shouted, "Father, what do we do? I can't hold it any longer!"

He looked at Rose and calmly responded, "If you are able, let's carefully bend and set it back down on the rug. The table can be repaired, Rose. Don't worry."

Carefully, she did as he asked. The table had, literally, been balancing on unattached wooden legs. What kind of carpenter had constructed the furniture here? Feeling like her protective walls may finally give way to a wave of emotions, Rose exclaimed, "Don't worry?"

She fell into the nearest arm chair and began to cry. "I think maybe this is all too much for me, Father. I'm only twenty-one years old. I have no idea what I'm doing. This, maybe, was just a pipe dream I had envisioned. Not every hope and wish is attainable. I don't know if I'm ready," she paused and continued, "And it sure feels like the house isn't."

Father Eli grabbed a dining room chair nearby and setting it down next to Rose, took a seat.

"You know, a quote I once heard said this, 'Strength is the product of struggle. You must do what others don't, to achieve what others won't.'"

He gave her time to digest his words and then continued, "There are many who have come before you Rose who were interested in the house. Before they barely began to sweep the floors, problems came about and they walked out the front door. You are something different. I see in your eyes the way you picture what could become of this place. Remember, "What God has called us to, He will equip us for."

He cleared his throat and lifted Rose's chin, so she had to look at him, "Believe in yourself. Don't let hurdles in the race hold you back. You have a town full of friends that hardly know you but believe in you. Won't you do the same?"

He slowly stood up and walked over to the legs of the table laying askew on the floor. He collected them, stacked them neatly next to the wall and looked at Rose.

"I'm going to leave you for the night, Rose. Walk through each room. Think about what I said and before bed, put all your trust in God's hands. My bet is you will wake up in the morning with a crystal clear answer to what your next step will be. I want you to know I will support you in whichever path you decide to take."

And with that Father Eli walked out the front door, closing it tightly behind him.

Rose stared at nothing in particular for several minutes. She was trying so hard to focus and really think about what Father Eli had said. It all was just getting to be too much. She wasn't strong. She always felt like a crybaby. When things became difficult she couldn't seem to take it. She didn't know the first thing about finances, running a business, and barely knew how to take care of a household. What twenty-one year old did? She was still learning life as she went. Feeling at her wit's end, she laid her head back against the throw pillow and closed her eyes. Rose searched for the words to a suitable prayer for help, but the only words that came were, "What should I do, Lord? Tell me." Only seconds passed before she was fast asleep, curled up on the armchair and still dressed in her dirty work clothes. After what had felt like only minutes, she woke to a dark room. Something had startled her awake though. She sat a bit longer, waiting. In the distance gunshots or something exploding sounded. Rose became frightened, but in spite of herself, ran to the window to look outside. What in God's name was going on? Again, BOOM, BOOM. She thought perhaps she was still dreaming. Nothing was making any sense. Suddenly, she saw far off in the distance, bright lights flashing simultaneously with each boom. Fireworks?

She ran out the front door, down the steps and toward the colorful flashes. She got all the way to a clearing near St. Mary's Church and looked up. Though still far off in the distance, she could see the beautiful light of fireworks in a star filled sky. She felt the explosion in her chest. She was in full entrancement by the blinding gold, blue, and pink flashes. She thought of Flynn. The night he took her to his honorary 4th of July party, she had watched him gaze at the fireworks. She knew then that she loved him and would always. Flynn. He wasn't here. But he was. She felt him. He wanted her to keep going. Keep strong. Complete what she had started. He believed, always, in her dream. Rose began to cry again, but for a much different reason.

She looked up to the sky and with the most loving voice, she said, "Thank you. Thank you for this. I'm going to start putting my trust in you. And start believing in myself too."

Rose ran back to the house and slept until morning in that same arm chair she had fallen into earlier.

CHAPTER 26

After that night, Rose was all about moving forward. She felt light on her feet and she trusted, now fully, that she was meant to continue on this path. Make her dream a reality. She had scheduled Chives O'Connor, who always brought along Samson, his old, Golden Retriever, to start fixing floorboards on the newly wrecked front porch along with other needed repairs.

The plumber and electrician were both set to come Thursday morning and pest-control, Friday. After all the internal repairs were completed, she could start thinking about the cosmetic changes. She had ideas. Lots of them. So much so, they kept her up at night. Though, keeping things crisp, clean and simple was always her style.

One thing she could begin, with the help of the flower sisters, was her little garden in the backyard. She planned to have a quick breakfast at the Crystal Café and then she'd stop at Wild Flowers to buy a few packets of seeds and starter plants.

Stepping into the café, she noticed it was rather quiet, unusually so. Mudsie came out of the kitchen through the swinging door and greeted her, "Hello sunshine, how are you this early morning?"

Was it early? She glanced at the clock on the wall. 6:00 a.m. Wow. No wonder only a few tables were occupied.

Rose blinked her eyes and replied to Mudsie, "I guess I'm just ready to dig into the day of work. Sometimes I can hardly sleep at all with all the plans I have running through my head." She laughed at herself. "You must think I'm crazy huh, Mudsie?"

"Of course, I don't. I wasn't much older than you when my husband,

George and I, opened up the café. It had been a dream of his all his life. I loved cooking and visiting with new folks. We worked well together, him and I."

Rose saw a fleeting, melancholy look on Mudsie's face. She hadn't seen this side of her before.

"George was called to the war only ten years after we opened Crystal Café. He died while trying to save another soldier. A total stranger, actually. But, in the military, whether you know the guy's name or not, he's your brother. You are there together on the battlefields fighting for the same cause. This young soldier was fighting for the safety of me back at home, just as much as his own family. And George likewise. It wasn't a question, when George witnessed this young soldier, by the name of Nicholas Brown, get shot in the stomach. He laid their wounded and scared, I was told. The only officer that jumped out from the bunker was my George. He hoisted this Nicholas Brown over his shoulder and ran. He even made it to the bunker, but as he handed poor Nicholas off to his team, a wave of bullets came through killing George, Nicholas and another soldier instantly." She sniffed into a handkerchief and looked out the window. Rose gave her time and quietly waited a minute before responding.

"I'm so sorry Mudsie. I didn't know," Rose told her, sympathizing.

Collecting herself and turning her tears off like the flip of a switch, she replied, "Oh, no matter, Rose. It was a long time ago. After George died, the only thing that kept me going was the café. I felt a comfort in continuing on with the dream he had made happen."

Rose, then confided in Mudsie and said, "My husband, Flynn, was called on a special mission to Afghanistan. He's to be there for twelve months. It's very dangerous and I pray every day and night for his safety."

Mudsie rubbed Rose's hand with her own soft, wrinkly hand, "Oh Rose, such a young girl to be an Army wife. But you're strong, sweetheart. You are timid and kind, but I see a strong side of you that is unwilling to falter. As for your husband, I will pray for him too, my dear."

After a moment, she stood up, "Well my goodness, all this fuss and I haven't even gotten you coffee. Do you know what you'd like for breakfast this morning?" Rose decided on something filling, being she never seemed to take the time to eat again for the remainder of the day. "I will have a cheese omelet with tomato, mushrooms and bacon. And an order of your homemade wild rice toast. Just coffee to drink, please." Mudsie gave her a wink and took her order back to the kitchen.

Though their conversation had affected Rose, normally she would worry about Flynn until she became sick. But she refused now to return to that place. She was putting her trust in God to watch over him and to lead her in the direction her heart seemed to be taking her. She stared out the window, nervously playing with her napkin and thinking of her handsome husband. How she missed him.

It had felt like only half a minute and Mudsie was back to her table with her piping hot omelet oozing cheddar cheese, and two slices of buttery wild rice toast.

"Mmm, mmm this looks wonderful," Rose said, licking her lips.

"Looks edible huh, honey bun. Oh, I forgot the jelly. One second."

When Mudsie returned she set down the container of jellies and looked at Rose with a puzzled look on her face. "Rose, since when has there been a war in Afghanistan? I thought after World War II, things with the U.S. troops simmered down."

Wow, Mudsie must never watch TV or see the steady updates online. Or did she just block it all out mentally since her husband died in combat?

"Oh Gosh, Mudsie, there have been several wars and really just a need for regular patrol by U.S military forces. Actually, in many countries in the world. Before I came to Cherish I stopped looking online at all the headlines that came up minute by minute. It just made me sick."

"Online? Like a telephone line a person calls to hear news updates?"

Mudsie was looking even more confused now.

Rose brushed it off, realizing Mudsie was very *old school.* "Yea, kinda like that," she answered, deciding to let it go.

"Ahh, well, new-fangled things are always popping up. You enjoy your breakfast, darlin," and she went to take an order at the table across from Rose. The café was finally getting their morning rush.

Strange how old-fashioned and sheltered the town of Cherish seemed to be. She hadn't seen, even remotely, any modern amenities. No microwaves, no video games or DVD players, no laptops, no cell phones; *nothing* of the modern world. Even the cars were old collector cars. It must be some sort of law that Cherish was historically protected. That the *old school* feel needed to be maintained. It reminded her of Mackinac Island. She had visited the Michigan Island with her parents when she was a teenager. There were no automobiles allowed on the island. A few emergency vehicles, such as an ambulance and fire trucks were the absolute only exception. It was the law there. To date, it was one of Rose's favorite places to visit. Only bicycles and carriages pulled by well trained horses were allowed. She also thought back to her and her mom's trip to Colonial Williamsburg a few summers ago. Another historically protected part of Williamsburg, Virginia. Not only were automobiles not allowed down the streets, but all the original buildings, shops, pubs were preserved, and the workers kept in character; 1700s style. Another favorite trip for Rose. Cherish reminded her of these destinations. No wonder she loved it here!

Rose ate all she could of her omelet and toast and decided she had enough. Time to get to work. She left a $10 bill on the table and waved to Mudsie, who was busy running plates of pancakes and corned beef hash out to hungry customers.

Rose felt rejuvenated and walked briskly in the direction of Wild Flowers. It was time for a lesson in gardening.

CHAPTER 27

The previous owners of the house must've had some sort of garden in the backyard at one point, because there was a ten by twelve foot area surrounded by a short, brick border. The ladies would need to loosen the soil with their hoes and clear the overgrowth of weeds, but all in all, it looked promising.

Being Daisy was still laid up with a swollen ankle, Violet and Rose were taking on the job today. Rose had selected packets of carrot, yellow squash and green bean seeds. She purchased starter plants of Roma tomatoes, English cucumbers and herbs such as basil and rosemary. The flower sisters had advised her to start small. Gardens require a lot of work and upkeep. Rose also wanted the beauty of flowers around the property. As she had envisioned the first day, she opted for a rose bush that would bloom deep burgundy rose buds in a year or two. And, of course, two peony plants (her favorite) that would flower with a delicate, soft pink. Eventually she would have hanging baskets and window boxes overflowing with a variety of colorful blooms, but one step at a time.

They got busy pulling weeds first. After a few minutes, Violet looked at Rose. "You sure you want to take this on, sweet pea?"

Rose laughed, "Oh yes. I have to give it a try. I've always wanted a small kitchen garden. Now is the time to make it happen. I sure appreciate you taking the time to help me, Violet!"

"Oh, it's my pleasure. Who loves seeing plants grow more than Daisy and me? We get excited when someone shows interest in gardening. As you know, we can't get enough of it."

Rose smiled and went back to work, grabbing an armful of dead, viney weeds and adding them to a pile she had started. She thought this may be an opportune time to visit with Violet, getting to know her a little better.

"Violet, tell me about yourself a bit. Have you grown up in Cherish your whole life?" Rose looked down while she hoed a few roots loose from their grip in the soil. Violet kept working but responded quickly to Rose's question.

"Actually yes. To be honest you'll find many of the current residents of Cherish were born and raised here. Of course, a few left for a time, like myself, but found their way back." Rose questioned further. "Was it your nursing school that pulled you away?"

"Yes. After I graduated from high school, I was enrolled in St. Cloud State University in the nursing program. I had always loved helping people and I also knew college would take me out of this small town, and small town people. I thought the town too dull, the people too sheltered. I wanted to be adventurous. Spread my wings, so to speak."

"Well, good for you, to follow your own aspirations." Rose said, looking up from her work, wiping sweat from her forehead.

"The first year, yes. I was living it up I guess you could say. I was doing well in school due to my sheer drive to become a nurse. But thank God for that, because otherwise I was footloose and fancy free." Violet, uncharacteristically giggled at the wording she had used. "But, after year two, things weren't all they were cracked up to be. I mean the college life. I began to miss Cherish, my parents, Daisy and other people there. I stuck it out, but after I got my degree I returned the day after graduation. I needed to live that experience to make me the person I am today. I got a job almost immediately at the small clinic here in town. But four years had gone by, and well…things change."

Rose heard the sadness in Violet's last sentence. Again, a mystery lay still uncovered.

"Anyway, we better quit all this chatter and concentrate on our work. I have barely cleared this one corner of vines. Sorry, Rose. I kind of unloaded a bunch of old history on ya." Violet giggled, embarrassed.

"Oh, don't apologize Violet. I'm here to listen. I've been told I'm good at it. Anytime you want to talk, please don't hesitate to find me."

Violet looked up and met Rose's eyes and smiled.

The ladies worked all morning, only pausing for a quick sip of water here and there. When they had just begun hoeing the lines for seed planting, Chives O'Connor and Samson appeared around the corner of the house and were walking toward them.

"Good morning, ladies. I had some time, so thought I might get to work in the house. That ok by you, Rose?"

"Of course, Chives. Any time." Then looking at Samson, she spoke affectionately, "Hi buddy, how are you today?" She bent down and stroked Samson's golden hair and scratched behind his ears. He toppled over on his side inviting her to continue the attention she was giving him.

"I'm sorry, Sams, but I have lots of work to do," Rose apologized to the lazy old boy. Samson didn't mind. He stayed right where he was and stretched out in the sunshine.

Chives shook his head, "Well, I guess I can't count on any help from you today, huh Samson?"

He, Violet and Rose shared a laugh and went back to work.

At 3:00 that afternoon, Violet and Rose put down their hoes, took off their gloves and looked over the garden that would be sprouting tiny green plants in a week's time. "We did it, Rose. Before you know it, you'll have so many tomatoes to pick, you'll run out of recipes to use them in." Violet teased her.

Rose admired the dark, loose earth in front of her and the little markers at the end of each neat row, "Ah, Violet I can't wait."

The two, very dirty and very tired friends gathered their things and walked back to Wild Flowers. The garden supplies needed to be returned for now and Daisy had offered to make them all dinner since she wasn't able to help in the garden. It sounded like a good way to end a very productive day, Rose thought.

CHAPTER 28

Two weeks had gone by. Rose had given up on trying to call her parents. The number wasn't connecting, nor would a call to Maurice and Flora. Strange.

She had resorted to *snail mail* as it was called in this day and age. She sent a letter to both her parents' address and Maurice and Flora's, letting them know where she was, that she was safe and had, in fact, stumbled upon her dreams. She had promised to come visit real soon. It was the only thing she could do. She prayed they received her letter and were content that she was safe and following her own path. This all felt so out of the ordinary, especially for Rose. But at the same time, each and every minute of it felt real and meant to be.

Monday morning, June 23rd, she was meeting Father Eli and Chives for breakfast at the café to go over any last work that needed to be done on the house. Walking in, she spotted the two of them in a corner booth, sipping coffee.

"Can I join you fellas?" she asked politely.

"Oh Rose, there you are. Of course, take a seat," Father Eli replied, sliding over to make room for her.

"I am so anxious to see where we are at and what we have for the last loose ends that need tying up," Rose exclaimed. Father Eli took out his trusty little notepad and started going down the list. A neat checkmark was next to most of the items, she noticed.

"Well, Chives, are all jobs done on your end?" Father Eli questioned.

"So far, what has been pressing has been fixed, yes. It's an old house, though. You know where to find me if another board breaks." Chives said, winking at Rose. Father Eli continued, "As you know, Rose, the electrical work was completed last Thursday. The plumber will be installing new appliances and fixtures in both the bathrooms and the kitchen, tomorrow. Once that is done, your job is to decide on paint colors and invite some friends to lend a hand." Rose was both extremely excited, but felt kind of guilty, "Everyone has been lending plenty of hands already. I just hate to keep asking for help."

Father Eli could see she had been struggling with that, "Listen, Rose, not only do the people of Cherish want to help bring the house back to life, but you have become a friend to us all. It's not work that we begrudgingly are being called to. It's an enjoyable day with friends. And how fun will it be to see the inn completed and ready for its first signature in the guestbook huh?" They all smiled as if picturing it.

"Hey, it's looking so nice, it may be Samson and I that are the first guests," Chives remarked. Rose giggled.

Mudsie hustled over to their booth with menus, the coffee carafe and a cup for Rose. It didn't occur to Mudsie that anyone wouldn't want a cup of coffee.

Rose took it saying, "Thank you Mudsie. As usual the café is busy as ever." Mudsie wiped her brow with a cloth napkin, "You said it, sweet cheeks. I'm running around here today like a chicken with its head cut off. Which reminds me…we have chicken fried steak on special for lunch today." She laughed at herself and continued, "Now, what are we hungry for this morning?"

Rose ordered a cup of oatmeal with raisins, brown sugar and milk. Father Eli chose the poached eggs on toast and Chives decided on the meat-lovers scramble with hash browns and whole wheat toast.

"Sounds great, kids. I'll be back in a jiffy with your breakfast," Mudsie yelled, halfway to the kitchen with their order ticket.

Rose took a long sip of coffee and decided out loud, "I think I'll take a walk to the hardware store after breakfast and take a look at paint swatches. Anyone want to accompany me?"

"I'll leave that to you. I can pound a hammer and nail, but pretty paint colors aren't my forte, sis," Chives answered. "Plus, I should get back to the station."

"I think I may pass too, Rose, if you don't mind. I'm working on my sermons for the week and also have a wedding to prepare for this Saturday. I'll swing over to the house in a day or two to check on your progress," Father Eli assured her.

Rose nodded, taking no insult to their declining her invitation. They both did have other obligations.

After they had finished a mighty filling breakfast, Rose insisted Mudsie give her the bill. It was the least she could do. And it was true. Everyone, especially her few closest friends here in Cherish, were doing far more than ever expected. She felt she'd never be able to repay them for their kindness.

FLYNN

"Collins, you look great, man! What have they been feeding you in the hospital there? You look better than before you got shot!" Sanchez joked as Collins walked into the galley.

"Yea, yea, I know it, Sanchez. What are you gonna do to make yourself more attractive? Might take a full on beating to accomplish that."

Flynn was happy to see the banter between military brothers. Collins did look good. Good and healthy. He was patched up, wound stitched up and heading home at week's end. A strange part of Flynn felt a fleeting surge of jealousy. Though not enough to take a shot like Collins had endured. He was a lucky guy. A lucky guy who got to go home and see his young wife and three-year-old son, Liam.

All sixteen soldiers that had been crammed into the back of that Army truck with Collins's life hanging in limbo would never forget the way things had played out that day. But, here he was living and breathing and taking shit like a champ, as usual.

Flynn strolled over to Collins, shaking his hand and giving him a sideways hug. "I hear you are leaving here on the next flight out, hey brother?"

"That's what I hear." Collins grinned. He was both exceedingly happy, but Flynn could see a quickly passing melancholy in his buddy's smile.

He would no doubt miss the bond he had shared with his military brothers and sisters. Danger or not, war or not — they shared a camaraderie that could never be erased.

"Take care of yourself." Flynn let go of his friend's hand and walked away before anyone could witness sudden moisture in his eyes. Marty and Sanchez and many others bid farewell to Collins and sent him on his trip home, with prayers of safe travel.

Collins turned and waved one last time and hopped into the passenger seat of the jeep waiting to deliver him to the air base.

Flynn watched and wondered if he would ever see Jess Collins again.

CHAPTER 29

Rose stood outside on a step ladder rolling a fresh coat of buttercream yellow on the siding. Balancing a bit precariously, she lifted the roller against the wall and rolled up and down, up and down. The smell of fresh paint made her think of fresh starts, new adventures. She loved the original color and didn't want to change it. Just a clean, fresh coat would do the trick. Violet and Daisy were busy painting trim on the front porch a sparkling white, while Father Eli, Millie and Hank, from the general store, helped Rose with the application of yellow. Chives was on a taller ladder with a roller and Hank and Millie's sons, Russ and Richard, were perched even higher on scaffolding. Rose worried they might fall and get hurt, but Hank assured her this wasn't their *first rodeo* and laughed.

Things were sure coming together. Mudsie showed up after the noon rush with lunch for the work crew. Rose dug blankets out from the linen closet down the hall and laid them on the lawn and front porch. She made a mental note to get more chairs for the porch soon, but no one seemed to mind taking a seat on the blankets. Mudsie handed out wrapped BLTs. She also served cups of potato salad and sliced homemade pickles. Rose brought out glasses and a pitcher of lemonade to wash down their lunches.

"Thank you Mudsie. This is wonderful," Rose exclaimed.

"Oh, sugar plum, it's really the least I can do. In my younger years I would've been up high with those young boys painting the tip of your roof bright yellow. Nowadays, I'm content to cook and serve my friends coffee and good food," Mudsie replied.

The sun rays shone down on the group of friends as they visited and admired the house. Rose sat next to Mudsie on the porch rocking chairs and a tear came to her eye. "Mudsie, I feel like, finally, I am where I'm meant to be. Like all the steps have led me here. I would be doing cartwheels down Main Street every day."

Mudsie sensed hesitation in Rose's tone and piped up, "But something's missing isn't it? some*one* is, rather?"

Rose struggled with finding the words, "It's so strange. I feel so happy that I'm ready to burst and yet my heart is completely empty without Flynn here to share the joy. You know better than anyone the contradicting emotions I'm dealing with."

Instead of just consoling Rose, Mudsie asked a question. "What is Flynn like? Why does he love you so much?"

Strangely, Rose was happy to talk about Flynn. She hadn't opened up to anyone for so long. It felt good for someone to know how special this man was, *is*. She looked at the sign out front that would someday show her inn's name upon it, welcoming guests.

She took a breath and replied, "I spilled a milkshake in his lap."

Mudsie slapped her knee and laughed. "Isn't it funny what makes a man fall in love? There is never any rhyme or reason."

Rose smiled but kept on speaking without pause. "He waited for my shift at the diner to be done and asked my name. I hate that *love at first sight* myth. But I swear, it almost was. We spent at least an hour together every day after that. And when I wasn't with him, oh, I wanted to be. And he is so handsome, Mudsie. Dark hair, dark eyes, clean shaven face and he stood so straight and proud. And…you know how a soldier looks in a uniform." Both women nodded in agreement, smiling.

But Rose continued, feeling an open wound was healing a bit. "He took me to a 4th of July party, a simple BBQ really. Flynn and his fellow soldiers were being honored. He stood so proud — a willingness to risk his life for his country, for the people of the US. I fell in love with him right then and there. And kept falling day after day. I mean, I know we weren't married long before he was taken away from me, but I've only ever known a positive, gentle Flynn. His good heart is far more priceless to me than his good looks."

"Keep praying, Rose. He'll come back to you. And the two of you are gonna run this beautiful inn together. I can see it now. And ya know what? I can't wait to meet this good lookin' soldier myself," Mudsie promised.

With that, the two ladies crumpled up their lunch scraps and stood up, motioning for the group to do the same. Lunch break was over. Everyone stood up stretching after the short, relaxing pause in the work day. Chives grabbed his hammer and can of nails and walked back up the front steps. Hank and his boys hauled the ladders back to the east side of the house. It was the last side of the house needing paint way up to the eaves of the roof. Rose still wasn't overly comfortable with them risking their lives. But Hank, again, had assured her this was *old hat* for them all.

"Mudsie, you head on back to the café. I know it's busy there, and I can clean all of this up and get you your dishes and silverware this evening. Is that ok?" Rose offered.

"Of course, darlin. No rush. I have a few extra at the café as you can imagine." Rose smiled realizing that was very true. Mudsie went on her way, marching down the sidewalk to Crystal Café while Rose started collecting all of the plastic cups and plates from the porch and the blankets she had laid out for her friends to have their picnic lunches on. She couldn't help looking up at these people, these friends, that were working on her house. Not being paid, not being begged to do so. Who ever heard of such kindness in this day and age? Wasn't everything about money and getting what you wanted no matter who you stomped on? Rose could hardly stand to watch TV nor the news, with all its crime and corruption. As far as she was concerned, if there was a place like Cherish and friends like these, she never wanted to leave. This was home.

Interrupting her sweet day dreams was a loud crashing sound against the side of her house. Oh no, what has happened? Rose thought. Running around to the east side of the house, followed by others she found Hank and his ladder laying on the ground next to the house, a few pieces of broken yellow board next to him.

"Hank!" Rose yelled. Millie was crying and Russ and Richard came down from their ladders at lightning speed. Hank was unresponsive.

Violet, still remembering her nursing skills, nudged through the concerned crowd and knelt down next to Hank.

"Millie, please move back a bit. I need to take a quick look," Violet gently, but firmly urged. She listened to his breathing, felt his wrist for a pulse and with both hands lifted his head slightly feeling the back of his neck. "I think he hit his head hard and has been knocked unconscious. But we need to call Sully from the ER right away. Hank needs to be examined by a doctor. Daisy, run to the shop and get a hold of Sully as fast as you can. Millie, stay with Hank. It will be ok."

Violet looked up at Rose and mouthed the words "It's ok." For a moment Daisy looked at Violet with a questioning look on her face.

"Daisy. It's ok. We need the ambulance. And we need it now. Just go!" Violet ordered her sister. At that Daisy hurried away.

Rose was on the very urge of breaking down into tears as Millie had done. Father Eli calmly walked over to Rose first.

"Look at me, Rose. It will be all right. You have done nothing wrong. Things happen, and not you, or me, or anyone else can stop them." He held her shoulders, still looking at her with a look in his eyes that told her he was right. She felt she needed to trust him. It could have been any one of them, but she still felt wound tight like a drum. Her hands still trembling a bit.

Hank's boys were looking on with worry painted on their young faces. They leaned down rubbing their mother's back, making all attempts to be strong. After what seemed like only seconds, a siren sounded loud, and a small ambulance pulled up on the grass near the crowd. Rose could only assume the man that had been driving was Sully. Another paramedic followed him.

"Please, let us through, folks. We gotta get my buddy, Hank, on this gurney and over to the hospital ASAP," Sully said, sounding unusually calm. Rose guessed this wasn't his first time being called to the scene of an emergency, but he seemed almost aloof. Somehow his conduct took a sudden turn when he noticed Violet was assisting Hank.

She took her hand away from Hank's head as Sully began to position him for the gurney. Rose caught an unmistakable awkwardness between the two and the same agonizing sadness in Sully's eyes that matched Violet's so often. Was there a history here? If so, why would the two be reluctant to be together?

Rose shook the musings from her head temporarily. The focus needed to be on Hank's safety.

After Hank was safely loaded into the back of the ambulance with Millie at his side, Sully sounded the sirens again and sped off. At this point, Rose could take no more and sat right down in the grass putting her face in her hands. Daisy and Violet sat nearby, and they hugged one another. Richard and Russ left for the hospital and promised they would let everyone know what was found out.

"Rose, it's nobody's fault. Accidents happen," Chives said. Rose could hear the quiver in his voice though. What had happened was an accident, but it had shaken everyone. She prayed Hank would be ok.

"Let's get back to it, sweet pea. The work still needs to get done. We just have the lower bit of the east wall to paint yet. Then we'll have it licked," Daisy said, grabbing Rose's hands and pulling her up.

Violet added, "That's right. Hank is in good hands. We will hear soon." She looked in the direction the ambulance had sped away. "I think I'll take a stroll to the hospital. Just make sure the family is ok and that the doctors know the full details of the accident."

Daisy nodded at her sister and turned back to Rose. "Ok, Rose? Let's get back to it."

"You're right. You're both right," she agreed. Rose stood up, took a deep breath and continued her task of cleaning up the lunch mess she had left behind. Though it was no use fretting over what had happened, she also knew the sour feeling in the pit of her stomach wasn't going to go away until she knew how Hank was.

Time ticked on.

CHAPTER 30

The day's work had been completed and Rose's friends had gone home to wash up and get some rest. Daisy and Violet vowed to let Rose know if they heard anything about Hank. Rose was exhausted, both physically and emotionally. After she had taken a long bath and dressed in fresh pajamas, she walked downstairs to the kitchen. Chives had left her a 6-pack of bottled beer as a gift. He told her she needed to relax, that she was working too hard and kicking back in the evenings with a long neck would be just the ticket.

Rose agreed. Tonight, she needed just that. She grabbed the cold glass bottle from the refrigerator and with her bottle opener popped the top off and let it clatter to the floor. The golden liquid bubbled a bit when she took a big, satisfying drink. "Awwww, yes. I needed that," she said to no one.

Taking her beverage and a magazine from the living room, she went and sat out on the front porch. Rocking back and forth in her chair, she took sips of her beer and thought of her dad, Phil. He loved a cold beer after a hard working day like they had today. He also loved a cold beer when they would go on camping trips and roast hotdogs over the fire. Dad would always drag out his guitar and sing songs while the family would eat marshmallows and listen to his soothing voice. Her mom would be handing out little glow sticks to her along with the cousins, and full mugs of hot cocoa for them to sip on. They would then cozy up in their tent and Mom would tell silly stories while Dad began to snore.

Rose hadn't thought much about her parents lately. She had been so busy (maybe selfishly) concentrating on the house project and making it all come about. Maybe it was a combination of what had happened with Hank today and seeing his family and friends so distraught over his injuries and wellbeing. That, pairing with her time alone now and the light headedness the beer was giving her, she began missing her mom and dad. Wouldn't they love it here? The house, the town. Some day they would be here with her. Visiting her and Flynn and maybe their grandkids? Rose hoped so.

Taking the last flat sip of her beer she glanced down Main Street and saw Russ, Hank and Millie's oldest boy walking toward her. Rose's heart sank. All of the sudden she felt stone cold sober.

"Russ? Is your dad going to be ok?" Rose stammered.

As he came closer Rose could see his face clearer, and to her utter relief, Russ looked calm and happy.

"Yes. Oh, it's been a long day. He actually *came to* not long after we arrived at the hospital. And was coherent. He remembers slipping on his ladder, grabbing the siding, when the board came loose in his hand and he knew he was going down," Russ said, actually snickering a bit.

"Oh wow. How scary, Russ." Rose replied. "What are his injuries?"

Russ leaned against the front porch railing and pondered her question. "Well, it's all lots of mumbo jumbo to me. But they are making him lay low, and the lights need to be dim. The doctor said he had been knocked unconscious and likely had a concussion. Though his memory has been just fine. He also has bruises up and down his left side where he landed and a sprained wrist. But besides that, Doc said he can get back up on the ladder in a couple weeks." Rose nearly choked on her own saliva.

"OOOOOh no! No more of that business. The house is done, we are all set. No more people risking their lives over making my little inn look storybook perfect."

Russ and Rose laughed, both feeling a huge weight had been lifted.

Russ started walking down the front steps to leave. Rose called after him, "Russ, please tell your dad to get well and I want to thank you and your family for your help today. It means the world to me."

Russ replied, "I'll do that. You're welcome, Rose. Good night."

Rose sat back in her chair and felt all of her tight muscles relax. Within minutes she had dozed off and the last bits of sunlight faded.

CHAPTER 31

Now that all the work was done to make the house safe and in working order, the real labors of love began for Rose. A newfound friend, Stella, (or as her students called her, Mrs. Patches) helped Rose *patch* up drapes, quilts, and some furniture upholstery. She came highly recommended by Father Eli, and she was talented at her skill.

Rose was also happy to have made a friend a bit closer to her age. Stella was in her mid-thirties, a petite woman, brunette, and naturally very pretty. She was married to Mark, who was an electrician in Cherish and they had two young children. Max was four years old and Betty, just six months. Usually, the little ones accompanied Stella when she came to the house. Though the ladies got less work done with the frequent toddler interruptions, Rose didn't mind at all. She loved their company.

Stella was stopping by that afternoon with Max and Betty in tow. The drapes in the largest guest room upstairs still needed mending and Stella was bringing back the quilt she had patched up for Rose's bed. Rose looked out the kitchen window, waiting for their arrival. It was raining and she wanted to rush out and lend a hand. Finally, Stella's Hudson Jet sedan pulled up in the front of the house. Rose grabbed an umbrella and ran out.

"Stella, let me give you a hand!"

"Hi Rose, Oh thank you. The rain's sure coming down, isn't it?"

Max hopped out on his own and ran up the porch steps, hardly noticing the rain. Stella heaped the quilt into Rose's arms, while she unbuckled Betty from her car seat. "Ok, let's make a run for it, like Max bravely showed us," Rose yelled, smiling.

Max clapped when they were all safely dry under the protection of the porch ceiling. "All right Max, should we go inside?" Rose suggested while opening up the front door. Max was the first one in. He was never without energy, it seemed. Stella set little Betty down on a soft blanket she had brought in her bag and handed her a teething ring to chew on. Max had a few matchbox cars he pushed around on the floor.

"Rose, do you mind keeping an eye on them while I run upstairs? I want to take down those drapes and see what mending needs to be done. I can also run the quilt up and put it on your bed if you'd like," Stella offered.

"Oh, no, that's ok, Stella. I have to make up my bed this evening anyway. The sheets are tumbling in the dryer at the laundromat as we speak," Rose replied. Stella smiled then and hurried up the stairway.

Rose sat on the floor next to the kids. "So, Max, how are you today? Any new adventures this summer?" Rose questioned.

Max thought long and hard, finally replying, "Well, I saw a dinosaur at the zoo, Woze." Rose tried not to laugh at Max's version of her name. He still had a hard time forming his r's. So, she was "Woze" for Max, which she secretly loved.

"A dinosaur? You're kidding? What did it look like?" Rose asked dramatically.

Max started going into a long description of what was clearly an alligator, when Betty started fussing. Stella, having a mother's ear and eye always on full alert, yelled from upstairs, "I'll be right down, Rose. I think she's hungry." Rose picked up Betty and walked around the room. She swayed from side to side and pointed at birds out the window to distract Betty.

The baby had little rolls on her legs and a full head of soft, blonde hair. She had chocolate brown eyes and a little dimple on her left cheek. She smelled sweet, like baby lotion. Rose could snuggle right into her chubby little neck if Betty had been her own baby girl. Hopefully, someday she and Flynn would have one of their own. Betty became content with Rose, and they continued peering out the living room windows while Max pretended to be a dinosaur, running all over the room.

Stella finally came down with the drapes neatly folded over one arm. "Awww, Betty, you seem happy now huh? Thanks Rose."

"Of course. We three are doing just fine down here," Rose confirmed.

"Well, I will need to take these drapes home where my sewing machine is. There are far more tears and pulled stitches than I had thought," Stella sighed as she began to pick up Max's toys.

"Stella, why don't you go and work on the drapes. I can manage with Max and Betty. Maybe feed Betty well before you go? Bring in the diaper bag? We'll be fine, won't we Max?" Rose said, giving Max a thumbs up. Stella looked around contemplating the idea.

"Well, I probably could get these done in a couple of hours if the kids aren't there with me. Are you sure, Rose?"

"Absolutely! It will be fun. The sun's coming out. We can take a stroll out to my garden and see if anything's grown taller overnight," Rose suggested.

Stella took Betty from Rose and sat in the chair to feed her.

"Ok, Rose. If you insist. Thank you so much," and looking to Max she said, "Max, you be a good boy." After Betty's little tummy was full, Stella kissed the kids goodbye and wished Rose good luck.

Rose dug her little red wagon out of the storage room, wrapped Betty in her soft blanket and laid her down in it. She held Max's hand, and they took a walk around to the backyard to her vegetable garden. Betty watched all the birds in the sky and tree branches swaying in the breeze overhead. She drifted off to sleep within minutes. Rose and Max talked about the dinosaur he had seen and the night he went fishing with his dad. They hadn't caught anything, but Dad let him have an ice cream cone on the way home, even though it was right before bedtime.

When the three of them reached Rose's garden she showed Max her plants. "Max, this row here is my carrot row. These tiny, little, green plants are growing crunchy carrots below them. I have to water them often unless we get lots of rain like earlier today. Do you like eating carrots?" Rose asked. Max thought about it.

"Not weally, Woze. But I do like apples. Are you growing those in yo gawden?" Max asked excitedly.

"I'm afraid not, Max. But when my vegetables are ready to be picked, I'm going to have you come help me pick them. And after we have washed them all, I want you to try just one small bite of each. I bet you will love them all. Even the carrots," Rose explained.

Max looked very interested and reached down to pull a carrot sprout. Rose gently pulled him back. "No, no Max. They aren't ready to be pulled just yet. They need time to grow. We need to be patient. All good and beautiful things take time. Ok, buddy? It just will take some time and patience."

Max looked up at Rose's face and said, "Ok, Woze."

"While sister is sleeping Max, let's you and I take a little walk. I have a little path that goes through the woods, over a wooden bridge and ends in the park. I could push you on the swing. Sounds kind of fun doesn't it?" Rose suggested.

Max took her hand tightly in his own and agreed. "That sounds good to me, Woze. Have you ever been there before? Is there a slide too and monkey bars?"

"I've only taken walks and seen it. I haven't had any kids come to visit me yet and I'm not a mommy yet, so I can't take my own kids." Rose simply responded.

"Well, I can come over anytime you feel like taking someone to the park. I don't mind," Max told Rose, hoping he made her feel happy. Rose grinned at the perfect innocence of youth.

"Well, thank you Max. I will keep that in mind. Look, we've made it. Show me how you go down the swirly slide." Max bolted as fast as his little red Keds could take him.

Rose watched Max go down the slide multiple times, helped him go across the monkey bars and pushed him on the swing. After thirty minutes of nonstop activity, Rose suggested they take a little break.

She and Max sat down in the grass together while Betty napped. Max leaned against Rose after a bit and she suspected, though he wouldn't admit it, he was ready for a rest too.

She let the children sleep while she sat watching the townspeople mill around the park, kids playing, families enjoying picnics together. Rose closed her eyes, feeling content and happy, with the shimmer of sun rays warming her skin.

FLYNN

Dear Rosebud,

I have given up on the mail delivery system here. No letters have come. I would love to hear from you, but I know there must be a good explanation for the absence.

I don't know why, but the last few weeks I've been thinking of our future with little ones. Do you ever? You seem like a natural mother. So nurturing, so loving, so FUN! I can see you pushing a little blonde girl, who looks just like you, on the tire swing we are going to have in our big yard. Our little boy and I, tossing the baseball back and forth nearby. Guests from the inn wandering out and joining in the fun as if they were close friends. Your dad, sitting at a picnic table nearby, while your mom brings out the last of the food for the barbecue. Everyone laughing, visiting and enjoying the day.

It sounds so "Leave it to Beaver", but really, what's not to like? Here, I have time to think. And truly think about what I yearn for.

This is what I want. Nothing extravagant and certainly nothing lavish. I want the simple life.

Oh, I miss you Rosebud. My God, you haunt my dreams, and I would give away ten years of my life to hold you right now. I dream other things about you, but I won't make this letter R rated. Ha.

I hope you are well.

Love,

Flynn

CHAPTER 32

"**D**aisy, do you know anyone who is giving away kittens? Or sheep? I need some animals around," Rose asked.

"Sheep? That is a very specific, random request. And anyone else would be puzzled by it, but me? Nah," Daisy responded to Rose's surprise and elation.

"Do you remember Sully, the ambulance driver, who came and scooped up Hank after his fall? He raises Babydoll sheep. Cutest things you have ever seen. I assume you want them just for pets. Or for the general *English countryside* feel correct?" Daisy winked at Rose.

Rose laughed, seeing that her friend knew her well. "Yes, I guess that is true."

"Well, let's go pay Sully a visit. I'd bet he has a batch or two of kittens in the barn too," Daisy said, leading Rose out the back door of Wild Flowers.

"Hop in, sweet pea. Your first ride in our old jalopy," Daisy laughed.

"Fine by me. This will be fun," Rose replied.

Daisy turned the key in the ignition while the old truck rattled to life. She shoved the stick shift into place, and they bumped down Main Street, taking a left onto a country road. The road wound between rolling, neon green hills, and fields of corn and alfalfa. A few silos and picture perfect red barns graced the farmsteads they passed. Rose wasn't expecting this so close to town. Only five, maybe seven or eight miles out of town was Sully's farm. Daisy made a hard left onto his dirt driveway and when they reached the barn she slammed on the brakes, putting the truck in park.

"Sorry, I hardly ever drive," she said, jumping out of the truck and slamming the rusty door shut.

Sully was in the corral letting the baby sheep feed and play a bit. Spotting the ladies, he waved and began walking their way.

"Sully, do you have any little ones ready to go soon?" Daisy asked.

"I do, though I didn't know you had a pen and grazing area behind your shop for my sheep to live, Daisy," Sully laughed.

"Ha, ha!" Daisy sarcastically said, used to Sully's teasing. Turning to Rose, she continued, "You remember Rose, Sully? She is interested in adding a little charm to her inn. What could add that more than a couple of sweet, fuzzy Babydoll sheep?" Daisy asked.

Rose sheepishly smiled at Sully.

"I know it is a silly request, but my inspiration was a trip to Colonial Williamsburg. They have them roaming all over, grazing in perfectly green fields, penned in by white picket fences. The picture of a simplistic life."

Rose laughed at her ridiculous musings.

"Rose, you'd be surprised how many folks purchase my sweet little sheep for just that reason. Let's be honest, what other use are they other than being cute, simple creatures?" Sully remarked and added, "let's go take a look at a few."

As if showing off, the tiny little sheep were bouncing around the fenced-in corral and playing tag with each other. Rose thought it was funny they almost seemed to be smiling, or was she imagining that part?

"Here," Sully said, offering Rose and Daisy bottles to feed the lambs. All six came running for the warm bottles of milk. Sully reached down and grabbed two under his arms and moved them to separate stalls so that Daisy and Rose could feed them without interruption. One of the Babydoll sheep was black, the other white. They had tight, fuzzy little puffs all over their bodies and the tiniest little sound came out of their pink mouths when they tried to bleat.

"Hold on tight to those bottles when they start to drink. They will yank them right from your grip. Feeding time is their favorite time," Sully told them.

This became very obvious when the lambs put the nipple of the bottles in their mouths and pulled hard, drinking aggressively.

"Rose, aren't they adorable?" Daisy said looking at Rose gazing at her newfound animal friends.

"Oh, so cute, Daisy," Rose replied.

"Sully, ya got any kittens in the barn you want to part with too?" Daisy yelled across the corral. Sully poured a bucket of water in one of the troughs and yelled back.

"Just take a look around, Daisy. I have ten, maybe twelve barn cats I'd be willing to give away if Rose wants them," he laughed. "Rose? What do ya say?"

"Perhaps, one, Sully. Some guests may frown if my house is crawling with felines," Rose teased.

"Ok, if you say so," Sully replied, faking disappointment. Then scratching his head looked in Daisy's direction and asked, "Say, Daisy, what has Violet been up to these days? I saw her the day I had to get ole Hank into the ambulance, but given I was a bit pressed for time, I didn't have a chance to say hello."

Rose glanced at Daisy with a puzzled look. Here was another clue to the mystery. Did Sully and Violet have feelings for one another? Had they dated in the past? Did they have a history? This was all news to Rose.

Daisy stifled a giggle and looked back to Sully, "Well, Sully we've been busy helping Rose and it has been crazy at the shop. You should swing by sometime though. I'm sure Violet would be happy for the visit. It's been months since you showed your face around."

"Ahh I don't know. I'm working the ambulance pretty regularly and this farm keeps me hopping both day and night. Just, tell her I said 'hi' will ya?" Sully asked.

The two women shrugged their shoulders and Daisy replied, "Of course I will."

Daisy and Rose bumped along back to town with two Babydoll sheep in the back of the truck. Rose decided to adopt both the white female and black female she had fed earlier. Sully graciously lent them an animal pen to haul them home in.

Also, laying curled up on Rose's lap was a sweet tabby cat, *Mrs. Bigglesworth*. Not the kitten she had been looking for exactly, but Sully assured her, this cat was made to be a resident of the inn. She was the perfect, lazy pet and would make great company.

Rose hated asking Chives, Russ, and Richard to work for her again, but she needed them to build her a small shelter for her lambs and a simple fenced area in her yard. She promised up and down that she would cook them all a wonderful meal afterward. Knowing the amazing cook Rose was, they had all agreed, happily.

Hank tagged along to supervise.

After completing the job, the friends all sat down at the picnic table in the backyard, spent from the day's work. With the help of Millie, Rose brought out the night's feast. She had prepared Cajun rubbed pork chops with a fresh corn relish. Her mom's famous recipe for homemade, gooey, three-cheese macaroni and cheese and maple syrup glazed carrots. She had also prepared wonderfully sweet rhubarb slushes for such an occasion. The taste was 4th of July in a glass, as far as Rose was concerned, which wasn't a far off date.

"This looks incredible, Rose," Russ commented.

"I agree! Do you need any other jobs done tomorrow?" Richard exclaimed, taking his first bite of pork chop.

The meal was enjoyed by all, as they listened to the new sound of sheep bleating in the background.

Sister sheep, Elsa and Ana, seemed to like their new home. Strangely, none of Rose's friends seemed to recognize the *obvious* character names from her favorite Disney movie, *Frozen*, but Rose thought it fit them just fine.

CHAPTER 33

Though she could hardly believe it, Rose was ready to open the house as an inn and welcome her first guests.

Word had gotten out quickly and she had two couples coming the weekend of the 4th of July to stay. She was so nervous. She could hardly walk down the stairs without tripping — could hardly pour coffee without spilling. There had to be a first time for everything. She would be just fine.

The house looked beautiful. Fresh, ivory paint covered the walls, the furniture had been repaired and reupholstered where needed.

Daisy and Violet made sure vases of flowers sat throughout the house. A large clear vase held a massive bouquet of lavender hydrangeas and was the centerpiece to her dining room table. Each guest room night stand had a dainty white vase filled with snow white baby's breath on it.

The wood floors shined like honey and the dark grains swirled throughout the boards. Arranged strategically were multi-colored rope rugs colored in crimsons, chocolate browns, and forest green. The light fixtures glowed and were dust free. The old, framed artwork shown like newly purchased treasures.

Rose had Chives build her a small counter cabinet in the foyer where her guests could check in and out. There was a surface for the guest book, a feather pen, and drawers underneath for receipts, room keys and for money safe keeping.

Just that morning Rose had made a batch of her mom's famous peanut butter oatmeal cookies and she placed a dozen of them on a jade green serving tray she had purchased at the general store. The smell of the goocy delights traveled through the house. Rose felt a true sense of pride and happiness as she looked around the house. When she heard a chime from the newly installed doorbell, she rushed for the front door.

An older couple stood on the welcome mat with two small suitcases. "Welcome Mr. and Mrs. Nelson. Please come in. I'm Rose, the owner and with whom you spoke to on the telephone," Rose said, greeting them.

"Yes, Hi Rose. I am Charles, this is Mary. We've traveled for hours and were hoping for a nap before we venture out for a walk and some lunch," Mr. Nelson stated.

"Of course, let me get you a room key and a couple of towels. And please try one of my fresh baked cookies if you'd like," Rose offered.

Both Mr. and Mrs. Nelson took a cookie from her serving tray and took a nibble. "Mmm, these are delicious, Rose. I'd like to add this recipe to my collection if you're willing to share it," Mrs. Nelson asked. Rose laughed shyly.

"I will write it out for you and include it with your check-out documents." Then motioning to the stairway, she said, "Please, come this way and I'll show you to your room."

"This is a lovely house, Rose. I love the decor and the special touches you give it," Mrs. Nelson complimented.

"Thank you Mrs. Nelson. You really don't know how much that means to me." Rose replied.

"She notices everything, let me tell you, Rose. Mary has worked as head manager at five different inns throughout her working years," Charles said, looking proud of his wife.

"Well, that is nice to know, Mrs. Nelson. I may have to sit down with you and get some tips on how to run this place. I am very new at it, as you could probably guess."

"You look like you were made to run this inn, dear," Mrs. Nelson said with a wink.

After the sweet couple had been shown to their room, Rose let out a long breath that she must've been holding during their entire conversation.

It will get easier, Rose, she told herself. *How delightful were those folks? And to ask about my recipe even? Mrs. Nelson must've just been acting polite.* At any rate, her first guests had checked in, tasted her baked goods and were resting in one of the guest rooms. How wonderful. It wouldn't be long, and the second couple would be arriving.

Rose was dusting the banister when the doorbell chime sounded for the second time that day. She scurried to welcome the couple, opening the door.

"Welcome. And won't you come in? I'm Rose an…"

But the tall, frigid man with a mustache cut her off, "We aren't here for pleasantries Miss. Our son wouldn't allow us to stay with him and his new wife while we visit, so here we are, staying in an overpriced, old house." His wife looked at Rose with a silent apology in her eyes.

"Mr. and Mrs. Hawthorne, I certainly can show you directly to your room without delay if you wish," Rose offered.

"That would be ideal," Mr. Hawthorne agreed with a sigh.

When guestroom #3 had been unlocked and Mr. and Mrs. Hawthorne shown in, Rose seemed to have the breath she had let out earlier, stuck tightly in her chest again. I *guess not all guests are gonna enjoy my greetings or my cookies.*

She made it her personal goal to make Mr. Hawthorne smile before his stay ended. There had to be a way to break his shell and find what must give him some joy. It was a tall order, but why not try? He was Rose's guest, and she wanted each of them to walk out her front door feeling glad they had come.

CHAPTER 34

Early Friday morning, July 3rd, Rose sipped her coffee while she started prepping breakfast for her guests. She had a few small bunches of dill and chives from her garden. Having the opportunity to use her herbs in recipes now filled her with a child-like pride. Also set out on her butcher block was a dish of a dozen eggs, pie dough she had prepared the evening before, browned breakfast sausage and grated cheddar cheese. She was putting together her mother's quiche recipe.

Rose stopped, while cracking an egg into a small bowl, and thought of her husband. He loved this recipe. She made this exact quiche recipe often for Flynn. It was his favorite! He would know what she was preparing when he came down the stairs and smelled it baking in the oven. His hair would be askew, his eyes puffy with sleep, but still he was the most handsome man she had ever laid eyes on. Before he even poured himself a cup of coffee, he would look through the glass oven door, smile and kiss her on the forehead. "Good Morning, Rosebud," he always said. "Oh Flynn, I miss you." Giving herself the brief moment and no more, she went back to her task at hand.

In addition to the quiche for breakfast, she would also roast some thinly sliced breakfast potatoes in the oven with the fresh chives and dill. In small fruit bowls she would dish up diced peaches and blueberries with a light squeeze of lemon on top to heighten the tangy flavors.

While the savory quiche baked in the oven, Rose went to the linen closet to collect cloth napkins and tablecloths to set the tables out on the front porch. A memory of her and Flynn's breakfast at the Old Rittenhouse Inn the morning after they were married, came to mind while she stepped out the front door. As she laid the tablecloths over the tables and smoothed them with her hand, she could picture Flynn sitting in the chair across from her sipping coffee and looking out at the sparkling Lake Superior. A morning, with her love. A morning she would never forget. He sure was hijacking her thoughts this morning. Though, this wasn't a rarity.

A voice from in the house startled her, ending her daydream. Rushing back inside, she found Mr. Hawthorne standing at the bottom of the stairs with his hands on his hips.

"Miss, is coffee not served promptly at 7:00 a.m.? And we'd like to eat up in our room rather than out in the blinding sunshine. Not to mention the overbearing scent of all the flowers hanging in pots above our heads. It's enough to make a person lose their appetite all together."

Rose smoothed her blue skirt and took a deep breath, replying, "Of course you can take your breakfast up in your room, Mr. Hawthorne. When it is finished I will bring up a tray for you and your wife. Why don't you have a cup of coffee in the sitting room while you wait? I'll just be a minute with the coffee. Do you take cream or sugar?"

To which Mr. Hawthorne answered, "Black," and walked to the sitting room.

Rose returned with not one but two cups of coffee. She handed one to Mr. Hawthorne and though he didn't indicate he wanted company, she sat down in the chair next to him, sipping her own cup of coffee. She took a chance and tried to strike up some type of conversation, "Any special plans tomorrow for the 4th of July?"

"Not really," he answered shortly.

"They have a wonderful parade running down Main Street starting at noon if you're interested. I have chairs we can set out by the road. Your son and his family are more than welcome to come and sit out front with us," Rose said, trying hard.

Mr. Hawthorne looked out the window for a moment before answering, "We'll see. Matthew most likely will turn up his nose at any show of patriotism or celebration of it."

He looked at his watch and stood up from his chair. "Please bring breakfast up when it is finished. And more coffee too." He turned and stiffly walked up the stairs. Rose heard the oven timer go off. Feeling frustrated, but even more determined, she went into the kitchen and started dishing up breakfast for her guests.

CHAPTER 35

Mr. and Mrs. Nelson, in typical fashion, enjoyed their breakfast on the front porch with a smile and all the polite compliments they could come up with. The couple was a pleasure and the perfect guests. But Mr. Hawthorne was a challenge and Rose couldn't give up on it. When she had been watering her rose bush out front, she saw Mrs. Hawthorne resting in one of the rocking chairs on the porch. Rose laid down her watering can and walked up the steps toward her.

"Hello, Mrs. Hawthorne. Is there anything I can get you? An iced tea perhaps, or a book to read?" Rose offered.

"Oh, thank you, but no, Rose. I appreciate your kind hospitality and want to offer my apologies for my husband's behavior," Mrs. Hawthorne said, motioning for Rose to take a seat in the rocker next to her.

She continued, "My husband became calloused and quiet after the war. He had been sent to Germany and, as you can imagine, saw many terrible things. Jon took his job as a commander very seriously. But he also had a heart of gold. All the pain and agony he witnessed took a part of him away and left it right there on the battlefields. What's worse is my son, Matthew, blamed him for being away all those years. Their relationship has had many struggles."

She wiped a tear away.

Rose felt a bond with Mrs. Hawthorne. She reached out and took her hand, saying, "And you are caught in the middle aren't you?" Mrs. Hawthorne looked away but nodded.

Rose sat silent for a moment and began again, "There is nothing good about war, but there is always hope in the healing. Don't give up on Jon and your son, Matthew. Time can heal all wounds."

"Thank you, Rose. That means a lot." And with that, Mrs. Hawthorne stood up from her chair and walked down the front steps and took a walk through the gardens, stopping to admire each plant as they reached for the sun.

Rose hoped for a time when she and Mr. Hawthorne could talk once more before they checked out on Sunday morning. She had some things to say.

That night, Rose tossed and turned with nightmares. She saw Army soldiers riding in a covered truck, racing through a sand filled, dusty city with no sign of life around them. The truck sped faster and faster. Though Rose couldn't tell what they were driving away from or driving toward, she felt a sudden jolt bringing her into the back of the truck among the crowded men and women.

All were in full combat attire. Rose was sitting among them — sweaty, dirty, exhausted and scared. Before she was able to peer under any of their helmets to identify someone- the truck slammed to an abrupt stop.

She heard footsteps approaching outside and a spoken dialect she didn't understand. Suddenly, gunshots! Like the loudest fireworks you can imagine ricocheting at every angle. A soldier next to her jumped up in panic, yelling to his comrades to save themselves. Seeing his face finally, from under his helmet, she gasped. As the soldier jumped out of the vehicle averting the enemy's attention, their truck was finally able to speed away. Rose screamed in her sleep, no sound coming from her lips.

The soldier. NO! He sacrificed himself.

Waking, drenched in a cold sweat, Rose remembered, now, the face of the soldier.

Mr. Hawthorne. A young Jon Hawthorne.

CHAPTER 36

The 4th of July parade started promptly at noon, as promised. The old, well maintained, police cars and fire trucks sounded their sirens loudly, for all to hear. Violet and Daisy rode on a float decorated with oversized flowers and trees crafted of paper mache and fabric. They also placed tin pots here and there, filled with fresh flowers. The two of them were dressed patriotic in red, white and blue, and threw handfuls of candy to all the children watching.

Chives and Samson drove his old Model-T, which had been parked out front at his gas station the first day Rose came to Cherish. Samson wore a bright red bandanna around his neck while Chives threw out small boxes of Cracker-Jack. Kids and adults alike reached high in the sky when a box of the sweet, crunchy snack came flying in their direction.

Rose watched clowns riding on bicycles and horses of roan, black and buckskin colors. Many Main Street businesses had floats. Rose was particularly happy to see Hank and Millie riding on a float for The General Store. Richard was driving the old Chevy pickup truck that the float was being pulled by. Russ sat in the passenger seat throwing out packages of Big Red gum and Tootsie Pops. Hank looked great. He was smiling and waving to fellow patrons of Cherish, no sign he had survived an accident that certainly could've cost him his life. Rose glanced at his wrist and saw the cast up to his elbow. But besides that, and a few yellowed bruises, Hank was the big, gentle giant she had met weeks ago.

There were several athletic teams taking part in the parade also. The high school football team wore their jerseys and strutted down Main Street waving to giddy young girls while they tossed a football back and forth between each other. The high school band even marched in full uniforms complete with white gloves and tall hats pinned with a white plume. Rose hadn't seen members of a marching band wearing such distinguished attire since she was a little girl. The young students must have been roasting in the uniforms, but they sure impressed everyone with their lines and military style cadence.

Rose felt an ache in her heart, though laced with pride, when the National Guard and retired veterans marched by, carrying the colors.

She hadn't noticed Mr. Hawthorne had come out the front door of the inn until the moment she saw him standing at attention saluting his fellow soldiers. She scanned the front porch and toward the spectators by the road for Mrs. Hawthorne. She finally spotted her sitting on a blanket with a young man and woman. Both appeared to be in their mid-twenties, Rose thought. Assuming it must be their son, Matthew, she strolled over to casually introduce herself.

"Hello Mrs. Hawthorne. Are you and your guests enjoying the festivities?"

Mrs. Hawthorne smiled and proudly answered, "We certainly are! Rose, please let me introduce my son, Matthew and his wife, Emily."

She turned then to Matthew and Emily, saying "Rose owns and runs this beautiful inn we've had the pleasure to be guests at."

"Nice to meet you, Rose," Matthew replied, softly shaking her hand. Emily, likewise, smiled and greeted Rose politely. After they had exchanged a few pleasantries, Matthew and Emily excused themselves, deciding to take a stroll further down Main Street to get cotton candy from the corner candy store.

Rose sat down next to Mrs. Hawthorne, "How is Mr. Hawthorne doing? I see his patriotism is certainly still very much a part of him. Have he and Matthew spoken much today?" Rose didn't want to pry, but she could sense that Mrs. Hawthorne needed a friend to talk to. Before speaking, Mrs. Hawthorne glanced back at the front porch where Jon had stood during the parade.

"They shook hands, casually spoke of the weather, President Kennedy's current operations and the new color TVs that have been introduced. It's all very superficial, though I guess this is nor the time or the place to engage in deeper conversation."

Pausing and watching the last of the parade turn the corner she then made a wish out loud, almost forgetting Rose was even sitting beside her.

"I do pray someday Jon and Matthew can talk, really TALK to each other and make amends. Just start from the here and now. The healing would begin, perhaps…and I might have my family back."

Rose, again reached for her new friend's hand, giving it a quick squeeze.

"I am praying for the same outcome for you."

Letting Mrs. Hawthorne sit in peace and quiet, Rose stood and walked back to the inn. She glanced through the large living room window and saw Mr. Hawthorne, Jon, sitting in one of the arm chairs looking toward the street where the soldiers had been marching.

Rose took a breath and decided this was as good a time as any.

She pushed through the swinging door to the kitchen first, taking a pitcher of iced tea from the refrigerator and filling two glasses with the refreshing beverage. She sliced two wedges of lemon and perched them on the rims.

"Here goes nothin," she whispered to herself and headed for the sitting room.

There with his usual grimace, sat Mr. Hawthorne looking away from her as she entered the room.

"Mr. Hawthorne, I thought you could use a refreshing glass of—," Rose started to say, but her shoe caught the edge of the area rug and she fell to her knees, sending both glasses of iced tea in the air. The airborne beverages crashed into a pile of glass pieces, soggy lemon wedges and a cold brown liquid. Had Rose not been in complete shock with what transpired next, she would have cried in complete humiliation.

Mr. Hawthorne had sprung from his chair and was crouching next to Rose holding her arm in assistance, "Rose, are you ok? Let me grab a towel to help wipe this up."

She sat on the rug for a second to collect herself.

When Rose finally stood up and smoothed the rug flat, Mr. Hawthorne had found a towel (a placemat to be completely correct) to help clean up the mess she had made.

"Oh, please Mr. Hawthorne, I'll take that. I've made a complete idiot of myself. Thank you for offering your assistance though."

He conceded, handing her the placemat and taking his seat again.

As her attention and her eyes were concentrating on the tea soaked floor, Mr. Hawthorne began speaking.

"I owe you an apology for my behavior, Rose. You've been nothing but welcoming and polite to us. The truth is…after the war, I haven't been quite myself. Not like the old me, from years prior to the war. Honestly, I can't see how any soldier *could* come back from such a nightmare and start again, exactly where they left off. Rose, I saw things that I will never be able to unsee. I did things, was forced to, ordered to. I had to do my job and I would defend my country regardless of the cost. I had comrades, friends, that were killed sitting two inches away from me. The cost for them was the ultimate one. For me, I made it. I was lucky. It's just…"

He paused and swallowed the lump in his throat. "The truth is…it has put a real strain on my family." He stared at the floor, seeing nothing but his past and finally said, "primarily Matthew and my relationship."

Rose took a broom and dustpan from the hallway closet and ventured a word to Mr. Hawthorne, "My husband, too, is in the US military. He is away on a twelve month mission. I miss him terribly, Mr. Hawthorne. But my pride in him is beyond measure. As is my pride and sheer gratitude in each and every one of you that has risked your lives for us back home. I know your wife, and even your son, feels as I do. Of course, there is healing to do. But confide in them, lean on them. Start with just enjoying their company. If not for that, what were you over there fighting for? I believe time will heal."

She smiled a bit, "And who knows, maybe when Flynn returns, the two of you can get together and talk. Only soldiers that have been through war can understand fully what the other has been through. In my experience, talking about something that festers inside, helps ease the pain." Rose rubbed her sticky hands on the wet dish rag she held and nodded silently to Mr. Hawthorne before turning to the kitchen.

With that Mr. Hawthorne softened. Almost as if he was tired from carrying the heavy armor.

"Rose," he called after her. "I thank you. You've certainly given me more than a place to rest my head and a good meal to eat."

He started to walk up the stairs to his room before turning and adding, "By the way, would you mind giving my wife the recipe for that egg dish you served yesterday morning? It was delicious."

With that Rose ran to the kitchen with her dustpan piled high with sticky mess and gave a soft cheer. Her heart, again, was overflowing. She reached for her recipe box for two blank cards.

She wrote out two different recipes for two very different, but special, guests.

Her first.

FLYNN

Flynn walked the desolate city streets of Kabul. It looked deserted, though he knew better. At any time, a Taliban Kamikaze dumbie could jump him. The times he had walked this perimeter had been so many that his thoughts tended to wander. Today, he was a bit surprised even, they were focusing on his childhood, his mother and father. Mam and Pops he called them. They had such dreams for their boy. He had been an only child. Though they had yearned, especially his mother, for more children, Flynn was it. Joe's family, generation to generation, had hoped and almost carved in stone that all Mitchells would enlist. Cynthia had years of anxiety with the Mitchells' well-laid plans for her son. Cynthia reminded Flynn of Rose. Not in a creepy way. Rose was sexy, attractive, young and vibrant. Obviously, these were not the similarities. But Rose was kind like his mother, gentle like his mother, and had dreams like his mother. He wished they could have met. The two may have had a friendship that would make him smile.

Mam and Pops, I wish you were still here with me, Flynn thought while he rounded another street corner. Kabul was as dull, as depressing, and as lonely as the day before.

Flynn wanted to go home. His mind remembered people, friends, faces, places, but the thought of the beautiful Minnesota trees and lakes felt like a mirage now. Unreal.

CHAPTER 37

On a warm July day, while Rose was giving her sweet lambs, Elsa and Ana, their afternoon bottles, she started thinking about the day she and Daisy had gone out to Sully's farm. She had questioned Daisy on the ride home about Sully's interest in Violet. Daisy had kind of laughed it off, almost as if it's been something that has been going on for years.

But why wouldn't Sully ask Violet on a date if he had feelings for her? Maybe Violet had given him the impression she was not at all interested. Or maybe they had dated years ago, and it ended badly. It could be that she had dated his brother way back in high school and Sully just had always felt awkward asking her out.

Finally Rose looked at her two puffy babies, with whom she had taken to talking to, and asked Elsa, "I should let it go shouldn't I, Elsa?" Ana bleated loudly, surprising Rose and she laughed. "I know Ana, that was a terrible joke!"

Rose took the empty bottles back in the house, washed them in the kitchen sink, and planned to bake a little something for the guests who would be checking into the inn tomorrow morning. Settling on Flora's ever-popular Bumbleberry tarts from the diner, she started gathering ingredients from her refrigerator and pantry. Flour, butter, salt, sugar, cinnamon and lemon juice. Fresh strawberries, black berries, pears, and apples.

As she started scooping the cups of flour into her large glass mixing bowl, a thought came to mind. Rose decided to make another small batch of tarts for a special someone.

At about 4:00 p.m. her house was smelling of the warm, fruity pastries in the oven.

"Meow."

Rose turned to see Mrs. Bigglesworth had snuck around the corner and was rubbing up against her leg.

"Well, hi miss. I know you're hungry, but I don't think you like fruit tarts, do you?" Rose said, speaking in a cute, high pitched tone like she always did to animals and babies. Why did women do that, she wondered? Laughing to herself, Rose went into the pantry and got a tin bowl full of dry cat food. She placed it on the floor in the corner of the room for Mrs. Bigglesworth to enjoy.

Opening the oven door, Rose could tell the tarts were perfectly baked and golden. Purple and Red juices bubbled over the top of the pie crust nests. These treats had been such a hit at the diner every time Flora made them. Rose's dad, Philip, had such a sweet tooth and she would always put a couple aside to bring home to him after her shift.

She wondered what her mom and dad were doing this evening. She guessed Seinfield reruns or taking their gentle giant dog, Jack, for a walk. Rose smiled to herself, missing them very much.

Now, to figure out how to deliver a plateful of these to Sully.

CHAPTER 38

Rose stopped by the general store to check in on Hank and his recovery.

"Ahh, Rose. I'm back to normal. No worse for wear. Now I wish Millie would quit making such a fuss of it. Accidents happen," Hank sputtered. Millie rolled her eyes.

"I don't wanna hear it, Hank. I'm going by what Doc said today. You still need to take it easy for a bit. "Hearing that they had been at the hospital that day, made Rose think maybe Sully was working the ambulance today.

"Umm, say — was Sully working there by chance today?" Rose asked.

"He certainly was. Though, when we walked past his office, he had his feet on the counter and was leaning back in his chair catching some winks. Must not have been a busy one. Though, I guess that's a good thing when no calls come in," Hank answered. "Why, do you ask, Rose?"

"Oh, nothing really. I thought I'd bring him a plate of tarts also. Just a thank you for helping me learn to care for my sheep girls," Rose replied, coming up with a believable reason to visit Sully, without rumors surging through town. It was time for match-making.

"Well, I better be on my way. I'm so glad you are on the mend, Hank. Take it easy, ok. Bye Millie," Rose called as she walked toward the door.

Hank yelled back, "Will do, Rose. And thanks for the little pie things, or whatever you call them."

Rose laughed as she carried the other small plate down the road, turning on 1st Avenue toward the hospital. Someone had to be the cupid here. And who didn't like delectable treats, even if they were being used as a bribe to get Sully to talk.

The Cherish hospital and clinic was a small brick building with an attached garage in the back for the ambulance. Rose was used to hospitals like the Duluth Memorial Hospital. It was six stories high, and the campus and parking ramps covered the span of two city blocks. There, a map was needed to locate which door you entered, which desk to check in at, and then which elevator was needed for the floor you were visiting.

In the small courtyard, a basic wooden sign read *Cherish Medical Center*. A red arrow pointed toward the ambulance garage, and she could see a separate entrance there. She figured she'd take a chance and see if perhaps Sully was still in. Taking the walkway around the back of the building, Rose started to slow her steps, second guessing her presumptuous actions.

What am I going to say? And why is this any business of mine? Sully is probably going to tell me to mind my own business.

Thinking she had made a mistake, Rose stopped and turned back. After considering running before someone saw her, a man's voice startled her from behind.

"Rose? What are you doing here? Is everything ok? Are you hurt?" It was Sully. It appeared he was just locking up for the day and noticed her.

"Oh no, no. I am feeling great. Everyone is fine. At least I think everyone is fine. I guess I can't guarantee everyone is fine," Rose was stumbling over her words now.

Well, I made this into an awkward mess.

Sully smiled, confused, and looked at her plate of homemade tarts.

"Can I help you with something, Rose? Were you hoping to visit one of the patients in the hospital?" Sully asked politely.

She was going to just have to fess up. Here it goes...

"No. Well, the truth is, I was hoping to talk to you. I figured you don't get homemade baked goods real often out on the farm, working all the time, so I brought you something."

At this Sully looked a bit uncomfortable. He rubbed his hand across the dark scruff that was beginning to grow on his face. He was a decently attractive man. Nothing like Flynn, of course. Sully wasn't a distinguished handsome, but a rugged, worn from hard work handsome. He was kind but liked to crack a joke.

Unfortunately, he was standing across from Rose with a perplexed look on his face and a hint of pink in his cheeks. Rose realized if she didn't speak up soon, this visit would turn from awkward to downright humiliating.

"Listen Sully, this isn't going the way I had intended. I really didn't think this through I guess."

Rose motioned to the bench nearby, "Do you have a minute to talk?"

She wasn't surprised that this didn't ease Sully's confusion, though he agreed nodding his head. Rose sat down on the bench with considerable space between her and Sully. Rose tore off the proverbial band aid.

"Sully, this is absolutely none of my business. You will probably want to tell me to buzz off, but I have to ask. Why haven't you asked Violet out?"

Sully let out a relieved breath and laughed. "Uff, I thought you were coming on to me or something, Rose. I know you are a married woman, and I was feeling sick thinking of how to turn you down. Thank God." He wiped his forehead.

Rose laughed too, and uncovering the plate of tarts, she offered one to him. He grabbed one and took a big bite, flakes of crust dropping in his lap.

"Those are so good!" Sully exclaimed, taking another bite. Chewing slowly this time he stared at the ground, thinking of how to reply to Rose's questions.

"The truth is, Rose, I have had feelings for Violet for…well as long as I can remember even noticing girls at school." Sully let out an embarrassed laugh. "I can't explain why after seeing her in my third grade classroom, wearing a blue dress and her long dark hair braided at her side, I was just drawn to her. It helped that she was very polite and kind. She was nice to me when some kids weren't. I was the farm boy who lived out in the sticks. We were great friends as grade school kids, but naturally, as we became teenagers we started looking at each other through a different lens. The problem is her dad started noticing. He was pretty strict about his daughters dating, but we couldn't deny the chemistry we had. We snuck around a bit so that we could be together. I was a gentleman, mind you, I never pushed anything.

But one evening when we were seventeen I wanted to take her out in my pick-up truck and star gaze. The night was perfect. A cool, but comfortable, September night. Nice and warm when I brought out the blanket we wrapped around ourselves. I had brought a thermos of hot chocolate and a bag of popcorn. It was innocent, Rose, even though I can feel your accusing eyes staring at me right now."

Rose laughed. "Well, it sounds like a perfect set up for romance to me."

"Anyway, we talked for hours that night about a possible future for us. It was Violet that finally leaned over and with a soft touch of her hand behind my head, she pulled me forward and kissed me. It was brief, but passionate too. I don't know, maybe it was the surprise, or warmth of her lips, but I felt fireworks go off in my stomach and my whole body flooded with heat.

It didn't last though. At that very moment, the worst of moments in this case, her dad pulled up in their station wagon and shined the headlights right at us. I stood up so fast that I fell over the straw bale we had been sitting on. I think at that point Gabe thought I not only was stealing a kiss from his daughter but was sipping on moonshine too." Sully crunched a maple leaf in his hand and stared at it intently.

"It was a wonderful night, but it didn't end well. Violet was ordered to no longer see me. She became quieter and bitter I think. After graduation, she left town for college, and I thought that was it. She was gone. The way Daisy talked, Violet was out there living her life and wanted nothing to do with our little town of Cherish anymore. She wanted the past to stay in the past.

You can imagine my surprise four years later when she walked past the ambulance garage in a nurse's uniform, a name tag pinned on the front and a ready smile for her first day of work at Cherish Medical Center."

"What did you do? Did you go say hello? Welcome back? What?" Rose was being pulled into the story more and more as it went on.

"I was stunned. I didn't know what to do. But, as time went on we would happen upon each other in the break room or checking on patients here and there. In time, we were friends again. We would take quick coffee breaks together, laugh when days were good, lean on each other when days were bad. But I had heard Violet wasn't the dating type. She had become a confident, single woman. She enjoyed her own time, her own hobbies. When she left her job at the hospital to open up Wild Flowers with Daisy, her main focus was on the shop and making a success of it. It has been years now since the day I first started looking at Violet as something more. But I don't want to chance losing her as a friend by telling her I still, to this day, have feelings for her. Does that make any sense? Probably sounds foolish wasting a life pining for a woman that thinks of me as a brother type."

"Do you know what her feelings are? I'm sorry, but I do think it is a foolish way to live your life. Sully, I know you are worried about rejection. Especially from a woman you have been in love with for many years. But–"

Sully interrupted "Hey, who said anything about being in love? I said more than just a friend. That I have feelings for her. Not that I am in love with…" But he couldn't deny it. "Ok, damn it. I am in love with her."

Rose spoke in a comforting tone. "Then, you are doing you both an injustice by not sharing your feelings with her. At least if she doesn't feel the same, Sully, you can let it go and move on. And it will be ok. But why not take the chance on something that could become a beautiful love story?"

Rose stood up and left the plate of remaining tarts with Sully to take home. "Think it over, ok Sully?"

He looked up at Rose and nodded. "Thanks Rose. And for the tarts too."

Walking home, Rose felt a warm feeling inside. Oh, how she wished for a love story for others, as she had with Flynn. If it was meddling in other people's business, she didn't care. Some things needed a little nudge, as she saw it.

FLYNN

Flynn was crouched down, resting against the brick wall of a once flourishing hotel. At present it was a hollow, crumbling down corpse of a structure. No more life, no more joy, shared within those walls. It didn't even depress Flynn anymore. It was another day. As usual his mind wandered as he stared into the nothingness of wreckage and death.

He was sitting in a diner booth back home. Duluth, Minnesota. The day at Fort Briggs had been a trying one. He had showed up late when his phone alarm hadn't gone off. Showing up to work wasn't just humiliating, he knew it was unacceptable. He didn't want to know what the consequences would be. When Sergeant Wilcox saw Flynn run past his office window, he stepped out onto the sidewalk and simply commanded, "Private Mitchell. In my office, now!"

Flynn knew what was coming. Being on time in the military is late and being early is on time. There was no in between. In the US military there were no gray areas. At that moment Flynn remembered making a mental note to set two back-up alarms from now on.

The day had been filled with up and down hill running, hundreds of push-ups, mopping the galley and cleaning toilets after Chili day, to name a few of his punishments. He looked and felt like death warmed over that day. He was hot and terribly hungry after he was allowed only water as nourishment.

"Oh, you don't look so good. Are you feeling ok? Let me grab you a glass of ice water." The waitress returned within seconds with a menu and tall glass of water. Flynn took it from her hand, accidentally touching her fingertips for a moment. A ridiculous feeling made his heart swell with the sudden touch. Until that moment he had been so exhausted, mortified with himself and thinking of nothing, but getting a meal and going home to bed. But he looked up at the waitress. She was petite, five foot two inches maybe? Crystal blue eyes that creased into moon shapes when she smiled. And her smile; he had never seen or felt such joy in the sight of one person's smile. It lit up her face. And for the first time that day, he realized he wore one on his face too. Tucking her blonde hair behind her left ear she asked, "What else can I get for you, sir?"

"I would love a chocolate milkshake. That will cool me down I think! Can I also get a Walleye sandwich with tartar and some pub fries? I'm starving." Flynn handed the menu back to his waitress.

"Of course. That will be out shortly." She smiled again before turning and walking toward the kitchen.

Flynn thought to himself, "How have I never seen this girl before. Marty and I have had breakfast at this diner dozens of times. It seems like she would be hard to forget. Ahh, I'm sure a girl like that has a boyfriend. No doubt about that." Flynn's smile faded and he distracted himself watching out his window at leisurely people strolling down the boardwalk, Lake Superior making a lovely backdrop.

"Ok, here you are sir. One large chocolate milkshake," she said as she handed the ice cold beverage to Flynn. He was startled by her approach to his table and when he turned suddenly he bumped her hand and the milkshake tipped and dropped directly into his lap.

"Oh my gosh! I am so, so sorry! Let me get a towel. I can't believe – ahhh." Her face had turned a deep red and she looked to be on the brink of tears when she ran away. For the moment he waited for her return with a towel, all he could think was *I hope she isn't too upset about this. It could*

193

happen to anyone. He hardly noticed the wet, sticky, cold mess in his lap.

"Here you go," the waitress handed him the towel and grabbed the empty glass and ice cream soaked napkins and turned away again. He noticed her face was no longer joyous and full of energy, but just plain humiliated.

Flynn had done the best he could at cleaning himself up but was fine. No harm done. When another waitress brought out his sandwich and fries, he was profoundly disappointed.

"Uhh, thank you. But what happened to the other waitress?" he questioned.

"Oh, I'm sorry. Her shift is over. She headed home."

Flynn thought it strange to end a shift at 6:45 during a dinner rush.

As the older waitress turned to leave, Flynn stopped her, "Can I get my bill? And I think I'll take my meal to go if that's ok."

It had been a brief exchange between the two that day. Normally something you'd forget about within a week without question. But he hadn't. Not one day went by that he did not think of that sweet, adorable waitress and her blushing cheeks. His Rose.

Flynn stood up and took a walk down the street. A broken down truck was sitting in the middle of a side road, windows broke out, tires flat, and the passenger side door missing. Strangely a skinny, sickly gray cat climbed out of the truck window and perched for a moment on the hood. Flynn walked over to it. "Hi there little guy. You are very lost if you are in this place. You should be sleeping on the end of a little girl's bed. Or chasing mice and bluebirds." Flynn scratched behind the cat's ear. "You won't find either here, I'm afraid. This is no place for any creature."

Feeling an overwhelming loneliness, Flynn smiled weakly at the cat and turned back the way he came.

CHAPTER 39

The months of summer seemed to fly by for Rose. There was never a shortage of guests through her front door. Some were like Mr. and Mrs. Nelson, happy-go-lucky. Some were a touch more like Mr. Hawthorne. Either way, she made it her goal to please each guest as best she could in the ways that made each and every one of them feel special and right at home.

After that first weekend of sharing her peanut butter oatmeal cookie recipe and her sausage, herb and cheese quiche, Rose had the idea that it could be her signature check-out gift to her guests. A special touch.

So, the trend kept on and people seemed to enjoy it. Typically, she would jot down recipes that guests had tasted during their stay. Her buttermilk pancakes with cherry amaretto syrup, her classic apple pie, Grandma's gooey caramel, pecan sweet rolls and Auntie Jo's rich seven layer chocolate bars. She wrote out savory recipes like Mom's famous slow-simmered tomato pasta sauce made with fresh Romas from her garden. Succulent pork prime rib with a creamy parmesan sauce, roasted duck stuffed with apples and oranges served with fluffy Minnesota wild rice. Flynn's favorite pan fried Walleye pike with a side of cucumber remoulade sauce. Swedish meatballs with a mashed parsnip purée. Even her favorite Reubens from the diner in Duluth. The list went on.

What Rose loved as much as owning and running her inn, was cooking and serving guests her family dishes. Then, leaving a handwritten recipe just for them along with a thank you note as they turned in their key and paid for their stay, felt so much more personal than a Holiday Inn.

With things going so well at the inn and Rose's decision to keep moving forward with the final sale, she thought a lunch meeting with Father Eli was in order. She called and asked if he would mind meeting her at the inn at noon, Wednesday, September 5th. She had no guests staying mid-week and she could make him lunch. He accepted, happily, and arrived ten minutes early the Wednesday they had scheduled.

Rose opened the front door, greeting Father Eli with a big hug.

"I'm so happy to see you. I've been so busy here, that I've been neglecting my dear friends. Please Father, come in."

"Thank you, Rose. The house looks radiant. What a transformation. And you certainly have added special touches. I've heard wonderful things," Father Eli complimented.

Rose beamed with pride, "Oh thank you. It's been lots of work and so much more joy. I can hardly believe it."

She led him into the sitting room, motioning to a chair, "Please, have a seat, Father. I'm just finishing up in the kitchen and we can have a bit of lunch."

The two friends, in popular guest fashion, sat and dined on the front porch. Rose had roasted a turkey that morning with fresh herbs, a butter rub and sliced the meat thin for sandwiches. She had piled turkey slices onto homemade croissants, melted brie and a homemade strawberry basil aioli spread. On the side (her favorite from growing up) cucumber and tomato salad with a cool, creamy, buttermilk dressing.

Father Eli loved every bite. "Are you sure you shouldn't be opening a full time restaurant too, Rose? All I hear about is the five-star meals you've been serving to your guests. Although, then Mudsie would have some competition on Main Street, and she might not care for that." Father Eli laughed at himself and as the two friends finished their plates of food, Rose spoke frankly.

"Father, we need to talk final numbers. For the house. I'm happy here, the house is in great shape and to my absolute, joyous surprise, has been steady with guests."

He set his napkin down on the table and thoughtfully replied, "I'm so happy to hear that. Are you certain, though, you don't want to give it through a slow season? Winter, that is. Bed and Breakfasts in Minnesota are a sure success in the summer and fall. But winter? Winters can be slow and lonely. Not to mention next to no money coming in."

Rose knew he was probably right but didn't want the chance to pass her by. "Look Father, I know I want to be here. I feel it in my bones. I know Flynn will want the same thing. If you aren't ready to sign on the dotted line, can we at least set a date to do so?"

Father Eli obliged, nodding and replied, "May 1st."

The two shook and let the moment slip away.

After clearing the plates and glasses from their table Rose suggested, "Father, would you like a tour of the completely finished product? Stella has done wonders on the drapes, quilts and furniture upholstery. I've added several other touches and Chives is most likely becoming irritated with my projects I've had him…ok, begged him, to do."

They both laughed as Rose motioned for them to start the tour in her favorite room, the kitchen.

CHAPTER 40

Rose had hoped she would be too busy to notice when the calendar page showed her it had come to September 18th, her wedding anniversary. One year ago.

That morning she took her cup of coffee and walked out to her little garden where she usually found comfort and serenity. The growing days were few now and the harvesting season was in full swing. She didn't feel like doing any of it today, which, for Rose, was very unusual.

She needed a day. Just *one* day. Her and Flynn's day.

She sat down and ran her hands through the squash vines and looked up at her apple tree, heavy with fruit.

She whispered, "Flynn…what are you doing right now? I hope that maybe you are thinking of me, as I am of you. I'm happy, Flynn, and I'm living our dream. But I'm running out of steam without you here with me," Rose began to cry softly.

"Please come back to me, Flynn." She laid flat down on the grass, covering her face with her hands and wept until she fell sound asleep.

Rose woke to a tap on her shoulder, and another. She sat up suddenly, disoriented. "Who's there?" she exclaimed.

"My sweet Rose, what are you doing sleeping on the grass in the backyard, when you have a comfy bed upstairs?"

It was Mudsie. Rose was still rubbing her eyes and trying to remember how she fell asleep in the yard, of all places. And then, the emotions hit her again, like a sledgehammer to the chest.

"Ooooh, I just want to be alone, Mudsie. I want to sleep the day away and forget. If just for ONE day." Mudsie sat right down on the grass with Rose and folded her in her arms.

"Dear sweet girl, I know. I KNOW. And here's the thing, it's ok. You do it. Lay your head on my shoulder, or on the squash plants over there or on a fluffy soft pillow in the house. It doesn't matter where. Take today if you need it." With that Mudsie rocked her back and forth, soothing her in a motherly way.

After a while, Mudsie spoke again, "Take today, Rose. Let the hours slip away. Let September 18th dwindle down to the last minutes before the clock strikes midnight. Be angry, be heartbroken, be whatever you need to be. But tomorrow — you wake up, get dressed and walk down those damn stairs ready to take on the world. And do it with a smile on your pretty face! Your soldier is staying strong and fighting to get back to you. You need to do the same for him."

With a little struggle, Mudsie stood up and said, "Dinner is in the kitchen, honey. Why don't you come in the house and clean up. I'm gonna give you one last hug and head on back to the café. But look at me, Rose," she waited, "it will be ok. I promise you."

And with that, Rose watched that short, round, tough as damn nails lady walk back around the side of the house and down Main Street.

Why did it seem that the people that had been through the most pain, and should be hardened to the world, were usually the most caring and selfless people?

Rose did as Mudsie had told her. She went into the house, ate the ham and cabbage soup Mudsie had left on the stove for her and after washing her dish, walked straight up to her bedroom.

She laid in her bed until the bright sun of September 19th shined through her window. The blue bird song outside coaxed her onto her feet.

Remembering what Mudsie had told her, she put on clean clothes and with a smile on her face and energy in her step, she walked downstairs and started making coffee.

CHAPTER 41

T he day after Rose's melt down, the day after her anniversary, started like any. She had done as Mudsie urged (strongly urged). She held her head high and plastered a smile on her face. In a small way, it was a relief to let September 18th pass. She felt free to move on with day to day life. She needed to concentrate on what she was doing there in Cherish and focus on what needed to be done at the inn.

The coffee was perking in the pot. She had given Mrs. Bigglesworth a dish of Purina in the corner of the kitchen where she always dined. With a cleansing breath Rose tied her apron tight around her waist and began jotting down her duties for the day.

Groceries-

> *Raspberries*
>
> *Blackberries*
>
> *Heavy whipping cream*
>
> *Olive Oil*
>
> *Parmesan Cheese*
>
> *Eggs*
>
> *Salmon*
>
> *Chuck Roast*
>
> *Dish soap*
>
> *Cat food*
>
> *Things to do-*
>
> *-Strip beds and run large quilts to laundromat*
>
> *-Make loaves of oatmeal bread for the week*

-Muck out Elsa and Ana's shelter

-Prepare check-in documents for the week's guests

-Find a birthday gift for Stella

"That'll do for now. I can't think of anything else at the moment. How about you Mrs. Bigglesworth?" Rose asked her feline friend.

"Meow," she answered, roaming around the kitchen.

"You want to go lay on the front porch in the sunshine, kitty cat? It's an awfully nice day out there."

After letting her out the front door, Rose smiled. Mrs. Bigglesworth had been a little bit of a troublemaker when she first brought her home from Sully's farm. She caught the cat climbing the velvet drapes in the dining room on more than one occasion. She walked into the kitchen one early morning to witness her up on the butcher block sampling the left over cheese biscuits from the night before. Suffice to say, no food could be left out any more. But all in all, Mrs. Bigglesworth had become company for Rose. Not that there wasn't steady traffic through the house with guests and friendly visits.

Mrs. Bigglesworth was a cuddle mate who always agreed with everything Rose had to say. And she certainly kept the mice away.

Not expecting any guests to check in, the *ding dong* of the doorbell startled Rose. "Who could that be?" she asked out loud. She was busy kneading bread dough for the week's meals and was covered in flour. Wiping her hands on a dish towel, she walked to the front door and opened it.

A young man, about her age, was crouched down petting Mrs. Bigglesworth. The tabby cat was loving the attention and curled around his leg like she was his new best friend. Noticing someone had finally opened the door, he stood up.

"Hi, I was wondering if you have any room at the inn?" he asked. Then putting a hand to his brow, embarrassed, he reworded his question.

"What I meant to say, as opposed to sounding like Mary and Joseph on the eve of Christmas Day, was - do you have any available guest rooms for the week?" Again, he looked down at his feet with a boyish half smile. An awkwardness, or shyness to him.

Rose laughed, "Don't worry about it. I love the Christmas story." His eyes met hers and he seemed to relax a bit.

"I'm Luke. I'm in town working on some of the reconstruction after the recent storm damage to local business and a few homes. It looks like we will be here for the week. I've been told you run a nice inn here. And more importantly, cook wonderful, hearty meals for your guests? The guy at the corner gas station had nice things to say about you."

"Well, I'm flattered that the town's people are spreading such rumors. Chives O'Connor is the cheery old guy you would have talked to. He's a friend."

"Oh, he was very welcoming and talkative. Introduced me to his dog, Stanley was it?"

Rose giggled. "Samson. He is also a friend." Then remembering why Luke was on her front step, she said, "I do have a couple rooms that are available for the entire week, if you'd like to take a look."

"Great! I can't sleep in my truck one more night," Luke replied, with obvious relief.

Rose showed him in and asked him to follow her up the stairs to the first room.

"Here we are, this is a smaller room with just a twin bed, small dresser and nightstand. But I think it is a comfortable space and close to one of the bathrooms. Will this be ok?"

Luke didn't care one bit. He wanted a bed, a meal and a hot shower. That would have equaled heaven.

"Yes! This will be just perfect. Thank you Ms...?" he hung on for her answer.

"Mitchell. Mrs. Mitchell. Rose." She started walking out of the room, grabbing for the door and smiled. "Make yourself at home."

"Thank you, Mrs. Mitchell, for your hospitality."

Luke sat down on the small bed, noticing then how extremely lonely a bed made for one looked. He had nobody, not family or a friend in the world. This place, this Rose, made him feel welcome and comfortable. Unlacing his work boots, he threw them both across the room with a thud on the wood floor. He stretched out on the bed and fell into a sleep his body needed, his mind needed.

It wasn't until he smelled the smokey, sweet smell of dinner being served, that he came to life.

Rose pulled the large roasting pan from her oven filling the kitchen with a delicious scent. She had made a homemade bourbon barbecue sauce and glazed a chicken with it. Typically, if she had a full house she would've made much more for dinner, but it was just her surprise guest, Luke, this evening. Letting the meat rest a bit before she sliced into it, she went to the refrigerator to grab salad fixings. Setting a few ribs of romaine lettuce on the counter and a small brick of parmesan cheese, she decided on a Caesar salad to serve on the side of the bourbon chicken. The fresh baked bread sat across the room on the wooden butcher block cooling. This would make for a simple, but lovely meal she thought.

While she whisked more olive oil into a bowl of what she was turning into a creamy Caesar dressing, she heard footsteps coming down the steps.

Then a light knock at the kitchen door, "Mrs. Mitchell? Mind if I come in?" Luke politely asked.

Rose froze but wondered why. "Of course, Luke. Please, come on in. I'm just finishing up dinner here."

"Oh, I know. The amazing smells actually woke me out of a dead sleep.

I see the rumors are true. This looks fantastic!"

"You haven't even tasted a bite yet," Rose laughed. Though she knew she had a talent for cooking, she would never admit it. Plus, the meals should speak for themselves.

"Anything that smells this tantalizing will taste even better." Luke closed his eyes and breathed in deeply the mixture of aromas. "Mmmmm."

Rose looked away, feeling guilty somehow. Luke was a good looking man, young, about her age. His hair was wet from having just taken a quick shower before dinner and he smelled of clean Irish Spring soap. His hair was the color of straw and eyes a dark chocolate color. His hands, she noticed, were calloused a bit from hard, laborious work. A sweet smile graced his sun tanned, boyish face.

"Can I help in any way?" Luke offered, glancing down at her salad fixings. Rose shook any feelings of wrongdoing from her brain. Luke was a man, yes, but a guest like anyone else. She was doing nothing wrong by making him feel at home.

"Sure, that would be great. Thank you. I just rinsed this lettuce here. If you would like to tear it up and throw into these two bowls, and shred a bit of parmesan on top, this meal will be about ready to serve."

"That I think I can manage. When it comes to cooking though, don't ask me to do much more than making toast."

The two laughed together.

Rose excused herself and went to set a small table on the front porch. While she set a checkered tablecloth down, a napkin and a set of silverware she felt strange again. Why? She was doing nothing wrong. Was she going to feel like this any time a young man stayed in her inn? How ridiculous and immature.

Deciding, though it best to remain a welcoming host, maybe a bit more business-like was a smart idea. She walked back into her kitchen to do just that.

"Oh, thank you for helping me with those salads, Luke. But I really should finish up here, myself. I have your table all set out on the front porch if you would like to go take a seat. I'll serve this to you shortly."

Luke's smile faded a bit, though he tried to hide the fact.

"Ok, thank you. I will see myself outside, Mrs. Mitchell."

Again, a feeling of guilt filled Rose. This time for feeling a bit of sympathy for Luke. Poor young man, always traveling alone, no one to call family or a friend really. Her heart went out to him.

Well, what she could do was make him feel welcome and feed him a few good, home cooked meals for the week, as she had done for every guest.

This guest was no different from any other that had walked through the front door.

CHAPTER 42

The next morning Rose found Luke sitting out on the front porch step, watching the sun rise. She hurried a cup of coffee and a simple raspberry muffin out to him.

"Good morning," she said from behind as she stepped out the front door. Turning with surprise he greeted Rose.

"Good Morning, Mrs. Mitchell."

Rose handed him the steaming cup of coffee and the warm muffin.

"I know it's not much, but you're an earlier riser than me."

Luke smiled, appreciative. "Oh, this is great. Thank you. I have to be heading off to work here shortly. We are only in Cherish for a short time and pretty much work from sunup til sundown."

Rose nodded, feeling she should excuse herself and get busy preparing for new guests arriving. But, with her own cup of coffee warm in her hand and the morning sun so beautiful, she decided to sit for a few minutes.

"So, where do you come from Luke?" she asked.

"Ahh, a little bit of everywhere I guess. I was born in Denver, Colorado, moved with my ma to Seattle, Washington, where her boyfriend lived, when I was eight. Not two years later, I moved again, and lived with my grandparents in Burlington, Vermont until I was eighteen. Then got lucky and found Carter Construction after graduation. Here I am, still with them. We travel quite a bit. I keep in touch with my grandma and grandpa and have a few football buddies from high school that I hear from once in a while, but other than that, it's just me and my truck traveling the roads of our great country." He answered as though he had given this spiel before.

"My childhood wasn't that of the classic fifties family upbringing, but here I am. I'm making a way for myself. God gave me good work, my health and a book full of blank pages to write my life's words in. I intend to make the most of every day, Mrs. Mitchell."

"How old are you, Luke?" Rose asked, though she didn't know why that question.

"Twenty-three next month. October 23rd."

Again, something tugged are her heartstrings. Luke seemed to be a polite, sweet and upbeat young man who wanted no sympathy.

"Well, I'd say you're doing good for yourself. You should be proud. I mean, we are all dealt cards, but it's all about the way you play the game, right?"

They both continued sipping their coffee and watching the sun eek its way higher into the sky. The town started waking up, little by little. Lights were being turned on, Closed signs were being flipped to Open on business front doors. Luke popped the last of his muffin in his mouth and handed Rose his empty coffee cup.

"Thanks Mrs. Mitchell. Time to head to work."

As he started down the front path, Rose yelled, "Have a good day, Luke, and please, call me Rose."

"You too, Rose."

He smiled a last boyish grin at her before jumping into his pick-up truck and squealing away.

Rose took a last sip of her own cup of coffee and stood up. There was much to do before more guests arrived. Check-in was 10:00 a.m. and the clock was ticking.

A new refreshing energy kept Rose jumping from job to job, room to room, meal to meal. The two families that had checked in were fairly private and said very few words. Mr. and Mrs. Carmichael were in town only for her mother's funeral which explained their somber mood. And the Heigel family, from Rastatt, Germany, spoke little English. What Rose had understood from the bits and pieces they told her was that they were on their way to Maria Heigel's, Mr. Heigel's sister's home in North Dakota and were needing a place to stay for a few nights. Their three children were quite tired after their trip overseas, though Rose noticed, very well behaved.

Rose stirred a large pot of potato and sausage soup on the stove top when her kitchen door opened.

"Well, hello sweet pea. I feel like I haven't seen you in ages. This place is keeping you busy as a bee isn't it?"

Rose kept stirring the thick, creamy soup, adding a little salt and pepper and torn spinach leaves. She looked up and smiled at Daisy, glad for the visit.

"Well, yes, I guess it is Daisy. But it's a good thing. I wouldn't really want it any other way." Rose grabbed several ceramic soup bowls from the cabinet and cloth napkins from the wicker basket on the floor nearby.

"Do you want to stay for dinner, Daisy? I certainly have plenty. I'd love your company." Rose offered.

"Well, Violet isn't home, which has become a regular thing in the evenings. So, I guess, if you wouldn't mind at all…I'd be delighted to join."

"Great, here. Help me set the table in the dining room."

Rose and Daisy set ten places on the dining room table for themselves and the eight guests that were staying at the inn.

While they waited for dinner hour, the two friends shared a glass of beer out on the front porch. The September night was so beautiful, and they hated to waste it.

"What's new at Wild Flowers, Dais?" Rose asked, taking a refreshing slug of her jelly jar full of the frothy, golden ale.

"Oh, you know, same old. This time of year, a few weddings, an occasional funeral, several fall mums and seasonal arrangement sales, bouquets for birthdays, lovers, sick folks, yadda, yadda, yadda." Daisy sounded burned out. Rose wondered what was going on at the shop.

"How is Violet? Anything happening with her?"

"She's in and out of the shop far more than she ever has been, Rose."

"Do you think she and Sully are seeing each other finally? Could that be it? Though why not just say?" Rose questioned.

"Ya got me! I would be giddy to see them together. It's a mystery. But, if something is going on between them, I can't understand all the secrecy. Love is strange."

Rose thought back to when she and Flynn had met and plummeted into full blown puppy love. She remembered being physically ill when she had a twenty-four hour day that she wasn't able to see Flynn, touch his face, taste his lips. It seemed ridiculous, but at the time the agony seemed beyond words. One really couldn't explain love.

Taking a long drink of her beer again, she thought about her husband. She imagined he was doing something far different than she was at this moment. Something dangerous perhaps? She hoped he was safe. She prayed he knew she clung to this wish like none other.

FLYNN

Dear Rosebud,

What do you know, we were given out another taste of the foreign beer we had enjoyed on baseball day. I'm nursing one as I write. And I wonder how you are spending your evening. Although, I suppose it's eggs and bacon time there. I always forget our times are way different. Either way, I'm gonna picture you sharing a bottle of beer with me, and we are toasting each other on the sale of our new inn. Maybe it will be called Rose's? Nah, I'm no good at that kind of thing. You will take care of the little details. Ahhh, it sounds like heaven to be somewhere like that with you.

Marty and I are keeping everyone in line here. Ha. You probably laughed out loud when you read that sentence. Marty is cracking jokes and as usual is the life of the party. If you want to call it a party over here. It's not. War is not. But it is necessary to lighten the mood whenever possible. Otherwise, we may go completely insane.

You should know, as I'm sure I've told you before, you keep me company here. You keep me hopeful. You keep me safe, Rosebud.

Keep coming to me in my dreams. It makes the lonely dark nights bearable.

Love always,

Flynn

CHAPTER 43

Dinner had been enjoyable, but brief. It seemed all of Rose's guests were tired and anxious for their time alone. Mr. and Mrs. Carmichael politely thanked Rose for the wonderful meal and retired to their room. The Heigel family went for a walk after dinner in search of something sweet. Rose had recommended they stop at the candy store on the corner before it closed at 7:00, but she wasn't entirely sure they understood her. Luke seemed dead on his feet after a very long day of hard work. But he opted on sitting out on the porch for a bit of relaxation before turning in for the night.

Daisy helped Rose clean up in the kitchen.

"Who is this young man, Rose? Does he know you are married?" Daisy nudged Rose and laughed while they stood next to each other washing and drying the dishes.

"Daisy! Of course he knows. Why would that even be a question anyway?" Rose replied.

"He looks at you, I don't know, in a certain way. Smiles at you when you aren't looking. These are things only a bystander would notice I suppose. But, if I had to guess, I think he wishes you weren't a Mrs." Daisy gave a little chuckle as she stacked clean bowls back in the cabinet.

"Really, Daisy. Don't be ridiculous. He's just a friendly young man. He has no one in the world. My heart goes out to him. But…nothing more than that," Rose assured.

Daisy watched her from the back cabinet as Rose glanced out the front window. She could see Luke leaning against the front porch railing breathing in the cool September air.

Daisy wondered if Rose realized she had been staring out the window at this guy for the last couple minutes while her hands sat idle in the dish water. Walking over, Daisy put an arm around her friend.

"Listen, sweet pea. Remember not to misjudge your deep longing for Flynn, for a new attraction to someone else. I see you noticing Luke's charms. And it is very evident he has a fondness for you. Things like this are, though natural, they can turn into an unwanted fire really quick," Daisy warned gently.

"Oh, please don't even say such a thing Daisy. I would never, ever have eyes for anyone, but Flynn. He has my whole heart. Yes, I'll admit Luke is a sweet, nice looking man, but that is it."

"I know, honey. Don't get worked up about it. I'm just being honest and telling you to be careful." Daisy wiped her hands on a kitchen towel and yawned. "I think I'm going to head home, Rose. Thank you for inviting me to join you all for dinner this evening. It was lovely."

"Of course. Come again any time, Daisy." The two friends shared a light hug and Daisy left.

Rose watched out the window and noticed Luke and Daisy were visiting on the front porch step. He smiled, she laughed, the two seemed to enjoy the conversation. Rose tried not to spy, but every once in a while she'd steal another glance. Perhaps, Daisy and Luke could be a match? She didn't see that coming. Strangely, she got a little ache in her stomach at the thought.

Was Daisy right? Did she look at Luke in a way a married woman shouldn't?

CHAPTER 44

The remaining days of the week went by rather fast, and September began to dwindle. A new, cooler wind whispered through the leaves on the tall oaks hanging over the inn. When Rose found herself with time on her hands, which wasn't often, she busied herself with anything she could. It kept her mind focused on the task at hand and not on other distractions. A few days prior, when Daisy had quizzed her about Luke, she had brushed it off. However, since then, she had noticed Luke had a way of looking at her that made the heat rise up her chest and show on her cheeks. It concerned her some. And it felt good too. The guilt ate her alive.

As she hung freshly washed bath towels on the clothesline, she thought of Flynn. Her handsome soldier. Oh, how she missed him. She missed the feeling of her hands through his hair, the familiar smell of Stetson cologne on his chest, his kind eyes staring into hers. Flynn was so strong and a sweet teddy bear at the same time. She thought about their evenings together, watching 90s sitcom reruns. She would pop some popcorn and he would give her a foot massage. She pictured her life and how perfect it had been for such a short time, and she became angry, sad, scared…confused.

A towel pulled loose from its clothespins when another gust of wind came up. It blew across the yard into the trees. Foolishly, Rose ran after the beautifully white bath towel, that was now covered in bits of grass and leaves. When she got to the other side of the yard, she saw someone holding the towel out to her.

Breathing a bit faster from the sprint, Rose gasped, "Oh? Luke? You're not working this afternoon?"

"Done a bit early today Rose. Here, I caught your fly-away for you."

He winked and handed her the towel.

"Ah yes. Thank you." The tips of her fingers lightly grazed his as she grabbed for the towel. The feeling sent an electric shock up her body. "Oh sorry!" She pulled away fast.

Luke looked at her with amused pleasure. "For what?" Though she knew they both felt it, for a split second.

"Thanks for grabbing the lost towel, Luke. I better go finish hanging the rest with extra clothespins this time. I will see you at dinner time."

Rose turned and walked briskly back to the white cloud of towels fluttering in the wind. She couldn't even think this time. Her head was a fog and the palms of her hands, clammy.

At dinner Luke was polite and tried visiting with the Carmichaels and the Heigel family, but he and Rose shared a few glances from across the table during the meal. Rose had served each guest a flakey homemade pasty for dinner with fresh applesauce on the side. Everyone was smiling and laughing and seemed to enjoy their meal which always brought a warm comfort to Rose. After dinner she cleared the table with Luke's help, though she had tried to kindly reject his offer of assistance.

"So, what brought you to Cherish, Rose?" Luke asked as he stacked dirty dishes on a tray.

"Hmmm, that's a question that could have a short answer or a lengthy one. Let's just say, I needed to get out of the city. I've wanted to buy an old house and transform it into an inn for as long as I can remember. When I saw this place, it was like I found home. I couldn't pass it up."

He smiled and continued with his task of collecting soiled dishes and dirty napkins.

"It doesn't take a rocket scientist to tell you are happy doing what you're doing. You light up just seeing your guests sit together enjoying a meal you made for them. It's a beautiful thing — this passion you have. I admire it. I admire you, Rose." This time when she looked up at him his eyes were serious. He stood still and kept his eyes on her. She busied herself, pretending the look he was giving her didn't have an effect. Hands shaking with the weight of the heavy plates, she retreated to the kitchen with the load. Luke followed with his tray, setting it down on the counter next to the sink.

"Thanks again for your help. You know your stay here doesn't require you to help with the food prep and the clean-up, right?" This time Rose tried to lighten the mood. The serious look Luke had given her in the dining room had rattled her. She desperately needed to bring them both back to inn owner and guest territory, polite acquaintance territory.

Lines were becoming blurry and in danger of being crossed.

Luke answered her remark with a simple, "Yes, I know." He stared at her with a hungry, lonesome look in his eyes, sad almost. As if he was used to losing things he loved. She turned to the sink and began filling it with hot water and dish soap. She hoped he didn't notice that her breathing had quickened. He watched her, and she didn't make a move to excuse herself from the room. After what felt like several seconds, Luke quietly spoke.

"It's been a long day. Thank you for the wonderful meal once again. Good night, Rose."

She turned and watched him push through the swinging kitchen door without a second glance back at her.

Needing some fresh air, Rose went for a walk after she had finished cleaning up in the kitchen. It felt good to feel the cool air in her lungs and the light burn in her calves as she picked up pace. She realized the chemistry between her and Luke was palpable, heart fluttering even. But she was a married woman. A married woman who adored her husband and was feeling these feelings only because she dreadfully missed him. She felt for Luke. He was so alone and had no one to come home to. Even if she was a single woman, she got the feeling Luke wasn't one that could stay in one place too long. The two young people had been introduced during vulnerable times in their lives. Both lonely and searching for ways to fill the void. The real, raw truth was — she loved Flynn and only Flynn, for life. No other. Her attraction to Luke made her fingertips tingle and her heart skip a beat, but that was the extent of it. Flattery and male attention.

She knew she would need to explain herself plainly to Luke soon, before he got the wrong idea.

CHAPTER 45

Rose went straight to bed when she got back to the inn, spent from emotional fatigue. Though sleep found her as soon as her head laid on the pillow, it wasn't a peaceful sleep. Her dreams were fitful. She dreamed of Luke as a child being tossed around from house to house by his own mother, feeling a sense he wasn't loved or wanted by anyone. She dreamed of her car accident. She dreamed of her parents back in Duluth, worried about her. And she dreamed of Flynn…

Rose found herself laying on a small cot set up in a makeshift hospital under a large canvas tent. She looked around, deeply confused and scared. Several other cots were lined up next to hers, some with people sleeping in them. Patients. Soldiers. What was *she* doing here? She noticed a few medics and officers walking among the beds, stopping by a few to check vitals and speak to the injured or sick soldier resting. This wasn't right, what was she doing here? Flipping the thin cotton blanket off her legs and sitting up she called to the nearest medic.

"Please, can you tell me what's going on? Why am I here?" Rose began asking anyone she could see including patients that happened to have their eyes open. No one answered her. No one seemed to even see her frantically running through the rows of cots, through the many unwell soldiers. Two officers and a medic stood next to a cot, and she noticed, as one of the officers looked at his watch, the medic nodded and pulled the white blanket over the patient's face. As the three men began to walk away, Rose yelled this time.

"Please! Where am I? Why did I wake up in a tent full of injured soldiers?" She began to cry. All at once she knew where she was and who the men had just covered with the blanket. Unable to stop her hands from pulling the blanket from his face, all her nightmares came together, and she screamed when she saw her husband's still face.

"NOOO! Flynn! NOOOO! This isn't happening. Please, this is a dream. I know this has to be a dream. Please! Someone help me!"

Rose woke up laying in her own bed at the inn. She was covered in a cold sweat, tears running down her cheeks. She was still whimpering uncontrollably.

"Rose, Rose — it's ok. You're ok." She heard someone say. She felt strong hands helping her sit up in bed. "Here, sit a minute. I will get you a towel and a glass of water."

She was disoriented still and trying to calm herself. It was dark in the room, and she was shaking so much her teeth chattered.

"Here, let me dab your head with this towel. You are ok, Rose. Everything is ok," the man's voice assured her. Finally, after her breathing slowed and she accepted it had been a terrible nightmare, she held tight to him, hugged him, thankful for the comfort. He smoothed her hair and rocked her back and forth.

"Rose, I heard you all the way from my guest room. You were crying for Flynn, saying you loved him and that it had to be a nightmare. Oh, the pain in your voice was the most horrifying and heartbreaking sound I have ever heard. I rushed down here right away."

Rose remembered it all now and began to sob again.

"Shhh, I won't leave you. It's ok, honey. Everything is going to be ok." He sat on her bed holding her, brushing strands of hair away from her face, drying her tears with the towel, whispering soothing words in her ear. "Try to calm down, Rose. You're ok. Flynn is ok. You can relax now."

Rose knew where she was now and that it was Luke holding her. She had no strength to feel guilt for it. She needed human contact at that moment, someone to hold her, console her.

His tender touch was so gentle, and he continued to stroke her hair and dab the towel to her forehead. Finally, Rose felt herself calm and her exhaustion took over. As her eyelids started to close, she felt Luke pull the blankets up around her. He sat with her for a while watching her tear streaked face begin to relax and then Rose felt him softly kiss her forehead and leave the room.

The next morning Rose blinked open her eyes, recalling, shortly after, the happenings of the night. She rolled on her side and groaned, seeing the glass of water Luke had brought her still sitting next to the alarm clock. The memory of the terrible nightmare rushed back to her, and she thanked God it had been just a dream. And she thanked God a second time for Luke staying with her through it. She knew though, this morning they would need to have a heart to heart. Though she was appreciative of his actions last night, some things needed to be said. Luke needed to understand where things stood when it came to her affections. They were friends and nothing more.

Oh, she hated hurting people. Especially one such as Luke. A rare, sweet man.

After showering and dressing in a simple pair of jeans and a green, cotton sweater, she made her way down the staircase. Rose thought it strange she smelled coffee. With it came an uneasy feeling she couldn't place.

The swinging door to the kitchen felt extra heavy, like she was not wanting to make the effort to actually enter the room. When she looked at the counter, she knew why. A freshly brewed pot of coffee sat hot with a single mug sitting next to it. A package from the bakery sat next to the coffee mug and a written note laid between the two.

Rose walked slowly over to where it sat and picking it up in her hands, she read…

Dear Rose,

I am glad to have met you and for being there when you needed someone last night. This week, you were there for me.

I saw a glimpse of what I hope to have with someone someday. And you made me feel welcome and at home. Something I am not accustomed to. I see your extreme love for your husband. Your cries to him last night would have assured anyone of the fact. Though I thought it better for me to leave before you woke, I hope you know I will never forget you. And I genuinely pray for your husband's safe return.

Your friend,

Luke

P.S- I decided to make you coffee and pick up a bag of assorted pastries from the bakery down the street. Your guests can make do with glazed donuts and blueberry scones for one morning. You, dear Rose, pour yourself a cup of coffee and go sit out on the front porch. It's a beautiful morning.

Rose's eyes burned with a new glaze of tears collecting. She hugged the note to her chest and felt not longing, but gratitude and an admiration for Luke. A man she knew for less than one week. But someone she would never forget.

Softly smiling, she poured herself that cup of coffee, dug out a glazed donut from the brown paper bag, and walked out to the front porch.

Luke was right, it was a beautiful day. One she didn't intend to waste.

CHAPTER 46

October in Minnesota is a photographer's dream. The leaves are in full color. Bright orange and fire-red maples, deep maroon oaks and amber colored poplars. Something about the new, cooler breeze created a scent in the air that made Rose want to spend most of her days outdoors.

She spent time raking the first fallen leaves from the lawn or sweeping loose, brown pine needles from the cobblestone path. Her squash and pumpkin blossoms had turned into beautiful round gourds now. She was incorporating them into recipes so often she was running out of ways to use them. Some, she decided, would do just fine being used as autumn decor around the inn.

Not surprisingly, the rooms were almost fully booked for the month. Tourists loved sightseeing at this time of year. It was a perfect time for couples looking for a romantic backdrop for a picnic. A nostalgic month for a family looking for adventure.

The color palette of leaves would make for an amazing canvas painting. In fact, it wasn't a surprise to Rose, when an artist traveling all the way from South Carolina, checked in.

Her name was Ada. A wonderfully, colorfully dressed, African-American woman. Rose knew she liked Ada from the moment they met. Ada hadn't even rung the doorbell on the front porch yet, but was floating through the yard in her long patchwork skirt, admiring which flora and fauna to turn into her next work of art.

That morning, Rose was walking out the front door to do her usual morning sweep. The pine needles had been relentlessly falling, covering the front path. It had become an everyday chore. She was startled by a stranger walking through the yard.

"Oh, hi there, can I help you, Ms.?" She asked Ada.

"Not yet, honey. I'm trying to find just the right place to set up my easel first," Ada replied.

"You're an artist? How fascinating," Rose said as she walked closer to where Ada was exploring the yard.

"I sure am. Been at it for umpteen years and still traveling the country to make my mark on every state if I can live that long."

Rose noticed there was a hint of gray in Ada's coarse black hair. But other than that, she looked strong and full of an intoxicating energy.

At the sheep's bleating welcome, Ada stopped in her tracks, "You have sheep here, honey? If my ears aren't playing tricks on me, I could've sworn I heard a greeting that could only have come from such an animal." Rose laughed as she accompanied Ada.

"Yes, indeed I do. I have a black Babydoll lamb named Ana and her sister, Elsa, who is white. They are my pets. Nothing more. Although, I have to be careful. I've taken to visiting with them each evening before I head inside for the night. We talk about our days, the good, the bad, and the mundane. But I'm afraid my guests are going to start thinking I'm a crazy lady," Rose teased.

"Not by me, I assure you. I ask babbling brooks and falling leaves for advice on how they want to be painted," Ada replied.

"Would you like to take a look at the back yard? If I was going to paint a picture, which I assure you would not be displayed at an art gallery, that's where I would choose to set up my easel," Rose said with a snicker and pointed the way to Ada.

The two strolled around the corner of the house to the backyard.

"I'm sorry, I should probably introduce myself. My name is Ada

Franklin. Are you the owner of this enchanting inn I'm staying in this week?"

Rose smiled and nodded her head. "Yes, I am. My name is Rose Mitchell. I'm glad you're staying with me this week, Ada. I sure hope that I will be able to see some of your artwork before you leave?"

Ada walked ahead of Rose and called back, "Well, let's see what we are working with back here then, shall we?"

When they reached the spacious backyard, it was as if God had sent a little golden sun ray through the clouds right at that perfect moment. It shined down on the Maples and Oaks and the auburn colors were almost glowing. The black iron table and chairs Rose had set up under the shade of the trees invited them to come take a seat. The orange pumpkins from Rose's garden peeked out from under the twisting and curling vines. The apple tree was full of sweet red fruit; a light dew still sparkled on the green grass. Today, the breeze was just a faint touch on the skin — nothing to upset an easel set up with papers or canvas.

"What do you think, Ada? Will this work ok?" Rose offered. She watched Ada dance around the yard in delight, studying each area. Finally, she sat down at the little table and announced to Rose, "Yes, my dear girl. This will do just fine. I'm going to sit a spell and drink it all in if that is ok?"

"Of course, Ada. I will be inside preparing a light breakfast. Please come in and ring the bell when you are ready to see your room."

Rose watched Ada admire the trees, the grass, and the big orange pumpkins that had come to be a chore to Rose as of late.

Some folks saw the beauty in every stitch of God's handiwork. Rose found herself anxious to see what her newfound artist friend would create.

CHAPTER 47

During her stay, Ada woke even before Rose and would take her paints, easel and canvas out to the backyard — sometimes, as the sun was still rising. Rose agreed, a sunrise did provide some beautiful hues of peaches and yellows that an artist could appreciate.

Wednesday morning, Ada's third day at the inn, Rose decided to bring breakfast out on a tray for the two of them. She hoped Ada wouldn't mind a break and some company for a bit.

"Good morning Ada," Rose greeted her.

Turning in surprise, Ada replied, "Well hello, honey. How are you this fine fall morning?"

"I'm doing great. I haven't wanted to disturb you these last few mornings because you seem so engrossed in your work, but I thought I'd take a chance today. You must be hungry?"

"How sweet of you. I think that would be wonderful. I'm stuck on ideas of how to capture this beauty in one perfect work of art, anyway. Let's sit a spell and have some brain food."

Looking a bit stiff, Ada stood up from her chair and hobbled over to the table and chairs under the maple tree. Rose set the tray down and handed a dainty cup and saucer to Ada. She poured them both coffee and Ada dropped two sugar cubes in hers and stirred.

"Well, this looks wonderful. What did you prepare?" Ada asked, admiring the dish in front of her.

"Oh, thank you. This here is a pumpkin bread with raisins and a little nutmeg and cinnamon for taste. I also fried some pork sausages which are in the covered casserole dish to keep warm. Please help yourself," Rose offered, handing Ada a cloth napkin.

"My goodness, child. I feel like I'm being spoiled. And I'm not afraid to say, I am starving." Ada announced as she reached for a slice of the pumpkin bread and buttered it. Rose smiled and took the cover off the dish of sausages, taking two with her tongs and putting them on her plate. The savory scent of browned pork seasoned with sage and ground pepper was intoxicating. Rose realized she was famished too.

The ladies were quiet for the first moment or two as they enjoyed their food and the ambiance of the beautiful fall day.

"So tell me dear, how long have you been running this inn?" Ada asked, admiring the house. "It is a treasure to have found and had the pleasure of staying in. I have to admit though, you seem quite young for taking on such a feat."

Rose finished the bite in her mouth and swallowed. She wiped her mouth with her napkin and setting it back in her lap, replied "Hmmmm, it is hard to even know quite what happened myself. It all came about so fast." Rose too stared at the inn with admiration.

"I guess all that I can say is, when I saw this house, I knew. I felt like I was home." Taking a sip of coffee, she sighed, "I've always dreamed of running a Bed and Breakfast and I love to cook and entertain. I just didn't know how or when I would find the place."

"Well, you sure have found it haven't you. It's picture perfect, my girl," Ada resonated, sipping her last swallow of coffee.

With that the two ladies stood up and began piling the empty plates and cups onto the tray.

"Thank you, again for a lovely meal, Rose. I best get back to work here though."

"Of course, Ada. It was nice visiting with you. Please let me know if you need anything else."

Ada nodded and picked up her paintbrush determined to get something on her snow white canvas.

The latter part of the week, Rose was so busy with guests checking in and checking out she hadn't had a chance to sit with Ada and visit again. She would bring her out a tray of breakfast or lunch or a simple lemonade, but that was the extent of their brief exchanges.

On Saturday morning, Ada requested that Rose come join her in the backyard when she had a few minutes to spare. Rose had her hands full of clean bath towels she was bringing up to a guest room but told Ada she could come join her in ten minutes.

"Of course, take your time. I just wanted a brief bit of your time before I check out." Ada slowly walked out the back door back to where her easel stood.

Rose delivered the towels to Mrs. Quill in room #3 and a carafe of coffee and two cups to Mr. and Mrs. Lowly in room #5. Sweat dampened her forehead, despite the cool breeze outside. She hurried down the stairs and out the back door to see what Ada needed. The day was getting busier by the minute.

As she walked closer, she noticed Ada's easel had been turned toward the inn and she sat behind it.

"Ada?"

"Hi there, honey. I have something for you. Come take a look." Ada requested.

Rose was unprepared for the painting Ada had created. She gasped, "Ada! I don't know what to say. Only that — this is a masterpiece. In MY heart anyway."

Ada had, at some point in her stay, decided to face her easel toward the inn and turn that view into a lovely painting. She had captured the tall two story house with its glowing yellows and whites. The giant oaks leaning over in protection of the house showed their dark cherry leaves. The small garden, with the spindly green vines surrounding several orange pumpkins peeking out, was a comforting touch. Ada even had painted the small iron table and chairs where they had shared breakfast a few days ago.

Rose could hardly think of something more wonderful and meaningful to her. Her dream had been captured on a canvas — the bright colors of the leaves complimenting the soft shades of paint on the inn, the faint details jumping out as much as the distinct focal points. Ada had even added a far off view of Elsa and Ana in their fenced area on the east side of the yard, grazing on the chartreuse grass.

"Ada, I really don't know what to say. It is breathtaking," Rose complimented and hugged her lovely new friend.

"Oh, child. It was a joy painting it. And simply a joy staying with you this week." Ada started folding up her easel. "I managed to paint a couple others, but this one I wanted you to have. Perhaps you can find a place for it in the inn."

"I know just the place. Thank you again, Ada."

After Ada checked out and left that day, Rose felt a little sad. She was a rare, lovely soul. Rose had felt a sort of bond with her. She chose to hang the painting on the empty wall space above the staircase where she would see it each and every morning when she walked down the steps.

It was a reminder to find the beauty in each day.

CHAPTER 48

October was closely coming to an end, which caused Rose to feel somber. Colorful leaves were beginning to fall to the ground. The plants in the front yard and in Rose's garden had become brown and brittle. Elsa and Ana spent more hours in the small shelter Chives had built for them, despite their natural wool coats. Rocking on her chair out on the front porch, Rose thought, "If only Octobers could last longer than the other months."

Despite the extra bite in the fall breeze, Rose decided she needed a few more mums for the front step and a couple seasonal flower arrangements to display in the dining room and guest rooms. After finishing the last bite of her buttered English muffin, Rose washed her few breakfast dishes and grabbed her purse.

The flower sisters would no doubt have exactly what she was looking for.

Daisy was out front watering the window boxes filled with Black Eyed Susans that looked as if they were ready for a winter nap soon.

Noticing Rose coming up the sidewalk, she waved and yelled, "Sweet pea! Where have you been? I swear I haven't seen you in weeks." Daisy set down her watering can and grabbed Rose in an embrace. "Let's not let that much time slip by again. I miss your pretty little face."

"Oh, I can't believe it's been that long, Daisy. It's been so busy at the inn, I can hardly keep up. Though, it has been a joy, just the same. I've met so many interesting and kind people," Rose replied.

"I am so happy about that, Rose. And the word in town is that your cooking is to die for. I tell you, Mudsie is getting a run for her money," Daisy laughed.

"Oh, no. Nothing beats Mudsie's award-winning recipes. She says she won't share them. But to be honest, I think it's because she doesn't have so-called recipes. I think she just throws everything together and has done it that way forever. She knows just the right amounts to toss into the pot to create the perfectly delicious dishes. I assure you, I am still an amateur chef," Rose confirmed.

"Well, either way. You are taking good care of your guests, it seems."

Daisy opened the glass door to Wild Flowers and motioned for Rose to follow.

"Are you just here to visit, sweet pea, or were you looking for some new plants?"

"Yes actually. Do you have any potted mums left? I'm also looking for a few seasonal arrangements for the guests rooms and dining room," Rose replied.

"Of course, come on in and we'll take a look," Daisy offered.

As usual, the shop was cluttered from floor to ceiling. *Was there a floor?* Rose thought. It was beautiful chaos, however. Completely unorganized, but the mixes of large wooden boxes filled with crimson colored mums and bouquets of black-eyed susans and cosmos wrapped tightly in crisp brown paper gave a warm, welcoming feeling to the shop, despite the mess.

Daisy scooted boxes to the either side of the room to make a path for Rose to walk through.

"Where is Violet today? Is she taking the day off?" Rose asked.

"Apparently," Daisy rolled her eyes. "She asked if I minded. To be frank, she has been leaving a bit too often for my liking. Though our busiest season is summer, we do still have several weddings and the occasional funeral we are decorating for. Violet knows this much. So, it's a bit of a mystery. Though you and I both have speculated."

Daisy started pulling out large potted mums. "Aren't these ones lovely,

Rose? Fire orange, for on your front porch! Just got these in. I think I want to carve a couple pumpkins and throw bright orange mums in them, the flowers coming out the top. Wouldn't that be adorable?" Daisy kept talking. Though Rose nodded, she wasn't fully listening.

"Yes, I like those. I'll take two that color." Rose pretended to browse around the shop. "So, no idea what Violet is doing with her time off, Daisy?" Rose questioned.

"Honestly, I am a little concerned that she is perhaps thinking of going back to work as a nurse. I have seen her walking in the direction of Cherish Medical and Chives said he saw her speaking with Sully outside the ambulance garage a few days ago," Daisy humphed. "Do you think she is wanting to give up on Wild Flowers, Rose?"

"Something tells me that isn't it, Daisy. Did you forget Sully's so-called feelings for Violet? Is it out of the question that they have been seeing each other?" Rose speculated.

"I can't imagine that Sully all of the sudden would break out of the shell he's been hiding under for years and just ask Violet out. I suppose it's possible. But, without any sign of promise, I can't see him crossing that line," Daisy decided out loud.

Had Sully taken Rose's advice and asked Violet out? Was that where she was off to? Rose prayed so. How happy she would be to see them as a couple.

CHAPTER 49

It wasn't long after that the mystery was revealed. Rose was having lunch at The Crystal Café with Father Eli, catching up on how things were going at the inn, when they spotted Sully holding the front door open for Violet as she entered. More than a gentlemanly gesture, it appeared they had come together. The pair hadn't noticed Rose and Father Eli and took a seat at a booth across the room. As small town folk often do, eyes glanced their way.

Mudsie brought over Rose's cup of cheesy potato and ham soup and Father Eli's plate of steaming stuffed peppers and sat down.

"Is it just me or did our boy Sully finally get sick of waiting," Mudsie whispered, speculating at the couple's entrance.

"Let's hope so, Mudsie. Wouldn't that be a blessing for the both of them?" Father Eli declared, attempting to douse the subject.

Seeing there was no gossip to be had, Mudsie stood up, grabbed two menus and walked over to wait on Sully and Violet. It appeared the two were enjoying each other's company, laughing one minute and deep in conversation the next. Though Rose was trying with all her might to keep herself from spying, her eyes kept darting in that direction.

"Are you a bit distracted today, Rose?" Father Eli finally asked.

Embarrassed, Rose apologized, "Oh, I'm sorry Father. I guess I am thinking of the many things that need doing back at the inn. I should probably get back there."

Finishing her last spoonful of soup and wiping her mouth with a napkin, she said, "Thank you for lunch. Stop by soon if you can, Father. I'd like to show you the painting I received from the artist that had stayed.

Remember Ada Franklin I was telling you about?"

"Oh, yes! I am anxious to see that. I will come by later this week. Maybe have a cup of coffee too, if you have any to spare?" Father Eli teased.

Rose smiled, threw on her tweed jacket and left the café. On her slow stroll home, she was sincerely hoping it wasn't obvious that she had been glancing at Sully and Violet while they were on a date. "How creepy would that be?" she laughed to herself.

Though she had intentionally used the excuse of her chores at the inn piling up as her distraction, it was a truth too. It just always seemed like something was needing to be done. Soon Flynn would be there with her. They could take care of everything and anything together.

Thinking of Flynn, as she often did, made Rose's heart ache for a moment. She was filled with joy for Sully and Violet's newfound connection, but it made her miss her husband all the more.

One would think you'd get a bit used to having your husband be away. And though the sting wasn't quite as fresh, the dull ache remained. Rose had learned, the best thing to do was to stay busy. And Rose did just that, starting with the many sets of sheets that needed washing, the bathrooms that needed scrubbing, and the rugs that needed shaking. After that, next on the list was writing the week's menus and making grocery lists for her shopping run tomorrow.

By seven o'clock, Rose was ready for a break. After taking a long, hot shower she threw her hair in a soft towel, put on warm cotton pajamas and went to the kitchen to find something to munch on. No guests were checking in for two days and sometimes she felt like treating the house as her own. Lounging around where she'd like, walking around with a bath towel wrapped around her head and listening to loud music if she pleased.

Rose cranked up the old radio. *Book of Love* by the Monotones serenaded the empty kitchen.

"Oh, I wonder, wonder who, who-oo-ooh, who, who wrote the book of love." Rose sang as she poured a glass of Merlot and took out a block of Sharp Cheddar to slice. Taking a sip of the dark purple liquid made her whole body warm as it went down her throat. Wondering what the *one person party* was all about, Mrs. Bigglesworth tiptoed into the kitchen and jumped up on a wooden chair nearby. The sweet tabby cat stared at Rose as she sang and rummaged in the cupboards for a box of crackers.

"Chapter one says you love her, you love her with all your heart, Chapter two you tell her you're never, nev–"

DING DONG! Rose's singing was interrupted by the doorbell. At least she thought she heard the doorbell. She turned the radio way down and listened for a minute.

DING DONG! It had been the doorbell she heard.

"Oh brother!" Rose yanked the towel off her head and with her finger tips tried to fluff her still damp hair a bit. Peering out the kitchen window she tried to see if she could spot who her visitor might be.

"Violet?" Rose questioned out loud, before opening the front door.

"Violet, hi. Come in. Don't mind my pajamas and damp hair. I was exhausted after a long day and decided to relax this evening. Would you like a glass of wine?" Rose offered, showing Violet in.

"Um, sure. I guess I could have one glass," Violet accepted, smiling. Rose noticed she was carrying a paper bag with her and wondered what it might be.

"Here take a seat, Violet," Rose offered, softly nudging Mrs. Bigglesworth off her perch.

"Sorry kitty cat! I didn't mean to steal your chair from you," Violet said to Rose's fuzzy pet. Pouring another glass of Merlot, Rose handed it to Violet. She placed some of the strong cheese she had sliced on a plate along with a few wheat crackers and blackberries. She offered some to Violet who took a piece of cheese and two blackberries and set them on her napkin.

237

"Oh, Rose. This is yours," Violet remembered, handing Rose the brown paper bag.

"It is? Did I leave something at the shop recently and forgot about it?" Rose questioned. But when she pulled out the empty, now clean, plate she had given Sully that had held the homemade tarts, she definitely remembered.

"Sully, told me you must've put some special ingredients in those tarts that made him brave enough to finally share his feelings with me. And I wanted to personally thank you for doing so." Violet winked, taking a long satisfying drink of her wine.

Rose laughed. "I'm sorry I meddled in affairs that weren't mine to mess with. But I am glad I did. And I hope you two are having a good time together."

Violet sighed, a long happy sigh, "We are."

Rose raised her glass to Violet's and clinked the two together, softly saying "Cheers to my magic tart recipe!"

The two friends shared the bottle of wine and lots of laughs in Rose's kitchen while Mrs. Bigglesworth sat in the corner enjoying a chunk of dusty cheese that had fallen from the counter.

Rose ran into Violet and Sully from time to time in town while she was running errands or when she would pop into Wild Flowers to say hello to Daisy and Violet. They looked like two love sick teenagers again. She envisioned how they had been years ago and she was happy she had meddled.

They were happy and it was well deserved.

CHAPTER 50

With the holidays nearing, Rose made the decision that she would like to host a Thanksgiving Day dinner for her closest friends of Cherish, and of course, any guests that may be staying, were welcome. She sent personal invitations to Father Eli, Mudsie, Chives (and Samson, of course), Violet and Daisy, Sully, Stella and her husband and children, Hank, Millie and their boys, if available. She also had an elderly man staying at the inn as well as a family of four. If all were able to attend, she would have a full house. And how wonderful and appropriate for the holidays.

As the days grew closer she set out pumpkins and gourds on the front step. Corn stalks stood up against the front sign post fastened tight with twine. Indian corn hung on a hook by her front door. The gleam of candles in glass lanterns graced the front porch and in trees in the yard. Rose loved the warm glow at night shining against large oaks and maple trees. It was a joy decorating for each season. She felt like a little kid, giddy, when adding the special touches.

Though excited to do so, the anxiety of hosting Thanksgiving Day was keeping Rose up at night. One week prior, she wrote out her menu in preparation. She would make the traditional roast turkey, mashed potatoes with gravy, stuffing, squash from her garden, cranberries and finger rolls. Stella had offered to bring an autumn salad of shaved Brussel sprouts and goat cheese. Mudsie was bringing freshly canned pickled beets to share and Millie from the general store, was bringing a few bottles of their homemade wine. Of course, the day wouldn't be complete without Rose's apple pie and a pumpkin one with homemade whipped cream.

She hoped that in between the meal and the day-ending dessert, the group might pass the time playing games, visiting, and perhaps even take an afternoon walk, if the Minnesota chill allowed. Her thoughts soon became plans, and then turned into the motions of the big day.

Rose stood next to her butcher block and massaged the turkey with slabs of butter and snipped sage, rosemary and generous amounts of salt and pepper to season. She pushed the roaster into the oven and set her timer for four hours. Mudsie was set to be at her house at 11:00 to assist with the last couple hours of preparation.

Rose's guests, the Miller family, were staying for a few days, but were going to a relative's house for Thanksgiving Day. Mr. Lunzke, however, had nowhere to go (as he voiced it). Rose insisted he come join her table for a hearty meal and a gathering of friends, right there at her inn. Without a better offer, Mr. Lunzke obliged. Rose did notice the beginnings of a smile on his face though as he turned to go back to his guest room.

"Oh, Mudsie, Thank you for coming early. You're a lifesaver," Rose said, showing her gratitude with a greasy, flour dusted hug.

"Oh, you silly girl. This is what I do best and I love it! Now, where do you need me?" Mudsie replied, ready to work. Rose pointed her toward the potatoes that needed mashing, while she went out to the dining room to finish place settings with her handcrafted name cards. Perhaps, people didn't notice all the small details she spent time on to make things special. But, still, it made Rose feel good. She had stayed up until midnight the night before cutting maple leaf shapes out of gold cardstock and delicately scrolling each guest's name on each. She even dusted each with a light layer of gold glitter. Chives would tease her and ask her why all the fuss, but her very first holiday celebration in the inn had to be extra special.

She looked around the room and smiled. She was so happy that all of her friends would be attending and perhaps, a newfound friend in Mr. Lunzke.

Dinner was to be served promptly at 1:00, so she waited. Each guest trickled in, starting with Father Eli who was always early. Chives and Samson came soon after, followed by the flower sisters, and the remaining guests. Everyone mingled and sipped on refreshments, while they waited for Rose's signal that dinner was being served.

Rose and Mudsie were sweating in the kitchen, finishing everything up. Mudsie sliced the turkey and piled it high on a white, oval platter, while Rose split steaming finger rolls apart, placing them in baskets covered with cloth napkins.

The potatoes sat in a serving bowl with a stick of butter melting away, the gravy was made, the cranberries prepared, the squash roasted and smelling earthy.

Rose downed a jelly jar of the wine Hank had made before she brought out the last of the dishes to the table. Her mom always told her a glass of wine kills the jitters and makes you a more enjoyable hostess. A *relaxed* and *pleasant* hostess. Rose felt a warm glow and decided she agreed with her mom. Thanksgiving without her and Dad? Or Flynn? Her emotions always seemed to be at odds with each other.

The day must move on. There were still many things to be thankful for and many were sitting at her dining room table.

Mudsie held the kitchen door open for Rose as she carried the turkey platter out to the table. All the guests had taken their seats and were anxiously waiting. Rose set the platter down in the center of the table and took her seat.

"Thank you all for allowing me to cook you a wonderful Thanksgiving dinner. I have had so much fun preparing it, with the help of Mudsie. Don't tell me if the turkey is dry," she teased. "But I think you'll find something that is edible. Now, shall we say grace? Father Eli, will you start?"

Everyone, including little Max, bowed their heads. After thanking God for the meal and for the time spent with friends, Father Eli said a special blessing for Rose's husband, Flynn and all of the soldiers in harm's way. That they may be safe and content knowing their families and their country were thinking and praying for them today." Rose nodded with a silent thank you to Father Eli.

"Ok, let me dish up slices of turkey. Mr. Lunzke (who was seated next to Rose), do you prefer white or dark meat?" Rose asked.

"Dark, thank you. With a spoonful of cranberries right on top," he said, searching the table for the cranberries.

"Here you are, cowboy. Here's the cranberries. My signature recipe. Hope you like em," Mudsie said, handing him the dish of burgundy, sweet smelling fruit. He smiled and thanked her. Rose watched the exchange between the two and smiled to herself, thinking *hmmmm, I wonder if Mudsie would ever let a man back into her life. Chances are, she would have no idea what to do with one anymore.*

The room was filled with laughter, conversation and the glorious sound of silverware clinking against china as the dinner was enjoyed. Rose received continual praise for the amazing meal she had cooked. Besides the obvious star of the show, the turkey, the other favorite dish seemed to be her roasted squash. Rose blushed accepting all the compliments but was secretly very proud of herself. While the children took naps, Stella offered to clear the table and wash dishes while everyone took a walk down to the park where the oak trees were still showing their beautiful fall colors.

Mudsie opted to stay and help Stella, as her back had been a bit stiff that morning. Mr. Lunzke, also, decided he wasn't much for long walks these days and sat out on the front porch for a breath of fresh, brisk air.

The cool Minnesota air was intoxicating. Rose walked with her friends down to Oak Bridge Park. It was only a mile down the way, and such a picturesque view. The temperatures were warmer than the typical late November twenty degrees, but hats and gloves were still needed. Rose rubbed her mittens together as she strolled down the path admiring the huge oaks.

"How are you liking the job of Innkeeper, Rose?" Millie asked as she tied her scarf a little snugger.

"Honestly Millie, I love every minute of it," Rose answered without a second thought. "I knew it would be a lot of work, but the joy I get from it far exceeds any and all labor involved. How about you and Hank? Have you always liked being owners of the general store?" Rose asked.

Millie took a second to respond. "When we first opened the store, we were so excited. A new town, a new dream, all our own. But, we have had some tough years. The picture perfect dream doesn't always pay the bills. But, the truth is, we accepted that and kept with it. Thirty years later, here we are and I guess I wouldn't want it any other way."

Rose smiled and the ladies continued walking down the path, auburn oak leaves crunching underfoot.

CHAPTER 51

December had provided several snowfalls so far and the shimmer of the white on the ground gave Rose a child-like admiration. It was her favorite time of year — magical somehow. She had hung a beautiful evergreen wreath on the inn's front door bound by a burgundy velvet bow. She had wrapped the front porch railing in the same evergreen and added a string of twinkling white lights. She had added a few festive touches inside as well — a few seasonal plants she had purchased from Wild Flowers and another string of white lights wrapped the stairway banister. She had found a beautiful tiny porcelain nativity set at the general store near the gift section and purchased it. She had set it proudly in the foyer for all to see. Other than that, the only thing left was the tree.

"Mudsie, did you and Mr. Lunzke have a *moment* on Thanksgiving Day?" Rose questioned Mudsie while they browsed the Christmas tree lot.

Mudsie, annoyed, responded quickly, "How do rumors fly about old farts like us? There is nothing exciting, nothing passionate, *nor* fairy tale about it. Yes, he enjoys a home-cooked meal. Yes, I offered to cook him one some time. This doesn't mean cupid is involved in any way, shape or form!"

Smiling, Rose realized she touched a nerve. Mudsie was indeed feeling something for Mr. Lunzke — Clark as she called him.

"Ok, it's no big deal. I was just curious," Rose responded, walking ahead of Mudsie, pretending to be taken with the balsam tree in front of her.

"Mmm hmm, of course you were, you little stink bug," Mudsie murmured.

The two continued weaving through what seemed like hundreds of trees. Rose wanted the perfect one. Mudsie's back was getting a bit sore and she was getting a chill.

"Sweetheart, these all look beautiful. Why don't you choose already?" Mudsie suggested.

"I'm sorry Mudsie. I'm so indecisive. I love the look of the long needle balsam fir, but the cute little ornaments I have don't stay hooked on as well. The scotch pine is nice, but I haven't seen any that are very big here. It has to be an impressive one to grace the inn's living room don't you think?" Rose added.

"How about this one?" Hank and Millie's son Russ offered from within the trees to her left.

"Ahh, I think it's you Russ, though all I see is a forest of pine here. Are you hiding?" Rose laughed.

"Hello." Russ peaked around the side of the large pine he was holding up straight for her to inspect.

"Oh, yes, you're right Russ. This one is a perfect gem. I love it! Good choice. Are you working the lot?" Rose asked.

"I am. Dad thought it'd be good for me and Rich. A little extra holiday money, ya know? I'll go ahead and trim the trunk for you and deliver it if you'd like, Rose? I have my truck here. Rich and I can bring it and set it up on our way home."

"Oh, that would be ideal Russ. I was wondering how I'd manage that tree into the house by myself." Rose smiled at her tree choice. Then not seeing Mudsie, she went in search.

"Mudsie? Did I lose you in the maze?"

"Over here, doll face! I needed to sit a spell."

Finally, after a few twists and turns Rose spotted Mudsie sitting atop a snow bank a plow truck had made around the tree lot. Rose laughed.

"Hey, if this gal needs a rest, she'll find a place to take a load off."

"Ha, ha. Fair enough. Let's get you up and go get you something warm to thaw your bones shall we?" Rose grabbed Mudsie's frail arm and hoisted her upright. They had festive plans for the evening.

Rose, Mudsie, Violet and Daisy gathered together at the inn to decorate Rose's Christmas tree. She had set the large Frasier fir in front of the window in the living room. Violet and Daisy strung three long strings of multi-colored lights on the tree, while Mudsie sat and attached metal hooks to ornaments as Rose hung them delicately on the tree branches. Rose thought back to the many years growing up and how her mom had made this night so special for her. Usually, she and Dad would go find the perfect tree, while Mom cleared the area in the living room and set up the tree stand. By the time they had returned with the tree, both cold and shivering, Mom would have a warm pot of chili or stew on the stove waiting to be sampled. After they trimmed the tree together, Dad would usually sit in his recliner after a big bowl of stew and nod off. He would say he was checking his eyelids for holes. She and mom would laugh, but they always ended the night reading about the Christmas story. Rose remembered a collection of Christmas books Mom would drag out every year, but the one about the very first Christmas, about baby Jesus, was always her favorite. Hanging the last ornament on the tree, Rose felt a rush of loneliness well up inside though she decided to let it pass. The evening had just begun and she wanted to enjoy it with her dear friends.

The ladies sipped on Chardonnay and Eggnog. Rose had set out hors d'oeuvres such as baked brie, with an orange cranberry sauce and crackers, shrimp cocktail, deviled eggs, cucumber sandwiches and her rich, homemade fudge. By far, Rose's favorite tree was a decorated, colorfully lit, Christmas tree. Whenever she told anyone that was her favorite tree, they told her that didn't count. Well, it counted for Rose. Since she was a toddler, she was in awe of a brightly lit Christmas tree when the sun went down and the snow sparkled outside in the moonlight. Her mom had an old record player and the family would sit and look at the tree while listening to Bing Crosby and The Carpenters sing the classics. She missed home, as much as she loved Cherish. At Christmas time, her childhood home came to mind. Throughout the night, the longing thoughts wouldn't let up.

"Sweet pea, are you ok this evening?" Daisy asked her.

"Oh, yes, I'm fine Daisy. Just kind of thinking about home, ya know. Doesn't the Christmas season do that to everyone?" Rose replied.

"It does. Our parents have been gone for years now. But you're right, this time of year brings the memories rushing back. Our dad was always busy working, but on Christmas Day, we got him for the whole day. He would go sledding with us. He would put together our toys Santa gifted us. He would eat popcorn while we all watched *Rudolph the Red Nosed Reindeer*. It was a rare treat for us.

Mom — she was always busy in the kitchen making her usual Christmas dinner — beef roast, mashed potatoes, green beans and always sweet rice pudding for dessert. Every year, it never changed. But if it had, I think we would have all been unhappy. That's what makes Christmas so nostalgic. The family traditions," Daisy said, reminiscing.

"It sounds wonderful, Daisy." Rose replied and went into the kitchen to refill a tray with cucumber sandwiches.

Why am I missing home all of the sudden? I am living my dream. It's just because it's Christmas time. I'll go see Mom and Dad soon. Rose kept trying to rationalize her feelings. Kept trying to minimize them.

By week's end, she could see nothing was helping. It was time to take a week off and go visit her parents in Duluth over Christmas.

She only hoped Father Eli would lend her his car.

CHAPTER 52

The week over Christmas, Rose had no guests scheduled. She had made up her mind that now was a perfect time to go see her parents. Father Eli graciously had agreed to lend her his car for the week as he had several Christmas services and would be sharing Christmas Day dinner with Hank, Millie and their boys. Hearing that Hank and Millie were hosting filled Rose with such joy. It wasn't that many months ago that Hank nearly lost his life. Though Rose had always felt somewhat responsible for allowing him to climb those ladders to the tip top of her house just to get the white trim perfect, Hank told her he'd do it again in a heartbeat. And knowing Hank, she'd see him up on a ladder again soon enough.

Chives had been invited as well as Mudsie, the flower sisters and most likely Sully too. She smiled thinking of the same group that had been at her house on Thanksgiving Day. A day she wouldn't soon forget.

For a second, she wondered how Mr. Lunzke would be spending the holiday. It crossed her mind to ask Mudsie about it but changed her mind remembering the last time she brought up his name to her. Rose smiled to herself as she continued to pack a suitcase for her time away.

Slowly coming down the stairway, she looked up at the picture Ada had painted of the inn. Seeing it lit only by a faint gleam from the Christmas tree lights made her feel a fleeting sting in her heart. She wondered why.

It was early Friday, December 23rd. She had wanted to get an early start and have time to help mom with any remaining preparations for Christmas. Last minute shopping, cookie baking, or just sharing a glass of wine and catching up. She didn't care. But, seeing her tree glimmer in the warmth of her new home, she set down her bag.

One more cup of coffee while I sit for a moment and enjoy the peace.

Stopping first at the record player, she set the pin and heard the crackling of an old favorite by Perry Como begin to play, and she listened to the lyrics fill the empty room...

"I'll be home for Christmas, You can plan on me."

"Please have snow and mistletoe, And presents by the tree."

"Christmas Eve will find me, Where the love light gleams."

"I'll be home for Christmas, If only in my dreams."

As she sat in the dark room with only the flicker of multi-colored Christmas lights shining, she looked at her large dining room table at the other end of the room. She saw herself holding up a wine glass proposing a toast, while Father Eli smiled at her in a proud parent way. Chives was sneaking a piece of turkey under the table to Samson, thinking no one noticed. Mudsie, out of habit, dishing up mashed potatoes and gravy for the hungry guests, but pretending not to notice Mr. Lunzke smiling at her. Her good friends Violet and Daisy held their wine glasses, clinking them together and saying "Cheers" after Rose's toast. Max was dropping food all over the floor (which Samson enjoyed) and little Betty slept through all the commotion in her little bassinet set up in the corner.

Rose smiled at the empty table and empty chairs as if they were still full of that energy and joy she and her friends shared. In the true meaning of that day, she realized she was immensely thankful for her friends, her *family* in Cherish. She was so anxious to see her parents and spend some quality time, but this was home. And she hoped, perhaps, Philip and Evie would come often to visit her. This could be a second home for them. They were welcome, always. And she hoped they would be proud of her.

Rose finished the last sip of coffee and stood up, taking one last scan of the room. Everything was taken care of. Violet and Sully would stop daily to care for Elsa and Ana and feed Mrs. Bigglesworth too. Rose told them where to find the hidden key.

She didn't know why she felt such an emptiness inside.

"If only in my dreams." Perry Como's voice cut out and the record was skipping, no more songs to be played. Rose turned off the player and shut the wooden lid.

Unplugging the Christmas lights, the room went completely black. She grabbed her bag and walked out to Father Eli's car.

Always looking out for Rose, Father had filled the gas tank, threw an ice scraper and blanket in the back seat and reminded Rose several times to mind the Minnesota winter elements. "Take it slow. There's no need to rush."

To Rose's surprise there was a small, wrapped gift sitting on the dashboard. The tag read, *Merry Christmas, Rose. This is meant to be an early gift to keep you safe in your travels. Please open it before you start your journey. Sending my blessings, Father Eli.* Rose, again, was stunned by her sudden feeling of sadness mixed with total gratitude.

Doing as the tag directed, she ripped off the green and red wrapping paper and removed the top of the box. Inside laid a silver chain necklace with a pendant showing the image and description of Saint Christopher, patron saint of travelers. The bond she had formed with Father Eli during her short time in Cherish was profound. Her gratitude for the things he had done for her thus far, unmatched. And now this? What a kind gesture and a gift she would always keep close by.

The chain was connected safely in the box by a few tightly fit plastic bands. She had wanted to stop at the café to say goodbye to Mudsie, so she would ask to borrow scissors while she was there to remove the necklace and wear it securely around her neck. She admired the pendant for another second and closed the box tight, laying it on top of her bag.

Again, the feeling of sadness burned in her chest when she entered the Crystal Café. She took a seat at one of her usual booths looking out to Main Street. Mudsie ran out of the kitchen after a few minutes carrying a small paper bag.

"My sweet girl, I know you want to get on the road, but I wanted you to take a little something to eat on the trip. I've packed a ham, egg and cheese sandwich on sourdough toast and a container of chopped cantaloupe. I have filled this Styrofoam cup with coffee to keep you alert. And my coffee will certainly do just that," Mudsie said with a wink. Rose concurred.

"Yes, yes — we can all agree a person could put a spoon in a cup of your coffee and it would stand up on its own!" Rose stood up from her seat and gave Mudsie a long, tight hug.

"Oh, Rose. Quit being so emotional. It's one week. And your parents certainly deserve to have you back for that long," Mudsie said, making light of the moment. Why was it then that she saw just the slightest glimpse of sadness in Mudsie's eyes as well.

"Ugh, you're right. This is silly. I will see you next Friday, Mudsie. Give the rest of the folks my love."

Rose waved goodbye.

She was on her way down a road heading north. It felt right and it felt wrong too. Either way, she was leaving and as she looked in her rearview mirror, Cherish was getting smaller and farther away.

CHAPTER 53

Rose wasn't hungry, but she did sip on her strong, fragrant coffee while she drove. She remembered turning left off the five mile road she had taken to Cherish, but she didn't recognize the field in which she had crashed and abandoned her car last spring. Perhaps, covered in snow, things looked unfamiliar.

No matter, she knew she was headed in the right direction. At least she thought she knew.

Thoughts of Flynn kept her company on the lonely drive. She thought of his positive outlook on everything in life. How he could make her feel better no matter what was going wrong in her life. She thought it exceptionally ironic. A man, who knew at any given time, could be shipped over to a third world country where he knew he'd have to sleep on a sidewalk in full gear in hundred degree weather and only occasionally have the opportunity to bathe. These discomforts became insignificant to the fact that he and his comrades didn't know if they would live to see the next day while protecting the local people of that country.

It seemed the world was spiraling out of control. Yes, every era had their issues, but was it just Rose, or had the news headlines of tragedy become the norm? Picturing Flynn, as he was living in Afghanistan, sickened Rose as it always did. She had taught herself to somehow change her train of thought and did just that.

She thought of her inn. Of the work she and her eager friends had done to make it a success. She had several guests with multiple praises for the experience she had provided them. The beautifully decorated and comfortable rooms, the delectable meals they had enjoyed, and of course the special touch she had of welcoming them as friends. To her, the goal was always just that.

Oh, how she longed to bring Flynn back with her. As happy as she was at the inn, she knew her heart would grow to burst with him there with her. Flynn would love joking with Chives, snapping a few beers and helping him fix cars at the station. He would enjoy the company of her diverse, but enjoyable friends. Flynn had a knack for finding the best in someone, just by taking the time to visit with them. Rose thought maybe some of that rubbed off on her in the little time they had been married.

She sighed. He was simply a lovely person. A lovely person, she loved and missed deeply.

Setting down her coffee, Rose noticed the gift Father Eli had given her sitting in the passenger seat. In her rush this morning, she had neglected to bring it into the café to have Mudsie clip the ties that were holding the chain in place.

"Oh Father Eli, I'm sorry. I adore the gift, but it will have to wait," Rose apologized to a Father Eli who was now many miles away.

Glancing a second too long at the closed box, she had no time to avoid the deer that had jumped directly in front of her vehicle that was going sixty miles per hour down the highway.

Rose screamed and cranked the steering wheel to the right.

"God, *please*, not again!" The words seemed to tumble out of her.

The car plummeted off the road moving fast down into the ditch, the billboard sign unavoidable.

The last thing Rose saw flash in her mind was a vision of her and Flynn rocking in the chairs on the front porch of her lovely inn. They were smiling and looked happier than ever before.

Then…blackness.

CHAPTER 54

The relentless tapping on her shoulder had become aggravating. Had she fallen asleep again in her garden and Mudsie was prodding her awake? This time, Rose just wanted to sleep.

"Mudsie, please. Let me be. I'm so tired. And you said I could take the day, right? Please, please, just let me sleep for now," Rose begged. *Why was it so important that she woke up? Can't a girl just nap when she very much needs the rest?*

Rose was becoming more and more irritated but found it impossible to actually wake up and order Mudsie, or whoever was disturbing her, away.

Her head hurt a bit and her body felt stiff. Her mouth was dry. She craved a sip of water. But she was so disoriented and dizzy that she became nauseous. It felt as if an eye mask, or a blind fold had been tied around her eyes and a disturbing sensation of wires tying her down to her bed. She had to be stuck in a nightmare. Something wasn't right. With all the stress and emotions during the holidays, she summed this up to another bad dream. It had to be.

Ugh, just wake up, Rose. For God sake! You are sleeping upstairs in your beautiful antique bed, with the soft, mended quilt, upon you. You are going to get dressed, go down the stairs and prepare coffee before leaving for your parents' house in Duluth.

Though…hadn't she already done that? She felt a panicking confusion. *What was going on?*

The nausea was making her stomach churn and her head started to pound. Rose kept telling herself to just wake up. This nightmare was not something she wanted to continue with. But try as she may, her mind and her eyes would not obey. If she tried to speak, she found she couldn't form the words. If she attempted to sit up, her body was so weak, she crumpled back down again. *Was she even trying to do these things at all? Please, just wake up, Rose.* This pleading conversation she was having with herself, which felt like several minutes, was suddenly interrupted.

The soft touch of a hand on her forehead soothed her a bit, calmed her and she heard the faintest sound of a whisper in her ear.

"Rosebud, can you hear me? I want you to try and tell me that you can. We've been waiting a long time to hear your beautiful voice. I'm home now. But I want to look into my wife's eyes and talk to her. Can you try hard to wake up Rosebud?"

She kept hearing this soft voice, a man's sweet voice. Flynn's voice.

From one nightmare to the next! Now, her dreams were torturing her into thinking her husband was the one trying to wake her. What was going on? She became dizzy and somehow reached her hand up to her head to rub her temples.

There was Flynn's voice again. This time he seemed to be talking to someone else. Then, more soft whispers and an aggravating beeping sound.

Nothing was making any sense to Rose and her head kept throbbing. She massaged her forehead with her left hand.

Clearing her throat, she attempted a word, "Flynn?"

Her throat burned as she said his name, her tongue bone dry, but something forced her to try again.

"Flynn? Are...you...here?" She pulled the cloth from her eyes and slowly opened them. The room was far too bright and everything looked fuzzy. She quickly closed her eyes again. Pain throbbed in her temples.

"Dim the lights, she's trying to open her eyes. Rosebud, it's me, your soldier. Do you remember me? I'm here holding your hand," she heard Flynn say. After a bit, she slowly opened her eyes again. She kept trying to focus on figures in the room, but the dizziness was overwhelming. Was that actually Flynn, here in the flesh? She had a hard time believing the vision in front of her that was starting to come into focus. And certainly, none of this made a bit of sense.

She saw Flynn sitting next to her bed, or a bed — someone's bed. She thought she recognized her mom and dad standing close by and there was a woman wearing blue scrubs on the other side of her bed pushing buttons on a machine that kept beeping loudly. A man in a white coat stood next to the lady in the blue scrubs. Was she in a hospital bed? And why? Suddenly the events started coming back to her…

She had been on her way to Duluth to visit her parents for Christmas. On the way, she remembered swerving to miss the deer that had suddenly appeared out of nowhere in front of her vehicle. The next bits were unclear, though she remembered losing control again, rushing fast down into the ditch and seeing a billboard sign directly in front of her. And nothing else after that.

Oh no! Father Eli's car was ruined, no doubt. And where was she, and how was Flynn here? She decided, in order to get any answers, she must force some words out. But her throat was so sore.

"Flynn? What is going on?" she softly asked.

Flynn put his hand on her forehead and leaned down to kiss her gently.

"Oh, there you are, Rosebud. We have been waiting so long to have you back," he answered. Though, it seemed like his voice almost cracked when he answered her. And why did he say they had been waiting so long?

"Flynn, did I crash into the billboard sign? Is Father Eli's car totaled? Why am I in a hospital bed?" Rose questioned.

Flynn looked at the doctor for a moment and then turning back to Rose, he gave her a short, but devastating answer, "Oh Rose, during the rainstorm you swerved off the road and crashed into an oak tree back on June 1st. You've been in a coma now for almost seven months."

CHAPTER 55

After Rose had been told that she had been in a coma, laying in a bed at Duluth Memorial Hospital for the last seven months, she concluded she was having another nightmare. This was a relentless punishment for something. Why was she going through this?

Initially, seeing her husband safe and sound made her emotionally overjoyed and she cried and squeezed his hand with the only affection she could muster up thus far. Being the Flynn she knew and loved, he smoothed her hair from her face and kissed her cheek and told her that everything was going to be just fine now that she had woken up.

But…woken up? They had waited so long? Hit a tree on June 1st? How could this be her reality?

She needed to get back to Cherish and show Flynn all that she had built there. The friends she made, the beautiful inn she called a home. He would be so anxious to dig in and help her now that he was back from Afghanistan.

Back? Safe and sound? In one piece? Her perfectly wonderful husband was home? Her throat was so dry and it hurt to talk, but she tried.

"Flynn? You're back? You're…" Rose swallowed and tried to continue, "You're ok?"

Flynn softly cupped his hands around his wife's cheeks and looked into her eyes, "Yes, Rosebud. I lived through months that I hope to never have to endure again. The worst of it was being away from you. But now I am here. And you, my love, are too. I am so happy!"

Rose too, was (beyond words) overjoyed. A day, she thought, may never come to pass. Lifting her hands slowly to Flynn, she weakly pulled him into her chest and hugged him with all the strength she had.

Oh, the things she had to share with him about Cherish. The people that had become a second family. She and Flynn could move together and run the inn as a couple. All the pieces were coming together.

Rose was excited to tell Flynn all about it.

"Flynn, please, can you get me a glass of water or something? My throat is so dry. And I have things to talk to you about."

After bringing her a cup of water, Flynn held it to Rose and helped her with the straw.

"There, how is that Rose? Feel better?"

"Mmm yes, so much better. Thank you, hon. Can you sit by me? I want to visit with you." Rose asked.

"Of course, Rosebud." Flynn replied, taking a seat on the edge of the bed next to her.

"I have to talk to you about our inn. I know it was a bold move, but in my heart, I knew you were pushing me to go forward with our dream. I felt you in each decision I made even with you thousands of miles away," Rose said. She was gaining a little more volume in her voice, than the faint whisper from earlier.

Flynn looked at the doctor again, and at Philip and Evie who looked more concerned than before.

"Can we have a few minutes of privacy, guys? I wanna catch up with my sweetheart. It's been a very long time since we had the chance to visit," Flynn asked everyone politely.

Evie came over to Rose's side and squeezed her shoulder, "Love you, honey. I'm so thankful you came back to us," Evie said as a tear fell on the hospital blanket covering her daughter. Philip blew a kiss to her from across the room and followed Evie out the room. The doctor and nurse followed her parents out. Flynn closed the door quietly and Rose noticed he stood for a moment at the closed door as if he needed to take a breath or try to find the words he needed to say next.

Flynn sat down on the hospital bed next to Rose. He took her small hand in his and looked closely into his wife' eyes.

"Rosebud. Oh, my beautiful wife. I am so happy to see you. And your voice is something I have prayed to hear for many months."

Rose smiled and held tight to his warm but rough hand. He didn't look the usual healthy, clean cut guy she was used to seeing. Living through war does that to a person she decided. Though, she hoped he was still her same Flynn, after all was said and done. And she was excited. Such anticipation to speak with him about the inn — their new home, bubbled up inside of her.

"Oh, Flynn. Did you hear what I said? I have gone ahead and made our dream a reality. I know you will love the inn. And what's better, the people of Cherish are the salt of the earth, my friends. They helped me. Oh, when you meet Father Eli and Mudsie and Chi—"

"Rose, baby. Listen, you have been in a coma for seven months. You have been since you decided to take a drive on June 1st. You left your parents' house, drove fifty miles south and with the hard rainfall, swerved to miss an oncoming vehicle. Losing control, your car plummeted into the ditch and crashed into a very large oak tree. The front of your car was crunched like an aluminum can. Your airbags went off but you still hit your head hard, broke ribs and had several lacerations and bruises. In truth, we are very lucky to have you still here with us."

Looking away for a moment, Flynn swallowed hard. Rose wasn't completely coherent, but he seemed to need that extra ten seconds to find the next words.

"But…the truth is, though it be harsh, since that moment you have laid in this bed and haven't woken for a moment. Not one moment, Rose." Flynn told her with sincere sympathy in his eyes. "I'm sorry sweetheart. I know this must be confusing and scary and it's hard to hear. But it's the absolute truth."

Rose stared back at him for several moments, finally responding, "Listen, Flynn. I know in my heart and soul that Cherish is a place. A lovely, small, but *exceptional* town. A town I was led to. I can't accept that my friends were figments of my imagination. Or that my lovely, yellow with white trim inn, is an… *illusion*! My pets? My gardens? My recipes, My guests? Flynn, please, please. You have to believe me!" She began gasping for air as tears streamed from her stinging eyes.

With the last sentence Rose's head started to pound like a giant mallet on a bass drum. Then, becoming extremely faint she laid her head back on the pillow. Contradicting symptoms took over and she was finding it hard to concentrate or breath normally.

Flynn pushed a button next to her bed and a doctor and two nurses now entered her room.

"What happened Mr. Mitchell?" The doctor asked while the nurses looked closely at the beeping machine again.

"She is having some difficulty accepting what has happened. She is telling me about a town she visited and friends she's made. Is this a defense mechanism? Or simply an ongoing dream she has had throughout these several months?" Flynn asked the doctor. He was attempting a hushed tone, but Rose could still hear him. Her ears seemed to be working quite well now.

"We will schedule another CAT scan tomorrow, to eliminate any signs of bleeding. But I also recommend, now that Rose is awake, we start having a psychologist come for short visits. Try to reach her in a way maybe none of us can," the doctor suggested.

Flynn looked beaten down again. He had looked so relieved and happy earlier. Somehow, his face was filled with utter concern again.

Rose hoped that, perhaps, if she fell back asleep, she would wake up from this strange, cruel reality. Nothing felt right here.

She was scared and desperately wanted to be back sipping coffee on her front porch.

CHAPTER 56

Rose was busy twisting pastry dough into little heaps that resembled a woman's braid formed into a bun. She had loved making cardamom rolls with her mom growing up and figured it would be a fun tradition to do during the holidays at the inn. The smell of yeast and citrusy cardamom filled the kitchen. She could also smell the faint scent of the smoldering logs in the fireplace as they warmed the inn, and her favorite scents of the balsam fir Christmas tree gracing her living room.

As she finished brushing the last roll with butter, she heard a knock at the door.

Wiping her hands on her apron she walked to the front door and opened it with a welcoming smile. A confused frown replaced it seconds later. Rose didn't understand the scene in front of her.

Mudsie and Father Eli were standing in front of her with a doctor and nurse who looked familiar somehow.

"Hi Mudsie, Father. What's going on? Can I invite you and your friends in for a cup of coffee?" Rose stuttered.

"I'm sorry, Rose. But they say you need to leave here. The inn, Cherish, us. They say you need to go home now," Mudsie instructed in a tone Rose had never heard her speak in. Rose looked at the doctor, the nurse and Father Eli as she silently waited for an explanation.

"It's true, Rose. It's time to leave now," Father Eli didn't have that kind look in his eyes. Rose's heart was beginning to beat out of her chest.

"What's going on? I am home. Why would I need to leave? Someone give me some answers!" Rose demanded then.

The doctor and nurse stepped in front of her dear friends and made a motion to grab Rose's arms. Rose reached for her door yelling, "Leave me alone. This is my home. You can't just rip someone's life apart!"

She was crying as Mudsie and Father Eli turned and walked down her front steps and disappeared into thin air.

Rose fell to the freshly painted floorboards of her porch and held on to anything she could find. She found a metal bar attached to the floor and held on tight, screaming for the doctor and nurse to leave her alone.

"Please, please go away! You can't just take me from my home! Please stop, please…"

Rose woke in her hospital bed holding onto the side bar tightly and was still whimpering when she heard Flynn's voice.

"Honey, please calm down. It's ok. It's just a dream. You're safe here. I'm here holding your hand. Don't worry anymore," Flynn attempted to soothe her. "Rose, it's ok."

Calming herself some, she laid her head back on the pillow, scanning the room. Now, remembering fully where she was and why, she whispered…

"No. No, it's not ok."

Interrupting the new silence, the door to her hospital room opened and a server brought in a tray of food for her. Flynn took the tray, the bottle of water, and thanked the server.

"Here we are, Rosebud. You're wasting away to nothing. This looks like a tasty dinner that I think you'll like. I call dibs on your brownie though," Flynn teased, trying, as usual, to lighten the mood.

Rose sat up as best she could, as Flynn pulled the table close to her lap and set the tray of food on it. It certainly smelled good and looked appetizing too.

"What is this Flynn?" she asked. "Only Minnesota's most famous tater tot hotdish," he replied.

She smiled, thinking of when Mudsie had served the same hotdish to her and Father Eli during one of their project planning meetings at the café. Flynn looked pleased when she reached for her fork and took a heaping bite. The taste was bland and the meat chewy. She tried a couple more bites before setting down her fork. "It's not bad really. But it certainly isn't like Mudsie's. She had a special recipe with a homemade gravy that had fresh herbs and vegetables swirling in the mix." Rose looked at the floor, picturing herself sitting in a booth at Crystal Café.

"Oh, I can smell it now. And see Mudsie's tired, soft hands delivering a plate full to Father Eli and myself."

Her melancholy smile faded.

Realizing Flynn was giving her a look of concern again, she stopped speaking. Flynn spoke after a minute.

"Rose, we've had tests done. You're healthy. Physically, your doctor says you have healed entirely. The psychologist claims you are recovering wonderfully and that you seem to be mentally moving forward. Why the fabrication of this town, these friends, an inn you call *home*?" Flynn stood up and paced the room.

Since she had woken up from her coma, she had been kept in the hospital a month for recovery and to be closely monitored. Like Flynn, she wanted to leave this bright, cold room. Of course, she wanted to escape the constant disturbance of beeping noises, doors opening and closing at all hours, strange smells, uncomfortable beds and medical staff poking and prodding her. But, in order to do that, she apparently had to admit or *accept* that this life in Cherish was all a dream. A wonderful, though not real, fantasy.

She knew in her heart, she would *never* be able to do it.

"Flynn, can you take my tray away? I'm not hungry. And I just want to be left alone right now. I'm sorry," Rose asked. She laid back down and turned on her side facing away from Flynn.

He took her tray and kissed the top of her head, but he didn't say a word as he closed the door behind him.

FLYNN

Rosebud,

I am writing to you because it got me through the very hardest times in Afghanistan. This isn't a letter I will give you, but still, it comforts me when right now I don't know what to say to you.

When I heard of your accident I wasn't able to come home right away. You can't imagine the devastation I felt knowing how seriously injured you had been and I couldn't be there! I know it sounds absolutely ridiculous saying this, but during those months of war, this was the hardest thing, by far, that I had to endure. Your mom and dad sent word almost daily, though I wasn't always able to check my emails every day. It was terrible and took years off my life, I swear.

Rose, you are my life. You kept me sane when I was over there. Finally, when I was allowed to fly home to you, it was late September and you were showing no signs of coming out of your coma. Along with your parents we sat with you almost around the clock. We read to you, your dad played his guitar and sang for you, your mom talked to you about her book club and new recipes she wanted you to try.

It was almost harder seeing you live and breathe in the hospital bed when you weren't really "living". Does that make sense?

My sheer surprise and happiness when you woke up gave me a joy that surpassed even our wedding day.

But it seems you still aren't "well" and I don't know how

to help you. It tears me apart to see you so unhappy, Rosebud. All I've ever wanted to do is make you happy.

How do I do that and still help you accept this reality? It breaks my heart to see you this way, Rose.

But Cherish isn't a real place and there is no inn.

Please know, I am here to help you through all of this, whatever you need. I am here.

Love always,

Flynn

CHAPTER 57

For the next two weeks, Rose slept around the clock. She didn't feel like taking walks, she didn't care much for conversation. She would force down glasses of water and meager amounts of food, amounts an average woman would call a light snack. She couldn't stomach it. As dramatic as it sounded, the heartache seemed to spread to her stomach, bringing back a fresh nausea almost daily. Her headaches were so relentless, her doctor had no choice but to prescribe heavy sleeping pills, just for relief.

Flynn and her parents were, of course, beside themselves. They had waited months for her to wake up and after such relief and the sheer joy of seeing Rose open her eyes and speak to them, this was a frightening road no one was prepared to travel.

Sometimes Rose tried to converse with them, but it felt so rehearsed, so damn fake! How can you not share what is in your heart with the people that mean the most to you, without feeling like a looney tune? Without them looking at you as one? So…

She didn't try.

And after the initial high, things began to go downhill, and neither Flynn, nor anyone else knew how to stop it.

CHAPTER 58

Evie sat next to Rose reading her a newspaper story about the new Canal Park Diner that Maurice and Flora had rebuilt after the fire. The photos included in the article showed they had kept the old-fashioned diner vibe alive.

Rose noticed the counter with short, spinning stools sitting in front. The silver milkshake machines sat next to the clear pie cabinet filled with giant caramel rolls, beautiful apple pies, coconut cream pies and old fashioned cake donuts. Coffee mugs sat on shelves above, and the specials were written in chalk on a board just overhead.

A photo of Maurice and Flora standing in front of the newly built diner, was also featured in the article. It brought Rose a rare joy seeing them so happy.

"Have you and Dad been there yet, Mom?" She asked Evie.

"We have. It's a brand new, clean restaurant, smelling still of paint and plastic booth seats. But boy — the same yummy, greasy food is still served hot every day. Dad and I have only been there twice since they reopened. We found it kind of hard going there with you laying in a hospital bed, rather than running plates of eggs and bacon out to people at the diner," Evie told her. "But now we have you back, Rosalie Jane. And I have never felt such an answer to my prayers in all my life."

The two hugged. Evie cried, while Rose became stiff again — closed off, as had become regular practice.

When the doctor came in for his usual check-in, Evie excused herself from the room, giving her daughter a faint smile.

"So, Rose, how are you feeling today? Any headaches, stiffness in your neck, dizziness?" he asked while checking her vitals.

"No, I feel great, Dr. Evans. Is there any estimation on a date I will be released?" Rose asked.

"Soon I think, Rose. Physically there's no reason for you to be kept here. Your broken ankle has been healed for a long time and your cracked ribs as well. All tests show your brain function is near perfect for any woman of your age..."

Rose interrupted, "But?"

Dr. Evans stopped looking at her chart and sat down next to her. "Listen Rose, I think we will give it a little more time. I want you to be sure you are fully aware of what your true reality is. Head trauma can cause many hallucinations and having been in a coma for several months can confuse a person into thinking they have lived another life. Please know, I am not trying to be insensitive, but we need you to try and accept what has happened. That this is your true reality and your time in this town called Cherish was all a dream. I'm sorry, Rose. I understand it must be very hard. Take things a day at a time."

He squeezed her hand and left the room, leaving Rose to her thoughts. She wasn't ready to let go. Did she have to?

Things still didn't make sense. Not knowing anywhere else to turn, she bowed her head and prayed to God. Rose always prayed in a way she imagined she would visit with a friend. Maybe that wasn't the proper way. She didn't care. She felt the closest to God speaking to him from the heart.

Well, she was going to speak from the heart this time, but he may not like it.

"God, why can't this be real? Why does this have to be taken from me? What am I to take away from this? What am I to learn? I am TRYING to understand where you are coming from. Why you are putting this new challenge upon me. But none of it makes sense!" She slammed her fists on the bed and began to cry. It was a cry that made her chest ache and her body heave. After several minutes, she closed her eyes again and whispered.

"I guess...that's the point in trusting in You. I gotta say, it sure isn't always easy."

Rose felt some relief in lashing out at God. And surprisingly she felt He was ok with it.

At that exact moment she saw Father Eli's face and remembered what he told her...*Rose, sometimes God leads you down unknown paths. They may be scary or unsettling for a bit. The trick is to trust in his plan. In the end, if you always ask him for the guidance you need, everything will turn out perfectly.*

CHAPTER 59

Rose woke to a dark, eerie hospital room. The digital clock showed it was 2:00 a.m. She wasn't really sure why she had woken and laid back on her pillow staring up at the black ceiling. Finding it impossible to fall back asleep for several minutes she decided to go to the restroom and fill her water cup. She was wide awake and yet felt in a daze.

The cold water trickled into her cup slowly and she imagined her watering can raining water on her peonies and roses at the inn. Watering her vegetable garden, nurturing each plant as it grew, eventually providing fruit and vegetables to use in her favorite recipes.

She reminisced with a smile the day she had brought little Max and angelic Betty for a walk to her garden. How she and Max had talked about plants and what they needed to live and grow. She laughed to herself thinking of how he called her "Woze".

But after a minute of staring at her overflowing cup of water, her smile faded into a frown. Rose looked up and saw her reflection in the mirror. She hardly recognized herself.

She had become so thin, dark circles were visible under her eyes, skin a pale gray. Her hair — stringy, her lips — dry and cracked. Her hip bones stuck out a bit and the tie of her pajama pants were tied tight around her waist to keep them from falling. Flynn was right in pushing the tater tot hotdish and ice cream on her. But nothing sounded appetizing.

What troubled her the most about her reflection in the mirror was the sadness in her eyes that could no longer be hidden.

Rose took her water cup and opened the restroom door, switching the light off as she walked out.

"Ouch!" a man yelled as she ran face first into him, spilling her water down his shirt.

"Ooh, who are you? Get out! Don't hurt me." Rose exclaimed.

"Oh, Rosebud. Why are you always spilling beverages on me?"

It was Flynn. Rose then stupidly realized a mass murderer wouldn't sneak into a hospital with plans to locate her room and kill her. *Why did everyone's imaginations turn into horror movies when it was dark and the middle of the night?*

But she still hugged Flynn tight in complete relief.

Then, stepping back she looked up at Flynn.

"You scared the hell out of me," she said, giving Flynn a joking slap on his shoulder.

"Why on earth are you here at this hour, Flynn? I told you to go and get some rest. That hard bench couch is nowhere to get some solid sleep."

Flynn softly grabbed Rose's thin face with his rough hands, a glimmer of tears in his eyes.

"Rose. I know. You did and you're right, my back is still sore from that couch. But this is important. What I have to say couldn't wait. Rosebud listen, I want you to tell me about *Simpler Times.*"

Rose dropped her cup and the remaining water splashed on her bare feet.

"What did you say, Flynn? How did you hear? How do you know? I never told you the..." Rose attempted saying.

Flynn started speaking to protect his wife from hyperventilating. "Rose, come sit down." He helped her to her bed and turned on a dim lamp nearby.

"Rose, do you know what *Simpler Times* is?" Flynn asked her.

Her throat had become dry and she reached for her now empty water cup. Flynn grabbed it and walked to the restroom. She sat and stared at her hands in her lap, wondering if she was perhaps dreaming again. Flynn returned, handing her a fresh cup of water. Taking it, she took a sip and set it down on her side table.

Rose smoothed her thin blanket down over her legs and looked at her husband, replying, "That's the name of our inn, Flynn. I had it painted in black Victorian letters on the white wooden sign out front. But I know — I am *positive*...I never mentioned that detail to you or anyone else. Hardly any details were shared. How can you know?"

Flynn looked into Rose's eyes and spoke softly, "Rose. I saw it. A clear picture, as if I had been there in person. It was a two-story yellow house, with white trim and a front porch also painted white. On it sat two rocking chairs near the front door and on the corner of the porch was a bench swing. There was a cobblestone path leading up through beautiful flower bushes. And a sign, crystal clear with the name *Simpler Times* hand painted on it. You painted it didn't you?"

Rose pulled Flynn tightly into an embrace and cried. She closed her eyes and knew who had sent her husband the message.

CHAPTER 60

From that day on, Flynn and Rose had made a pact to keep Cherish and Simpler Times a secret between the two of them. Rose was gaining weight and a healthy pink color returned to her cheeks. She took walks through the hospital hallways and had coffee breaks in the cafeteria with Philip and Evie. Only late in the evenings when very few people were around, did she and Flynn talk about her times in Cherish.

Rose had started by telling Flynn about her drive. The night she had all she could take of war on the news and that her worry for him was making her crazy. She told him about the miles she drove and the downpour that was relentless.

She told Flynn about how after her accident, she had started walking and found a road sign leading to a town named Cherish. She remembered how her feet were so sore and her mind concerned about where she might end up. She told Flynn she walked into an old-time gas station and met Chives, the owner, a grease-stained shirt wearing handyman that would help anyone out. Rose recalled being hot and thirsty and buying a ten cent glass bottle of Coke from him. She couldn't mention Chives without mentioning his side-kick, Samson. Oh, trusty, gentle old Samson. He fit the true cliché of — *a dog is a man's best friend.*

She told him how she had stayed at Wild Flowers with the *flower sisters*, Violet and Daisy. How their flower shop was a mess, but a beautiful one, full of color and whimsy. She laughed about the afternoon the two sisters brought Rose lunch and how Daisy stepped on a rotten floorboard and sprained her ankle. Flynn didn't see the humor quite like Rose did. But telling of memories sometimes didn't hold the same emotions as the friends had shared together in the real moment. She even confessed that she had played cupid and had caused two friends, Violet and Sully, to reveal their true feelings for one another.

She told him about Stella and her family. About little Max and Betty and the day she had them all to herself. She confessed that talking one on one with Max about her garden and snuggling little, sweet Betty made her excited to start a family someday. Flynn smiled and had said he was ready when she was.

She told him about Hank, Millie and their boys. The general store they owned and how they had graciously helped her paint and work on the inn with her and her new found friends.

She shared stories about her guests like Mr. and Mrs. Nelson, a.k.a. the perfect guests. Also, about Mr. Lunzke and how at the Thanksgiving table she had witnessed a potential spark between him and Mudsie. Rose wondered to herself what became of the two lonesome elders.

Rose was anxious to tell Flynn of the experience she had had with her guest Mr. Hawthorne. How from the minute he had checked in, Rose could tell he had built a hard shell to keep all emotions at bay. She told Flynn how she had found out only a bit of what he had experienced during World War II from his wife. Rose had made it her goal to find a way, if only a tiny fraction, to break his shell and let him know she had been affected by war, but in the way his family had. How he needed to let them in. Flynn had nodded his head as if knowing the pain Mr. Hawthorne had endured during the war. He held Rose's hands in his and smiled with a pride she knew he possessed for her. He always told her that her heart was worth more than pure gold.

A brief mention of a carpenter named Luke that had been her guest for a short time, was all she shared. It wasn't something that she wanted to dig into and her conscience told her that that was ok. She had been faithful and felt love for only Flynn, always. Though, a little tiny ache still tugged a bit at her heart at the mention of Luke's name.

Rose expressed her admiration and love for a special guest, Ada Franklin. She told him of the breakfast they shared under the shade of the orange Sugar Maple in the backyard. She told him of the priceless gift Ada had given her, a painting of the inn. A work of art that had captured the essence of *Simpler Times.*

She even shared with Flynn details about the pets she had adopted. Her sweet girls, Elsa and Ana, whom she asked advice from and took to having long visits with before bedtime. She also told him about Mrs. Bigglesworth — her catty attitude as well as her morning snuggles. It almost surprised Rose when her eyes moistened at the thought of her tabby cat. She hadn't realized that she missed her so.

Rose spoke of Mudsie and Father Eli but remembering the two of them always brought fresh tears.

Flynn could tell that Mudsie and Father Eli were special to Rose and he always asked more questions, genuinely interested in how they had touched his wife's life. Rose told him that Mudsie had cooked some of the best meals she had ever tasted. Fluffy, cheesy omelets, tater tot hotdish, cabbage and ham soup, and homemade cranberry sauce on Thanksgiving Day. She described Mudsie to a tee. That she was an older gal, short, round and brassy. But that all who knew her would tell you she possessed a true heart of gold and had never stopped trying to make her customers, each and every one of them, feel welcome. They talked about Mudsie opening up about her own soldier, George, who she had lost in World War II. And how Rose was so grateful for their bond and friendship.

Rose spoke of Father Eli. He being the hardest for Rose to discuss without falling into tears. From day one, he had taken her under his wing and watched over her. It was he who walked up the path to find her in full admiration of the big yellow house that would become her inn. He had led her safely that first night to Daisy and Violet's shop for a safe place to stay. He had helped her find her dreams, had nurtured her gumption, and had even helped her find the strength to continue when she was falling apart at the seams. He had been like a father, of sorts, to her. The irony of the higher power he served, wasn't lost on Rose. In fact, it made perfect sense to her. He was special. She'd never fully let him go, nor forget his kindness.

After the days turned into weeks and telling her stories to Flynn felt like natural reminiscing, it was clear Rose was moving forward.

Oh, she had nights sometimes she would wake with tears in her eyes after dreaming of preparing meals in the inn's kitchen. or meeting new guests at the check-in counter Chives had worked so hard to build for her. She remembered he had even etched a small rose in the center of the surface. He had told her it was for her, the founder of *Simpler Times*.

She would smile at random moments thinking of the laughs she and the flower sisters had shared.

She would become quiet and thoughtful when a priest or pastor would pass her in the hospital hallway and smile at her. Father Eli? she would wonder…though she knew the truth.

And somehow, she had come to accept things as they were. Although Rose refused to forget, she was ready to move on.

Doctor Evans did a thorough exam and spoke in private with Rose.

"Rose, physically you appear to be back to your normal, healthy twenty-one year old self. It also seems mentally, too, you have recovered. Tell me, is there anything else that troubles you about being back in the real world? Any concerns you may have?" Doctor Evan, genuinely asked, leaning toward Rose a bit.

Rose wasn't afraid to leave the protection of these walls nor the care of the staff. Though they had gone above and beyond to bring her back to life, she knew they could do no more for her.

Rose replied honestly, "I'm ready and excited to leave, doctor, but please know how grateful I am for your care. I owe you my life. Truly."

The day after their meeting, Dr. Evans told her family that Rose was the picture of health and that it was high time she was released.

Philip and Evie had been there at her side when she was given the green light to leave. They cried and embraced their daughter.

"Oh, angel cake, we prayed this day would come. Now that it's here, I don't know what to say. All that I know is, I'm so grateful you are ok." Philip hugged his daughter like never before and then let his wife have her for a moment.

Evie had always been so protective and a touch possessive of her daughter. She was her best friend and her only sweet child. She had a hard time letting go. But something in her wanted to see her little girl spread her wings and live the life she imagined to the fullest.

"Ohhh my Rosalie. You make me so proud. I am soooo excited to see what you and Flynn make of this life. And I can't wait to stay in the inn I know you will own someday. I can picture it now. A front porch for you and me to sit and visit, sip lemonade and smell the steaks the guys will be grilling nearby." Evie brought her hands to Rose's cheeks and lightly held her daughter's angelic face close to hers. "I love you, honey. We will talk soon."

"Love you too Mom, Dad." Rose felt so blessed when looking at these two she called Mom and Dad.

After a few moments she turned to her husband. The person she would follow through good times and bad, for better or worse. It's funny how they had said the very words in their vows not so long ago. But already as newlyweds, they had endured so much together. Somehow the strains on their fresh marriage hadn't diminished but strengthened it. Rose's heart felt like it would overflow knowing she was walking out these hospital doors holding the hand of the man she loved. In her mind, she thanked God for blessing her so.

After the doctor had left the room and her parents said their goodbyes, the room was quiet. With their lives ahead of them, Flynn and Rose smiled at each other as they grabbed her packed bags and walked out the front doors of the hospital.

Flynn opened the car door for Rose and set her bags in the back seat. They both got into the vehicle but sat in silence. Flynn didn't start the car or turn on the radio. The moment felt surreal. Only moments had gone by, Rose figured, but it felt like hours as she and her husband, just the two of them, stared out at the open world in front of them. Flynn finally broke their hypnosis.

"Oh, Rose, I forgot. Here is your purse. They took it from your car before towing it to the salvage yard," Flynn mentioned, handing her the brown leather handbag from the backseat.

"Oh wow, it looks great. I guess one thing riding in the car didn't feel the effects of the accident," she laughed in spite of the seriousness of such an ordeal.

She rummaged through the purse. "Oh, right, still no cell phone. Can you believe I had forgotten my phone that day, Flynn?"

She stared out the window and remarked softly, "though I'm not sorry I did. No matter what truly happened that day, I am thankful for what it brought me. Maybe it was a dream. Who knows, maybe I time traveled? Cherish certainly was trapped in the 1950s. Or perhaps it was a wonderful gift God hand delivered. Whatever the case may be Flynn, I'm glad it happened."

As Rose continued to rummage through her purse, she gasped, dropping it on her lap. She began to cry. She let the tears stream down her face freely. Flynn became alarmed until he could see her holding something to her heart.

"My gosh, Rose--what is it?" he asked.

Rose opened her hand and held out a silver chain with a pendant showing the description and image of St. Christopher, the patron saint of travelers. Without any further explanation Rose kissed Flynn and with a fresh energy exclaimed, "Let's go and find our dreams, Flynn."

He turned the key in the ignition and they drove away, together.

EPILOGUE

Rose wiped her hands on her apron and filled a glass with water. She carried it out the front door, down the three wooden steps to Flynn who was putting up a white picket fence around their yard. The sun had been beating down on him all morning while he relentlessly worked. He was dripping with sweat. Rose took off her apron and wiped his forehead with it, then handed him the glass of water.

"Oh, thanks Rosebud. I am melting in this July heat," he confessed. Flynn drained the glass and set it aside, then putting his hands to Rose's growing belly, spoke sweetly.

"How are you feeling today? The little ones doing ok in there?"

Rose smiled. She and Flynn had found out they were pregnant a month after leaving the hospital and learned they were having twins only a week ago. Both were elated with the news. They had also been in full agreement to wait until the day the babies were born to see what sex they would be. It felt natural and old-fashioned. A true blessing either way.

"Flynn, how about taking a break and walking down to the café for a bite? I'm hungry. These babies are hungry," Rose said, rubbing her belly.

Flynn laughed and conceded. "Let me run inside to wash my hands."

He ran up the steps and into the house while Rose admired his work on the fence that, when finished, would border her rose and peony garden out front. She ran her hand over the light pink, tissue paper soft petals and thought of her time in Cherish.

A bee landed on the nectar filled flower bud and she pulled her hand away, allowing it to follow nature's course. Nature's course. So much trust in such a small creature.

Flynn ran down the steps and grabbed her hand. "Ready? I realized I'm famished too." The two walked down the sidewalks of Main Street, admiring their new home. Arriving at the Cast Iron Café, Flynn opened the door for his wife, "After you, babe." They found a booth in the front with a clear view down Main Street, their inn just in sight.

The waitress (though not Mudsie) was pleasant and cheery.

"What can I start you off with to drink?" she asked.

Flynn smiled at Rose, answering the waitress, "How about a couple of milkshakes?"

"That's not funny," Rose scolded Flynn, but laughed just the same. The waitress walked to the kitchen with a confused look on her face.

Flynn and Rose looked out the café window in silence. Both thinking of their future together. Both anticipating the two babies they were about to bring into the world. And of the road that brought them to this perfect small town and onto the doorstep of what they had hoped for all along... Simpler Times.

Made in the USA
Monee, IL
05 June 2023